MYSTERY
TIMES
TEN
2013

Other Books in This Series

Mystery Times Ten 2011
Mystery Times Nine 2012

MYSTERY

TIMES

TEN

2013

With Stories by
Linda S. Browning • John Jasper Owens
Faye Rapoport DesPres • Cyndy E. Lively
Selaine Henriksen • Wendy Sparrow • Tom Irish
Georgia Ruth • Megan Green

Bonus Stories by KC Sprayberry and Paula Gail Benson

Edited by MaryChris Bradley

Buddhapuss Ink Edison, NJ

Cover and Book Layout/Design by The Book Team
Editor, MaryChris Bradley
Copyeditor, Andrea H. Curley
Library of Congress Control Number: 2013951348
ISBN 978-0-9842035-8-1 (Paperback Original)
First Printing November 2013

PUBLISHER'S NOTE

Buddhapuss Ink LLC and our logos are trademarks of Buddhapuss Ink LLC.

www.buddhapussink.com

Foreword

WELCOME TO the 2013 edition of Mystery Times. The stories in this book were selected by our panels of readers and judges from more than two hundred entries. Competition was fierce this year! The top twenty entries went on to our Editorial Panel, who selected the final ten. Through it all our goal was to celebrate those stories that our readers picked as the best.

To our judges: We couldn't have done this without you. It was nothing short of amazing the way your team churned through what appeared to be an endless stack of submissions; you were persistent, demanding, and dead-on in your picks. Thanks!

To our entrants we offer a grateful thank-you for joining in the fun. We enjoyed reading your stories. We laughed; we cried; we were impressed by the quality of your writing. Way to go!

And to our readers: We hope you find this year's picks as entertaining as we have. We gave special notice to the top three winners, but we love them all. Thanks for picking up our humble book. Now, find a comfortable chair in a well-lit corner and settle in. You're in for a treat!

MaryChris Bradley
Publisher, Buddhapuss Ink LLC

Contents

Bonus Stories

First Place

No Wake

Linda S. Browning

LAKE WATER is nasty. I'm a look-at-the-lake person and not a play-in-or-on-the-lake person. I live in a townhome on Lake Manchester in Tennessee. The lake is beautiful. I like to look at it. I have no desire to touch it. When I was a kid, I loved being in the water. It didn't matter whether it was a lake or a pool. Now there is no way that I would swim in a lake...my lake... any lake. I mean, fish and frogs poop, don't they? They have to go somewhere...and guess where?

My husband, Tom, and I retired to Fairlawn Glen eight years ago. When we started looking for a place to retire, I told Tom that Fairlawn sounded like the name of a cemetery. As it turns out, Fairlawn Glen is a great place for retirees; even though it is practically a residency requirement to keep a walker on your premises at all times.

Three years after we moved from Michigan, Tom dropped dead on the golf course on the thirteenth hole. Massive heart attack. Dead before he hit the ground. Dead man falling. I am sixty-eight years old now. Tom was eight years older than I. Still, it was a shock. Oh, I'm Leslie Barrett, by the way.

It was not a shock, however, that Tom had died while on the golf course. Tom was always on the golf course. I hated playing golf. I really tried to like it, but my Lord, golf is boring. It hadn't helped that Tom always insisted on starting out early in the morning. I don't like mornings. Tom knew that. Morning progresses like a disease. The acute stage is around 6:00 A.M. (agony is excruciating)...the chronic stage is around 8:00 A.M. (pain is only dulled by massive amounts of caffeine)...around 10:00 A.M., morning goes into remission. I quit playing golf when Tom forbade me to drive the golf cart.

There are warning signs on the road to alert the old people of "golf cart crossings," and the posted speed limit around here is only thirty miles an hour. This one time I decided that I could beat the approaching car, so I gunned it...as much as you can gun a golf cart. I beat that car by a mile. Tom wouldn't let me drive the golf cart after that. He said I was reckless.

Tom tried to get me interested in fishing for a while. It was kind of fun...

until I saw a snake. That-Was-So-Over. Do snakes poop? Probably. The snake was in the lake, of course.

I get bored easily. Since Tom was always out golfing, I was at loose ends. I know perfectly well that there are a lot of places around here where old people can volunteer their services, and the causes are worthy. The problem is that I do not now—nor will I ever—consider myself to be an "old people"…and when I work, I want to be paid.

Next, I tried the "Wellness Center." That's what they call the exercise club around here. I tried to like that too. They have every kind of exercise machine you can think of in there. The problem is, people keep touching them.

I "worked out" on a treadmill for a couple of months. I figured that I could push the buttons with a towel and never make skin contact. That lasted until some man next to me started humming. Really loud. HMMMMMMMM. HMMMMMMMM. For God's sake, just shut up and walk.

I abandoned the machines and moved on to the swimming pool, which glistened, pristine with chlorine. AHHHHH. I would swim for my exercise. After happily swimming for about three months, I was stopped short in the lobby in complete shock. Big as life stood a sign:

THE POOL IS TEMPORARILY CLOSED DUE TO FECAL CONTAMINATION.

What? Shit. Somebody pooped in the pool? That was it for me. Honey, there isn't enough bleach or chlorine in the world that could get me back in that water.

Thank God I met Belinda. I'm five feet two inches and weigh around 130 pounds. Belinda is close to six feet tall and weighs…more than I do. She is a couple of years older than I am, and she is my best friend in the entire world. Belinda may not be my physical twin, but psychically we are identical.

Belinda's husband, Frank, died two years ago. It was a sad time. To be perfectly honest, I didn't much like Frank. He was a big blowhard, a real know-it-all. Obviously the know-it-all didn't know what copious amounts of Scotch could do to a guy's liver. Scare up some onions 'cause that sucker was good and fried. Frank died. It was sad.

Belinda and I like to keep up on the local news. Concerned and involved citizens, you could call us. Or nosy and pushy mature (not old) broads, if you prefer. We look into curious situations and then make a big deal out of nothing. That is how it started last month with the lake dredging. Belinda and I attend all the scheduled townhome community meetings. It was at the meeting in March where it was announced that our lake was scheduled for dredging in June. Dredging? For what? This sounded exciting. So we gathered information from knowledgeable sources. We called Mrs. Towers.

Mrs. Towers is an eighty-five-year-old widowed lady (must be an epidemic) who lives in one of our townhome units. If it needs to be known, she knows it. We wonder about her sources; nevertheless, if you wanted the skinny, you asked Mrs. Towers. Evidently, the lakes are dredged every ten years as a matter of routine maintenance Maintenance? Of what? Water? How do you maintain water? It isn't like you have to mow it or anything.

It turns out that sediments and gunk build up in man-made lakes (I may not have mentioned it before, but Lake Manchester is a man-made lake... that doesn't make the water any less nasty), and there are machines that scoop out the gunk that collects at the bottom of the lake; then the gunk gets hauled off, and the lake is happy again. Still, the entire process was supposed to take an entire month, and there would be these huge machines and a bunch of guys... It was like waiting for Christmas.

• • •

LAST SUMMER we spent one entire afternoon watching a bunch of construction workers dig this enormous hole a couple of streets over. I had this theory that it was a mass grave (my imagination tends to run to the dark side.) I envisioned a white van (serial killers' vans are always white) pulling up to the freshly dug hole in the dead of night and the killer unloading his macabre cargo. Covering the bodies with a layer of dirt so the construction men wouldn't notice them, and the next morning all traces would be concreted over. It was brilliant. The victims were likely hookers. Serial killers always kill hookers (and then carry them off in white vans).

It turns out that they were digging a basement; it was fun while it lasted. It was fascinating to watch though. And the fellas were nice...

• • •

FINALLY IT was June, and we were into the second week of dredging. Every afternoon Belinda came over to my unit, and she and I, and Riff-Raff, would watch the dredging guys. They were set up at the marina across the lake because the beach allowed them access for the scooper machine. Riff is my four-year-old Maltese mixed with some other kind of small dog. Riff doesn't weigh but ten pounds, but don't tell her that. She's the size of a purse, but she thinks she's a killer.

My patio faces the lake across a large lawn. There are several docks lined up, and every one of them has a pontoon boat. Our lake is what they call a "no wake" lake. No jet skis, no motorboats with people water skiing... no sir. No fun allowed on our lake. Pontoon boats. Big whoop. They are like big, bloated bars of soap floating around with deck chairs. You hardly ever see one out on the lake unless it is over a summer holiday and the kids and grandkids are in for a visit. Waste of money as far as I am concerned.

Belinda, Riff, and I were sitting on my patio drinking lemonade. Well, Belinda and I were drinking lemonade. Riff had a bowl of water. Very clean water. So, we were sitting and watching the dredging guys. It really is interesting. They have this huge machine with a big scooper on a crane—like a steam shovel—and the entire machine floats. Don't ask me how. It must weigh a ton. Anyway, it putters around (leaving no wake, of course) scooping up stuff from the bottom of the lake and then putters over to dump the stuff in this huge bin. After every dumping, two men poke around in the gunk with some poking equipment to make sure they haven't scooped up any innocent bystanders. One time, after much poking, the two men hauled out this humongous snapping turtle by its tail.

This afternoon we were watching the dredging guys, and suddenly there was this big commotion around the dumping bin. Belinda and I perked right up. We thought maybe it was another turtle…but guys started running around like crazy. The man operating the scooper machine clambered down and climbed up to look in the bin. He started yelling and waving his arms. Belinda and I could see him. Well, I could. I had the binoculars.

Belinda and I passed the binoculars back and forth throughout the remainder of that afternoon. We saw several police cars and then, finally, a coroner's van. Oh my.

Before the police cars and the coroner van arrived, a bunch of the dredging guys started throwing up. I had to give the binoculars to Belinda. I can't do disgusting. Belinda can do disgusting. She was a nurse. I was a social worker. Give me a good, clean emotional crisis any day.

• • •

I FOUND a dead body once. I was working in home health and went to see Mrs. Weatherford. I knocked and rang the doorbell and then whoo-hooed upon entering. I whoo-hooed my way through the house into the bedroom. There she was. Mrs. Weatherford was on the bed facing me. Eyes wide-open, with blood trickling out one corner of her mouth.

I got out of there. I called the office on my cell phone—which back in those days was the size of a small suitcase. I spoke with one of the nurses.

She asked me, "Are you sure she's dead?"

"Yes, she's dead."

"Did you take her pulse?"

"God, no."

"The, how do you know she is dead?"

"Look," I said, "she's either dead, or she has the best poker face that I've ever seen."

Mrs. Weatherford was, indeed, dead. I was convinced that it had been murder because of the blood trickle. The nurses explained to me that the blood trickle was consistent with Mrs. Weatherford's medical condition and cause of death and all, so once I was convinced that it hadn't been murder, I lost interest. Oh, don't get me wrong—Mrs. Weatherford was dead and all, and it was sad.

• • •

WHEN BELINDA told me that a coroner's van had pulled up, I wrestled the binoculars away from her. *This* could get emotional. Two guys got out of the back of the van with a stretcher and one of those black body bags like you see on TV. Body bags are always black, and serial killers' vans are always white. It is important to be observant.

After the police cars and the coroner's van pulled away, the dredging guys went back to work. Belinda and I were jumping out of our skins. Riff was on point...barking in the direction of the marina. She could smell it. It was murder.

We called Mrs. Towers. She didn't even know about it. Belinda and I high-fived. We had finally scooped Mrs. Towers. We settled back and allowed our source to ferret out the details. We watched our community newspapers, but they never publish any real news. Everybody was sick of reading about the overpopulation of Canadian geese—as though we couldn't see them.

Mrs. Towers promised to keep us in the loop.

• • •

ONE WEEK after the big discovery, Belinda and I had just gotten our observation station in place when Mrs. Towers called.

The body had been identified as Abner Cummings. "Abner?" I said. "How do they know?"

"What?" Belinda interrupted.

I shooed her away with my hand.

"Uh-huh...uh-huh."

"What?"

I shooed again.

After hanging up, I relayed the news.

"The body has been identified as Abner Cummings..."

I had barely begun to tell her when Belinda sucked in her breath and turned pale.

"Belinda...what's wrong. Are you okay?"

"A-b-ner? How do they know it is Abner?"

"The medical examiner traced the ID number on his hip implant."

Abner Cummings lived in the townhome next door to Belinda. He was a nice old man. An eighty-nine-year-old widower. Abner was as sharp as a tack. He had very strong views and wasn't shy about sharing them. Abner also fell down a lot. His head was covered with so many stitches and staples that he could have gone to a Halloween party as Frankenstein's monster without need of a costume.

"Belinda, you are as white as a ghost; have some lemonade."

Belinda took several ladylike sips. When she had composed herself, she asked, "How did he die?"

"Well, I'd guess lying around on the bottom of the lake could have had something to do with it."

"Leslie..." Belinda said in a strangled voice. "This isn't funny. Abner is dead."

"I didn't realize you were...um...close to Abner."

"He was my neighbor."

"He was my neighbor too. But I swear you look like you might faint."

Abner Cummings had lived in Fairlawn Glen for thirty-five years. Abner moved into our townhome complex after his wife's death ten years ago. Belinda and Frank moved in seven years ago. As I mentioned before, Frank died two years ago. Do the math.

"Abner was lonely," Belinda said softly.

I finally got it. "Belinda...you mean that you and Abner...'"

"No, no, Leslie. Don't be ridiculous. The man was eighty-nine years old and I'm seventy, for heaven's sake."

"So? Were you and Abner...um...friends...while Frank was alive?"

"Of course."

"I can't believe that you've been carrying on with Abner Cummings all this time and didn't tell me!"

"I have not been 'carrying on' with anybody. And if I were...of course I would tell you."

I was only somewhat mollified.

"Sometimes we would sit on his patio and drink iced tea or something. He would get my mail if I was out of town and vice versa. I assumed he was still in Florida."

We all had made the same assumption.

Every November Abner flew down to Florida and spent the winter with his daughter. The last time I could remember seeing Abner Cummings was at the community meeting last September. It had been a fiery one because someone was there from the Tennessee Department of Transportation

(TDOT) to inform residents about the long-anticipated widening of two-lane Trendle Road to four lanes. Most people living out here are all in favor of widening the road. It is the only thoroughfare that connects Fairlawn Glen with the big city. The old people out here drive like…old people, and it is impossible to pass any of them. Every vehicle appears to be piloted by one of the Muppets.

Abner was strongly opposed to the four-lane, as it would require the destruction of the Baptist church that Abner had attended for the last thirty-five years. The church would be paid handsomely for the acquisition and another church would be built at a location close by, but Abner was morally outraged that his church would have to come down in order to accommodate the road. He was always distributing petitions. I heard that Abner had collected enough signatures on his petition (most were church members) to get some kind of injunction that at least would postpone the start of the venture.

"Remember how angry Abner got at the September meeting with the road people?" I asked.

"Yes…Abner is…was…very passionate about his church." Then Belinda surprised me by chuckling. "Remember what he said to that new guy who moved in last summer with that great big motor on his pontoon boat?"

"Oh my goodness, yes. That was so funny!"

Abner had started a ruckus with new-guy because the outboard motor on his boat was so big…horsepower and all. Abner lectured him about how "no wake" is allowed on Manchester…implying that new-guy was going to go roaring up and down the lake with his big motor. When new-guy denied that he had any intention of roaring, Abner had demanded loudly, "Well what's the purpose of having a big motor if you don't intend to use it?"

New-guy responded, "I can have as big a motor as I want to; I just can't go very fast!"

Belinda and I got the giggles with that exchange and had to leave the room. We laughed again now at the memory.

We watched the dredging guys for a few minutes until I said, "Okay, we have to assume that poor old Abner was murdered."

Belinda immediately started shaking her head. "Oh no you don't. You are not going to start running around promoting murder theories."

Which, of course, was exactly what I was intending to do. Belinda, bless her heart, always tried to balance my imagination with logic…but logic schmogic. Abner Cummings had been murdered. How else could he have gotten stuck at the bottom of the lake? It didn't make sense. It wasn't like he was found floating around as if he had fallen off a boat or something.

Where was the boat? Where were the witnesses? No doubt about it; it was murder.

• • •

"IT HAD to be his daughter," I announced two days after the gruesome discovery.

"Why do you say that? Life insurance or something?" asked Belinda.

"Exactly. We all thought Abner was safely ensconced in his daughter's home in Florida, and now we find out he has been 'sleeping with the fishes' all this time. Why didn't she report him missing? Something about this whole thing smells…and it isn't just Abner."

Belinda moaned, and Riff whimpered.

"We have to look at motive," I said. "The most likely motive for murder is money."

"How do you know?" Belinda huffed.

"I pay attention, Belinda. I read," I huffed back at her.

Belinda started tapping her finger on the side of her glass of lemonade.

"What is it?" I asked. I know this woman so well.

"Nothing."

"Don't give me that, Belinda. You've thought of something."

"Well, Abner's daughter is the only surviving relative that I am aware of, so she will have to come up here to clear out his home. Maybe we could watch for her and ask her some discreet questions."

"You mean like, why in the hell didn't you report your father missing?"

"Well, yes. Why don't we call Mrs. Towers and see if she knows anything."

I gave her a smug smile. "I already did. The daughter is supposed to be here tomorrow."

We decided that Belinda would keep an eye out for the daughter the next day and call me as soon as she spotted her.

• • •

I WAS on pins and needles all that night and the next morning. Belinda finally called me at 2:00 P.M. Shoot. Because I'd been hanging around the telephone waiting for her call, I'd missed an entire day of dredging.

I hurried right over to Belinda's, and we went next door. Knocking briefly, we *whoo-hoo*ed our way inside. The daughter, April, was in her late fifties or early sixties, and she was really nice. I had been all set to accuse her of murder, so I wasn't prepared to like her.

Belinda and I offered our condolences.

April sniffed back tears. "Dad was close to ninety, but to lose him like this…"

I very gently interrogated her…I was a social worker…I know how to be gentle. "We all thought Abner was in Florida with you. Didn't you wonder when he didn't show up?"

April told us that she and Abner corresponded by e-mail. Her father didn't like to talk on the telephone, so once he had mastered the art of e-mail, they spoke (so to speak) often. He e-mailed her last November to tell her that he had decided to stay in Tennessee over the winter, as he didn't think he was up to the trip. Abner reminded her that he *was* getting on in years.

"When do the authorities think he died?" I asked...gently.

"The medical examiner is guessing that Dad died five to six months ago. Cause of death was difficult to determine due to the circumstances—you know... The autopsy did show that he had a skull fracture. So they are thinking he must have been out on the dock and slipped and hit his head or something. After that, the hypothesis is that snapping turtles—you know, they can get really big out here."

Belinda and I concurred. I saw one crossing the road heading toward our lake one summer that was as big as a footstool.

She continued. "They think the turtles...um...grabbed hold of him; and once he got pulled under, he got hung up on one of those stumps that are submerged in the lake. Then the dredging equipment...dislodged..." The poor thing broke down in tears.

It's true that the bottom of the lake is littered with tree stumps. People who fish around here are always complaining about their lures getting hung up on them. And no, I have no idea how tree stumps get on the bottom of a lake...but obviously they do.

"Yes, dear." I patted her shoulder...gently. "We know."

When April had recovered somewhat, Belinda asked, "Weren't you curious when you never heard from him again?"

"That's what's really odd. Dad and I e-mailed back and forth all winter. His e-mails didn't stop until a couple of weeks ago...and...then...well... you know what happened then."

"Do you still have the e-mails, dear?" I asked.

She shook her head. "No, unfortunately. I delete e-mails almost immediately. But they should still be on Dad's computer."

Oh boy. We were closing in now.

"Where is his computer?" I asked.

"Leslie..." Belinda warned, but I ignored her.

We followed April into a back room where Abner had kept his computer.

"I don't know whether it is password protected, but I doubt it," said April.

"May I?" I asked...gently.

"Of course," she responded.

I settled myself at the keyboard and booted up the computer (that's computer jargon for I turned it on). The e-mail account was active, but there had been zero activity since last November. The last e-mail on record…and yes, I checked the trash place…was the e-mail Abner had reportedly sent to his daughter announcing his intention to stay in Tennessee over the winter.

April couldn't explain it. "Someone must have erased them…but why?"

"What about his regular mail?" Belinda asked.

"I went to the post office. They said Dad stopped his mail delivery in November…just like every winter." Belinda and I believed April was telling the truth. Something was verrrryyy wrong. A bit of further snooping revealed that Abner's utility bills were set up for automatic payment with his bank. A very tidy murder.

We left April to her lonely task.

Now that Belinda was on board the mystery train, we headed back to her place to make some discreet inquiries. Belinda called our source and brought her up to date on the case. Mrs. Towers was impressed with what we had uncovered. She told us that the police were still investigating Abner's death but were leaning toward ruling it accidental. She suggested we tell the police about the missing e-mails.

I called, and a police officer said they already knew there was no record of e-mails on Abner's computer… He was actually quite insulting about it… implying that we were pretty stupid to suggest that they hadn't thought to look.

That made me mad, so I said to the officer, "Well, if you are really smart, you will have a forensic expert examine the hard drive!" I know that computer data is never totally erased from a hard drive. I watch a lot of *NCIS* with that cute Mark Harmon. I really impressed Belinda with my knowledge of computer stuff. The officer pooh-poohed my suspicions by suggesting that the daughter was mistaken somehow…or…embarrassed that she hadn't kept in contact with her father."

When I hung up, Belinda asked, "What are they going to do?"

"Nothing," I harrumphed. "Absolutely nothing. They're going to write off poor old Abner as accidental turtle fodder."

"Oh my Lord!"

"Belinda, it looks like it is up to us to find out who murdered your boyfriend."

"Abner was not my boyfriend!" When Belinda gets excited, she sometimes shrieks like Edith Bunker…"Oh, never mind."

Belinda and I got down to the onerous job (well, not really onerous…I enjoy a good project) of listing potential suspects who had motivation to kill Abner. It wasn't a very long list. We ruled out angry husbands because it was unlikely that Abner was dallying his dilly in anyone else's dally. According to Belinda, Abner's dilly couldn't dally even if he had wanted it to. Of course, Belinda claims this was only supposition. I decided not to pry… A lady is entitled to *some* secrets.

We ruled out April. She was too nice to have been involved with murder. Belinda and I both pride ourselves on the accuracy of our bullshit meters, and we detected none.

We considered the new guy and his *big* outboard motor. Abner was well known as the no-wake Nazi, and he had gotten pretty hot under the collar at the meeting in September. It didn't sound like much of a motive though.

We decided to make a list of all the townhome residents. We immediately ruled out Belinda and me, Mrs. Towers, and…well, Abner, of course. Abner had had some heated exchanges with other residents during meetings… especially about the planned four-lane.

"Belinda, you said you have a key to Abner's place because you used to get his mail?"

"Yes."

"I have an idea. We didn't search his computer very well for clues. All we did was establish that Abner's e-mails to April stopped in November. We didn't look at e-mail history."

"I don't know, Les. It is a good idea though. Why don't you call that police officer and suggest they do an e-mail search."

I snorted in a very unladylike fashion and waved my arm dismissively. "Barney Fife could crack this case before any of those clowns even get close."

"Peek out and see if April is still over there," I instructed.

Belinda peeked. "Her van is gone."

"Get the key, Belinda. Let's go. If we don't move fast, she will disconnect the computer."

We hustled next door and into poor old Abner's den. I booted up (that means, oh, never mind, I already told you) the computer and clicked on the little man silhouette with ABNER next to it. Belinda pulled up a chair, and we started peeling back the layers of e-mails. We got bored. A bunch of e-mails back and forth with April (as she had indicated) and lame jokes from friends. He had e-mailed a lot with fellow church members. We opened those (for forensic purposes) and read them, but they were mostly comments about the sermons and choices of hymns. Those Baptists take their hymn choices very seriously. I'm Catholic. In and out in half an hour. Belinda is Methodist. I went with her once to one of her services. I'd rather play golf.

One e-mail in particular caught my eye. It was a heated exchange back and forth about the anticipated four-lane and the petitions that Abner was forever circulating. The e-mail came from some guy named Mitchell Gaines. This Mr. Gaines was obviously all in favor of the four-lane. He stressed the convenience for residents (finally, a chance to pass one of the Muppets), but he also mentioned (several times) the financial benefits to commercial enterprises along the road. This Mr. Gaines even pointed out that the Baptist church was more than forty years old, and the congregation would only benefit from the construction of a new church.

Belinda had been correct when she said that Abner was passionate about his church. His return e-mails railed against the capitalistic motivations of TDOT and the business owners along the route, who selfishly stood to make money from the sale of their properties.

"I wonder who this Mr. Gaines guy is. He sounds plenty upset," said Belinda.

"I've got an idea," I said excitedly.

"What are you going to do?" Belinda asked suspiciously. Poor Belinda, she is always so tentative.

I opened a new e-mail. "We are going to throw out a teaser to Mr. Gaines and see what we get."

I typed, "We know who you are and what you did to poor old Abner." I hit SEND.

"Oh my God, Leslie. Are you out of your mind? Delete it…delete it before it gets sent."

"Give it a few minutes, Belinda. If this guy answers, it will be a good indication that he is involved somehow."

We sat there for a good twenty minutes. Nothing. We got bored. I am no computer genius, but as far as I could tell, the message had been received.

"Let's go, Leslie. This is making me very nervous."

The computer dinged. We had mail!

I opened the e-mail, which said, "Who are you? Abner's dead."

"Oh my God, Leslie! Let's go… Let's go."

"No. Let's wait around for a few minutes. See if he sends another e-mail. Don't you think *you* at least owe it to Abner to find out what happened to him? See what else this guy has to say."

Fortunately, I had brought Riff with me (I always bring Riff with me—almost everywhere—that's the advantage of having a purse-size dog), so I didn't have to worry about getting right home.

Belinda's voice was nearing the Bunker shriek. "*I* don't owe Abner anything! I told you; we were just friends."

"Still…if I were murdered, I would hope you would at least try to find out who done it."

Belinda knew when she was beaten. With a huge sigh she capitulated. "One hour. We leave after one hour."

"Agreed."

We waited around for an hour. We were getting really bored. Riff was having a great time with all the fascinating new smells. I let her wander around. Who knew; maybe she would turn up some evidence with her doggy sniffer.

"He's not going to say any more, Les. Let's go."

"Give it a few more minutes…" I started, and then stopped with a sharp intake of breath.

There was someone at the front door.

"Oh my God," Belinda whisper-shrieked (if you think that is easy…try it).

"Riff…" I whisper-called to my dog. "Come here, Riff." Riff trotted right back to me, and I scooped her up.

Belinda and I crept out of the den. "It's probably just April coming back," I whispered reasonably. "Don't panic."

We were halfway across the living room heading toward the patio when the front door opened. We had neglected to lock it.

A great big fat man stood in the doorway leaning heavily on a walker.

Okay, I thought. This doesn't look too bad. Belinda, Riff, and I can easily take this guy.

The fat man stumped his way into the foyer. A younger man followed. Uh-oh.

"Dad, get out of the way," the younger man said in an exasperated tone. When he had shoved his way around the fat man, he leveled a severe gaze our way. "What's going on here?"

I was starting to get mad. I straightened up and leveled right back at him. "We know what you did to poor old Abner. The police will be here any second." Then I narrowed my eyes at the fat man and declared smugly, *"Mr. Mitchell Gaines!"*

The fat man started to blubber, "It was an-n-n ac-ci-dent." "Shut up, Dad."

"No… I can't s-stand this any longer."

"What happened?" Belinda whisper-shrieked.

"Shut up, Dad."

The fat man stumped his way past his son and leaned heavily on the walker.

"I own the strip mall off Trendle," he explained. "Abner wouldn't leave things alone… He just kept up with his stupid petitions and letters to TDOT. I've been losing money on that strip mall for years. Half of the stores are empty. I *need* the money from the sale of that land. We only came over that night to talk with Abner…to reason with him."

"Shut up, Dad," the younger man growled.

Riff growled back at him. I was so proud.

The fat man kept talking. "We got into an argument. I got so worked up that Brian was afraid I was going to have a heart attack. Brian gave him a little push."

"Dad…" Brian and Riff growled in unison.

"Abner just kind of crumpled. He hit his head on the corner of the end table. We could tell he was dead."

Belinda had been inching toward the patio door with two fingers pinching my shirt, pulling me along.

"We panicked," blubbered the fat man. "Brian took Abner down to the docks and threw him in the water. We figured he would be found in the morning."

The rest of it fell into place. I said solemnly, "When the body wasn't found, Brian hacked into Abner's computer and set up the e-mail trail with his daughter in order to stall for time. Then when Abner got dredged up, Brian erased the e-mails."

The fat man nodded. He gave a blubbering growl. "Damn turtles."

I frowned at Brian. "But you couldn't have known that April automatically purged her e-mails?"

"No." Brian gave me a creepy smile. "That was most cooperative of her."

Belinda wrenched open the door to the patio and practically threw me through the screen door. Brian immediately started break dancing his way around his fat father. Belinda slammed the patio door behind her and pushed the barbecue grill up tight against the screen door to slow him down.

"Run, Leslie!" Belinda shrieked. My best friend took off across the lawn, headed for the docks. She was running like a track star. I was close (well, not real close) behind her. I heard little whimpering noises as I ran. I shut up when I realized it was me.

We ran past Mrs. Towers, who was sitting in the middle of the lawn watching the dredging guys.

I heard the grill screech across the patio. I managed to bawl as I passed Mrs. Towers, "They're after us."

Belinda was hotfooting it down (what we called) the boardwalk. She was untying new-guy's boat from the mooring when I panted up beside her clutching Riff. I glanced behind us crazily. Mrs. Towers had wheezed her way up out of her chair and was trying to engage Brian in some sort of stalling maneuver by planting herself and her walker in front of him. The fat man was batting at the barbecue grill with his walker.

Belinda shrieked, "Get in the boat, Les!"

"But…but …" I sputtered.

"GET. IN. THE. BOAT," Belinda shrieked even louder.

So I GOT. IN. THE. BOAT. I gave Riff a soft toss, and then I jumped (well, I didn't actually jump. If it had been caught on a YouTube video, I imagine I would have looked quite comical.) in the boat behind Belinda and Riff.

By this time Brian had run around Mrs. Towers and made his way to the boardwalk.

"We don't have a key," I wailed. Belinda was already at the wheel. I heard the engine start up. I hurried to her side. "Where did you get the key?"

Belinda was already moving away from the dock. Over her shoulder she explained, "Frank and I used to have a boat. Everybody hides a key under the dash."

By the time Brian got to the dock, we were too far away for him to do anything about it. He quickly jumped (now, *he* did jump…murderous young show-off) onto another boat.

He never had a chance though. Belinda had chosen new-guy's boat with its big outboard motor. Sometimes bigger is better.

"Hold on to something!" Belinda shrieked. When we got farther from the dock, she floored it. Riff and I were crouched down beside her. I had one arm around Riff and the other wrapped around the pilot's chair.

VA-ROOM!!! It was glorious. Riff and I hung on for all we were worth. I rose up enough to peer behind us. Brian was following in his pathetic little no-wake boat. He never had a chance. I turned around and peered fearfully over the dash.

"You're going to hit the scooper guy!" I shouted. We watched the scooper guy jump out of his scooper machine and into the nasty, dredged-up lake water. I cringed.

Belinda maneuvered around the scooper machine like a pro. She zigged and zagged. She was fabulous. We were headed for the beach. Quite a crowd of dredging guys had gathered on the beach to watch the action.

"Stop… Belinda…stop!" I yelled. "We're going to crash."

"I can't stop!" Belinda shrieked.

"What do you mean, you can't stop!?"

"Frank only let me drive. He never let me dock."

Riff and I sank to the floor of the boat again. "Oh…great…" I moaned aloud. Belinda's dead, blowhard husband was going to get us all killed. I never did like Frank.

Belinda turned off the engine. "Get up, Leslie. We have to jump."

"Jump?! Are you crazy?!" The boat was already slowing down but was still wobbling toward the beach.

"You do what you want to…but I'm jumping!" Belinda clambered up on the side of the boat, and over she went.

"Oh God…oh God…oh God," I whimpered as I grappled my way up and over the railing. I clasped Riff so tightly in one arm that she yelped. I screwed up my eyes, pinched my nose tightly, and made a leap of faith after my friend.

I lost my hold on Riff when we hit the water. I came up flailing and gasp-ing. Riff paddled up to me and, once she was sure I was okay, headed for the beach. I dog paddled right behind her.

Belinda had reached the beach and was being helped out of the water by a couple of the dredging guys. Riff reached the beach and was furiously shaking water from her fur. By now I was on my hands and knees, gasping.

I was suddenly swooped from the shallow water. One of the dredging guys had me in his arms. Oh my. Sometimes there are advantages to being a small woman. Nobody had swooped up Belinda.

I was so weak that I had to wrap my arms around the dredging guy's neck and lay my head against his dredging-guy chest. Oh my.

Belinda had already directed the dredging guys to call the cops. We made our way into the coffee shop of the marina, where we awaited the police, wrapped up in big towels and sipping hot coffee. New-guy's boat was float-ing aimlessly just off the beach. Brian had long since given up the chase.

My dredging guy was holding Riff. Nothing is sexier than a big dredging guy cuddling a ten-pound purse dog.

Brian and his fat father were arrested. Belinda and I were famous. Mrs. Towers was so proud. We don't know what charges will be brought against the men. I suspect the actual death really had been an accident. Abner should have worn a helmet just to go out to the mailbox. Dumping him in the nasty lake water like so much turtle kibble, however…well, that's just wrong.

• • •

A FEW days after our adventure, Belinda, Riff, and I were back on my patio, sipping lemonade and watching the dredging guys. Riff and I had taken so many baths, we squeaked when we breathed. Like I said, lake water is nasty.

I had the binoculars trained on the scooper machine and watched as it puttered back to the gunk bin.

I muttered, "I wonder how many more people have gone missing around here?"

"Leslie…" Belinda cautioned.

When I lowered the binoculars and narrowed my eyes at her, I saw that she was grinning.

"Let's call Mrs. Towers," suggested my best friend.

LINDA S. BROWNING has been writing in her head since the age of twelve, sometimes simply to relieve brain overcrowding. After retiring from a career in social work and office management, Linda began testing the waters of the writing profession via short story competitions. Winning First Place in the Mystery Times Ten 2013 competition for Buddhapuss Ink fulfilled a lifelong dream of publication. She is currently working on a novel featuring the two characters from her winning short story, a fast-moving tale of mystery, adventure, and humor with series potential. She currently resides in a retirement community in Tennessee with her husband. Linda welcomes you on Facebook linda.browning.5817 and/or Twitter @LindaSBrowning.

Second Place

Femme Fatale

John Jasper Owens

DECLAN BELIEVED in the holy trinity—Carver, Hammett, and
Thompson—and in the other saints and relics of his hard-boiled religion.
He worshipped the ancient scrolls of *Argosy*, *Black Mask*, and *Manhunt*. He
adored the Cains, Burnett, and Ms. Highsmith. His soul accepted Appel's
New York more readily than it did Block's (though he conceded Block was
the better writer) and that *Green Ice* was more fun to read than *The Maltese
Falcon*. Ditto Hammett, with genuflection. The stained glass portraits in the
atrium of his church were of Scudder, Heller, Burke, Bosch, The Op, with
the most impressive—the one that caught the sunset's light—of Hammer.
He had made his pilgrimage to The Mysterious Bookshop and climbed the
spiral staircase.

He believed Hawk deserved billing over Parker, Mouse above Easy.

He traveled with Milo and Sughrue. In a mellow mood he might hang out
with Lew Archer or Pronzini's Nameless, and as silly as Bernie was, he was a
decent guy to have at the beach. But anyone who read Doyle or Christie was
just kidding themselves. Buy yourself a romance already and get out of the
way. He believed Shirley Jackson wrote as hard-boiled as anyone; so what
if there was nary a gumshoe, she still had an Edgar. He knew Leonard's
Westerns were really crime stories dressed up with Apaches and soldiers.

He believed Mick Ballou could always save the day.

And he believed in the femme fatale.

Even more when he met one in real life.

• • •

DECLAN SHOULDERED through the tavern door, moving from fog
to cigarette smoke, from the lamp-lit night into the shadows of his local.
He walked to the bar and waved at Danielle, who winked back and started
pouring. He leaned on a stool, glanced around…

And saw her.

No *way*.

Not in this dump, not on a nothing Tuesday night.

Not possible that she was sitting alone in a pool of yellow light at the end of the bar. Not with that honey-blond hair cascading down her neck and shoulders, not wearing that dress—candy-apple red and backless to the swell of her hips, sequins glittering, with just enough spandex to make it cling all the way to her crossed knees and a slit pointing up toward paradise.

Not in this lifetime.

Not staring right at him.

He looked down at his Scotch, took a sip, and then cut his eyes back to the woman. Definitely real, and definitely staring at him. How long had it been since Katie kicked him to the curb? Three months? That sounded right. Three long, womanless months, like a man doing ninety days in lockup. He felt his mouth go dry, so he pulled some more booze over his tongue. When he looked back at the blonde, she'd turned her attention to her own drink, something fiery in a martini glass, almost finished. She wasn't going to be sitting alone much longer, he thought, not looking like that with an empty glass in her hand. He marshaled his courage and sauntered over. She didn't look up until he spoke, right beside her.

"Buy you a drink?"

She acted startled but nodded, and he waved for Danielle. He pulled out his cigarette pack and flipped two into his mouth with a flick of his wrist.

Staring deeply into her blue eyes, he lit the smokes and passed one to her. She plucked it with two long fingers, placed it between her full red lips, and inhaled.

She went into a violent coughing fit, turning her head just in time for the cigarette to shoot out of her mouth and hit the approaching bartender in her ample chest.

Danielle slapped at it, panicked, accidentally catching it against her shirt and shoving it, tip first, into her breast pocket. She yelped as the ember burned, snatched Declan's drink, and splashed herself with it. Unfortunately, Declan liked high-proof neat, and her breast pocket bloomed into a badge of flame. She grabbed the seltzer gun and put herself out with a long spray, then stalked away, muttering.

"I don't know why I took that cigarette," the blonde said. "I've never smoked a cigarette in my life. You just looked so cool, I didn't want to spoil the scene. I'm Molly." They shook hands. "If you're going to smoke, would you go back down the bar?" She waved her hand around. "I really don't like the smell."

He stubbed it. "We need fresh drinks from a fresh bartender."

Molly was trouble; he could see that right away, could tell by the way her strap kept falling off that tanned shoulder, by how she smiled at him when she slid it back up. She was married, and the rock on her finger was so big he knew that whoever slid it on probably could've bought out the rest of the jewelry store along with it.

The hours passed easily, full of laughs and light touches, lean-ins to whisper, sweet breath on his neck. Declan had questions. Why was she here alone? Where was her husband? But he didn't ask. He knew this woman was one dangerous tomato and didn't want to hear any of her pretty lies. It got late in no time. Molly stifled a yawn, and Declan knew it was time to shove off, cut his losses. Put this night down as a treasured memory and a narrow escape.

The bartender was scrolling through channels on the overhead television looking for sports and flipped past a late-night showing of *Vertigo* as Declan and Molly glanced up.

"I love Hitchcock," they both said at the same time.

Declan's mouth dropped open.

"He uses all the classic noir elements." Molly went on, holding up and counting off on her blood-red fingernails. "The sexy, deceitful bombshell; the well-meaning dupe; the con—grift, whatever you want to call it; murder; twist ending. It's all there." She challenged him with her eyes, swirling her drink at the bottom of her glass.

He had to have her.

"You know," he whispered, "the working title was *From Among the Dead.*"

She kissed him.

"I live right around the corner," he whispered.

"Let's go to my place. My husband's out of town."

• • •

MOLLY RACED her vintage Corvette outside the city limits and over three hills, cresting, finally, above a home so big Declan wasn't sure where it even started. They flew down a gated side street with its own sign, through a second gate, between several gardens and sheds, past guest houses and vine-trellised towers, down into a concrete tunnel, at last ending in a spotless six-car garage floored in white tile.

Way over my head, he thought. She's a poisoned honey pot, and I should pull my paw out right now.

"Listen," he said, and she took his hand. Light, like a spider's touch. "I, um. Well." She was rubbing his wrist, leaning in to him. "You're married, and I just think...."

"Did you know," she whispered, her breath hot on his cheek, "that *Vertigo* is one of the five lost Hitchcocks?"

He snorted. "Yeah. *Rear Window*? Hello? Thirty years gone."

Their lips were an inch apart, and she whispered, "How long before Al appears?"

"Eleven minutes." He was going to kiss her then but got turned off by the amateur question. "Who was originally picked for Madeline?"

"Ooh." She kissed his nose. "Vera Miles." He went for her lips then, let his hands roam freely. She pulled away with a gasp, led him into the house. Over her shoulder she said, "And Miles posed for the painting. It's in the movie."

They never made it to the bedroom.

• • •

DECLAN AWOKE on a couch—shirt over a lamp, his pants missing. He stared at a half-empty bottle of Stoli in the kitchen before finding his shoes on top of the microwave. He'd normally have trouble remembering after a drunk like that but not this time. Molly was an angel to look at and a hellcat to hold. On the floor, on the couch—in the kitchen, apparently—Molly was the best ever. Ever.

Of course she was. She was a femme fatale, and that's what they do.

She came down the stairs, yawning and scratching her scalp, as he was pulling his slacks from beneath an iron-framed bookcase. "Breakfast?" she said. "I'm no good in the kitchen, but there's strawberries and croissants."

"I have to go."

She looked hurt. That look slashed at his heart, but he knew danger—married danger kept in a mansion—when it walked downstairs half naked offering strawberries and croissants.

"Coffee?" she tried. "I can make that."

"I'm surprised this place doesn't have its own Starbucks." He pretended to be interested in getting dressed. "Just take me home. Please."

On the drive back through the hills and down to the city, he glanced over at Molly once or twice. She was crying silently, her cheeks wet and glistening. He directed her to his car instead of to his apartment building. When he got out, she'd regained some composure. Her blue eyes turned hard.

"I am *not* a whore. Why are you treating me like one?"

Declan shrugged, looking off.

"I felt a connection," she said, blinking back new tears. "A mutual connection."

He stood straight and cocked his head. Wished for his fedora. "Pretty girl, you're dangerous. Married, rich—outta my league."

"I am not out of your league. Declan, please, can we just talk?"

"You wanna talk, vamp?" He hitched his hands on both sides of his belt. "Be back at the bar tomorrow night. Same seat, same time."

"I have yoga tomorrow," Molly said, "and then I volunteer at the homeless shelter on Lincoln."

"Um…well. You know where to find me. You or your goons."

"I *don't* know where to find you, Declan." She got out of her convertible. "And I don't have goons. You haven't given me a number or an address."

The new-morning sunlight cut through the downtown buildings, long streaks of shadow. Declan got weak when Molly got close.

"Donald Westlake," he said when she was so near he could smell last night's perfume.

"Stark, you mean?" She slid her arms over his shoulders, and he shuddered. "A forgotten genius." She licked his ear. He grabbed her arms, pushed her back to elbow's length.

"No. He wants to be funny."

"Wanted," she breathed, leaning to his lips. A car honked, and kids yelled just behind her. "*God Save the Mark* won him the Edgar."

"I was three," he said.

"I wasn't born. My parents hadn't even met."

He kissed her, God help him.

"Ever read *The Ax*," she asked softly into his lips.

"Beautiful book. Suburban noir. The protagonist picks and kills his rivals to get what he needs."

"That's a real man for you. Friday night at seven," she said. "Meet me here; we'll go back to my place."

I'm doomed, he thought as her Corvette sped to the light and squealed around the corner.

Doomed.

• • •

BETWEEN THAT moment and Friday night he considered exactly how he was doomed. Dying, with Molly standing over him with a gun? A classic, always in style. A life sentence for murdering her husband, while Molly walked free? Another favorite. Ditto previous, except it's a frame-up. That could happen. Him in a bus station, waiting for the dame with the cash who never shows up. Softer, a bit Fusilli. And then, you never know. Drug money? She dumps him overboard. Embezzlement? When the FBI came, he'd be…

The UPS guy punched his shoulder, snapping Declan out of it. The warehouse where he worked was suddenly loud all around.

"Sign, Declan. And how come when I mention this new girl you keep talking about, you go off in a trance?"

"She's a real slick chick, heavy on the sugar."

"Talk normal, Declan."

"She's too beautiful for me, too rich," he muttered, signing.

Kevin grinned. He stood tall and broad, and had no problem with women. "Just enjoy it while it lasts, my man."

• • •

DANIELLE, BACK at the pub and pouring him one, was even more direct. "You're not exactly chopped liver, Declan," she said, and leaned her cleavage over the bar. "I'd go out with you if you weren't so weird. You dress like a reject from the black-and-white movies. Lose the sports jacket and the fedora. Go a little hip-hop. You'd be cute."

Declan killed his drink, cut the brim of his hat at Danielle, and was out the door.

Molly pulled into the spot she'd been in three days earlier right on cue. She looked up at him, and her beautiful eyes widened. "God, you look handsome."

"Think so?"

"A real hunk of heartbreak, heaven sent. Get in."

He slid into the car beside her, rubbing his vision over those breasts and legs. He put his hand on her knee, and she put hers over it, guiding it inside her leg and up her thigh. "My place?" she asked, and punched the gas before he could answer. Then they were outside the city, going up and down, through the hills, cresting and dropping, his hand jostling farther up her thigh until there was nowhere left for it to go, so it stayed there, moving with the rumbles of the Corvette's engine.

At least this time they made it to her bedroom.

• • •

DECLAN AWOKE with the birds, Molly still asleep on his arm, her breath on his shoulder. *I love you,* he thought, *do with me what you will. Well, except for that frame-up thing. Prison would be horrible.* His shoulder twitched. Molly's eyes fluttered open, so near his, and he melted. Most of him, anyway. There was a part of him that did the opposite of melt.

"Hey," she said, and kissed his cheek. Then she glanced down. "Look, Declan. My husband's coming home tonight. I need to talk to him, you know." She cuddled to his chest. "Alone. He deserves that."

The husband, Declan thought. *Well, here it comes.* He launched a preemptive strike, testing his ground.

"You must hate him."

Molly laughed. "Good lord, no, I don't hate Alex; I love Alex. What's wrong with you? We've just grown apart; that's all. It happens. Why would

I marry someone I hated?"

"For the money."

Molly kept laughing, her palm over her mouth. She caught her breath. "This is my house, Declan, and it's my money. I'll make sure Alex is very comfortable from now on. I owe him that much."

"Because he's old and decrepit, and you want him gone?"

Her brows narrowed. "He's younger than you and works out a lot, which you should consider. You've got natural muscle, but some gym time would clear up that chest flab."

Declan pretended to sit up casually, but when his legs were over the bed, he spun his torso around and thrust out his arm with a finger extended into Molly's face.

"He's a brute," he yelled, "and the only time he ever touches you is to force himself on you!"

Molly reached out and grabbed Declan's finger, then twisted it back.

"Ow. Hey, stop!" Declan's arm bent, and he drew his naked body up to it. "Ouch!"

"Alex is five-two and built like a fireplug," she said. "And I make love to him whenever he wants, because he's a wonderful man." She squeezed his finger joint. "Don't disrespect my husband. He deserves a gentle letdown."

"He'll kill you with his bare hands," Declan croaked. Molly let go.

"He's a math professor and wouldn't hurt a fly. But I"—she latticed her hands and cracked her knuckles— "have a brown belt in Tae Kwon Do."

Declan stood up, practically jumping into his slacks. "I knew it," he said. "You're trouble. Trouble from the *get-go*."

Now Molly looked panicked. Declan turned to leave. "I'm sorry I twisted your finger," she yelled at his back. "I was just mad!"

Declan was halfway down the hall when he shouted, "I'm going home, and I'll walk if I have to." He heard bare feet behind him.

"Declan, please!" She tried to get around him, and he blocked her with his elbow. They reached the grand staircase, which dropped two floors—thirty feet—to the marble grand entrance at the bottom.

Molly leaped around him so she could stare into his face. She pedaled backward, still naked but for her white silk robe. She wouldn't fall; she was sure footed and on her own landing.

But Molly made a mistake.

She put two palms against Declan's chest—not a push but a "please stop" gesture—but Declan, still moving forward, was so much heavier than she. At the top of the stairs, Molly's right heel brushed against her left... She slipped and fell backward. Declan's hand shot out and caught her robe, spinning her like a top, but she was still falling. His other hand reached and caught, just barely, her arm above her elbow; and he hauled her up straight, her toes on the top stair and her heels hanging over.

They were both bare chested, and he could feel her heart thumping against his skin.

"Jesus, Declan," she gasped. "You saved my life." Her knees buckled, and he scooped her up, turning to carry her back to bed. He marched down the hall. "Declan?" she said, "Um, Declan? You should put me down, I think. Declan?"

And she vomited on his knees.

• • •

"YOU EVER stop to think that maybe you finally met someone as weird as you are?" asked Megan, his assistant, as she taped up boxes for delivery. A forklift sped by, and she straightened up. "So she's all hot and rich and stuff. Just be happy."

"We're not weird," said Declan.

"All I'm saying is that both of you buy two copies of each and every Hard Case Crime that comes out so you can keep them on separate shelves, one alphabetical by author and the other alphabetical by title."

Declan looked confused. "That's not weird."

"It's true love, Declan. Trust me on this."

An hour later Megan was trying to stack a pallet when she heard her boss walk up again. She looked at him over her shoulder. "You open your mouth and it had better be about work."

"Just humor me a second," he said. "Look. I saved her life the other day."

"What? She was having a heart attack, and you beat her in the chest with a Mickey Spillane?"

"No. Listen. Her husband's back in town, and she won't talk to me. But this morning some guy's knocking on my door with a brand-new Jaguar XK and a delivery. A debit card and a note says there's twenty grand on it." He glanced around and whispered, "It's suspicious."

"My electric bill is three days past due, Deck. Quit whining." She got in his face. "You hit the love lottery, so just be happy. But be happy away from me. You're a couple of freaks who bumped into each other, and that's all."

"She wants me on a leash," he said, "but she won't talk to me right now...."

"If she wanted you on a leash, she'd lease you a car and make you ask for money."

Declan shook his head, not listening. "A pretty, golden leash that she can yank taut"—he clenched a shaking fist—"at her merest whim."

Megan exhaled a deep breath. "Deck, I'm gonna give you a 'Declan is a loser' test, then you're gonna leave my ass alone for the rest of the shift. Let me think. Okay, name all the characters and actors in the gang in *The Usual Suspects*. First and last names."

"Duh, Kevin Spacey. He's Keyser Sose, but in the credits he's Roger Kint—'Verbal' Kint, I mean. Gabriel Byrne plays Dean Keaton. Benicio Del Toro is Fred Fenster—that's the first thing I ever noticed him in. Then there's…"

• • •

"…KEVIN POLLAK as Todd Hockney," Molly said, swirling her linguini, "and Stephen Baldwin in the best role of his life: Michael McManus. Why do you ask?"

Declan shrugged. They were at an out-of-the-way Italian joint. She'd finally agreed to meet him "for an hour or two—no funny business."

"Alex is hurting," she'd told him on the phone. "We need to be patient. But I have to see you." She had arrived in a tasteful blouse and long skirt, but Declan wasn't fooled. He knew what she was teasing him with just a few layers of cloth away. She'd deny him just as long as it took for him to do her bidding—until he was a stone corpse or railroaded into the joint.

He dabbed his eel in the wine sauce.

"You're playing me, Molly, and I need some answers." She put down her fork. "That night at the bar. You picked me out, gave me the long come-on look. Why me?"

"I explained this to you. I wasn't staring. I couldn't even see you. The only reason I was sitting in that bar was because I'd been at my optometrist, on the corner, and my eyes were dilated so I couldn't drive home."

"You dressed like that for the optometrist?"

She shrugged, smiling. "A girl likes to look good when she knows she'll be stuck in the city awhile. Heck, Declan, I like to look good all the time. Like my blouse?" She leaned forward. "Don't I look good right now?"

Oh, she wants to play, thought Declan. *We can play.* He leaned forward too and raised his eyebrows. "Define 'fair play.'"

"Declan, don't start." She was trying not to grin, but there it was; and he tried not to grin back, but there it was too.

"A 'fair play' is a mystery in which all the clues are laid out for the reader, so he or she can solve it before the story ends."

Molly leaned back; her blond hair cascaded behind her chair. "They're easy," she said to the ceiling. "You just look for the unusual fact."

Declan kept his shoulders forward. "Like, say, a one-eyed bulldog wanders through."

"Oh yes," she said. Molly glanced off into the restaurant's shadows—this section was empty. Her hands undid her top two buttons, revealing a delta of pink bra with a front clasp.

"And from then on you're just waiting for—I don't know—someone who keeps bacon treats in their left pocket," he said.

"Two paragraphs from the end. Declan, please stop." But she snapped her fingers on the bra clasp, and it disappeared into her blouse, revealing her sternum and two gorgeous crescents of swelling flesh painted in candlelight.

"Hoch?" he said, and her palms fell to rub her rib cage.

"The best. Stop it, Declan."

"I can solve him, sometimes."

Molly's torso snapped forward, her head dipped, and her hair fell like a sheet. When she lifted her chin, her blond locks parted around her nose, and thick strands curtained her eyes. "Liar. You're a bad boy to lie to me, Declan. A bad, bad boy."

He swallowed.

Molly leaned back in her chair and stared at him with her brilliant blue eyes. "Have you ever read," she husked, "*All*"—her hands dipped from her waist and disappeared halfway beneath the table—"*the Way*"—her hands went beneath the tablecloth, her body arced, and he heard her skirt rustle up—"*Down?*"

• • •

THREE MINUTES later Freddie went to check on his last table of the night. Didn't they know the restaurant was about to close? Man, he hated customers. The hot chick was alone, and she looked like she was gonna have a seizure or something. Her head was back, face toward the ceiling, and her hands were fists on either side of her linguini. The guy in the fedora was gone.

"Ma'am," he said, "will the gentleman be returning?" Christ, was her shirt open? She slapped a palm against her chest and spoke through gritted teeth.

"Coming," she said. Freddie thought the table moved. "Soon," she said, dry mouthed. "Coming."

Man, that chick looked nervous as hell, or whatever. Did the table bang against the wall? Freaky stuff, dude, he thought, heading back to fetch the check. Just don't skimp on the tip.

• • •

DECLAN CALLED her the next day. He couldn't help it. The restaurant was fun, but it was like handing a starving man one potato chip. Molly sounded stressed.

"We can't, not now. I have to deal with Alex."

"Are you sleeping with him?" He squeezed the phone.

"Declan, don't do this."

"Answer me!"

"Declan, he's my *husband*. He hasn't done anything wrong. I have. Please be patient. He's having trouble letting go. I'll call you in a few days." And she hung up on him.

Trouble letting go? Was that some kind of code? Molly's husband was back at the mansion, apparently getting all the strawberries and croissants he wanted.

What I need, he thought, is a gun.

Outside of fiction, Declan didn't know anything about guns; but he was popular in the bars around town, so eventually he got introduced to a guy who knew a guy, the end result being a pistol in his pocket. It hung heavy; and all he knew about it was that it was black and had nine bullets in the clip and a safety that went on and off. It was enough.

• • •

"YOU DID *what*?" Kevin the UPS guy was using his huge shoulders to shove boxes into his van.

"Her husband won't go away. He'll come after me."

He glanced down at Declan. "Every time I'm here you're going on about being caught up in some"—he twirled his index finger around his temple—"crazy pulp fiction thing, then you go out and," he whispered, "*buy a gun*?"

"Did you say pulp fiction?"

"What? I read." Kevin lifted a fifty-pound box as if it was tissue paper. "Jane Whitefield. Jack Reacher."

"Deck!" Megan bellowed from inside the warehouse. "Get your ass off the dock and initial these pull sheets."

"Declan, look," Kevin went on, "you ain't a tough guy. You know what happens when someone who ain't a tough guy packs heat? Toss the piece."

"Deck, I will come out there and throw your ass off the loading dock," yelled Megan. "I got work to do!"

Kevin climbed back into his truck and winked at Declan. "I just love your assistant," he said.

• • •

HOURS LATER, near shift end, the shipping phone horn sounded, and Declan picked it up. Molly's voice hit him, breathless and crackling through the relays. "Hey, baby! He's moving out! I'll be at your apartment tonight after Pilates. I'm bringing two DVDs, a bottle of wine, and no underwear. Let's celebrate!"

Declan thought about it from every angle, and from every angle it looked free and clear. Molly was his now; and soon he'd be knocking around that mansion, enjoying her company in the morning, her amazing library in the afternoon, and her body all night. It was perfect.

A little too perfect.

Molly and Alex were *good*. He couldn't even see the setup that one or the other, maybe both of them, had lain down; but he'd be ready for it. When he got home, he changed to go out, slipping his pistol into his jacket pocket.

He walked around the corner and into his favorite gin palace.

After running the usual buy-me-a-drink and let's-throw-darts gauntlet, Declan found a stool at the bar while Danielle poured him a glass of amber relaxation.

"You look snazzy," she said. "For you. Got your girl tonight?"

Declan felt a bump as someone sat on the stool beside him. "Shot of Jameson," the man said, then spoke to Declan. "So you're my wife's new man. She said you'd probably be here." He paused. "Dressed like that. I'm Alex. I wanted to meet you."

Declan turned, and there was the little math professor, very handsome, in a herringbone shirt, bulging to the seams with muscles.

Mother of mercy, he thought, *is this the end of Declan? My gun!* He reached inside his jacket, but the little guy laid a strong hand on his forearm.

"Oh, I've got it." Alex tossed a bill at Danielle and told her to keep it.

"Wow. Thanks. So you're Molly's husband," she said, leaning her boobs on the bar.

"Soon to be former."

"You look sad."

"Well, my marriage is over," he said to her cleavage. "Sure, she bought me a great house in Shillelagh Hills, set me up with a chunk of money; but Molly's so special. A wonderful woman. That's what I came to tell—"

He turned toward Declan, but he'd vanished. There was just an empty stool, turning slowly.

"I think he locked himself in the men's room," said Danielle. She came out from behind the bar. "Declan," she yelled toward the bathrooms, "get out here and talk to the man!"

The door opened a crack, and an arm snaked out, with a pistol at the end. He fired at the ceiling, and the bar erupted in screams. He swung the gun back and forth, and people hit the ground, diving for cover. Alex dropped on top of Danielle. Luckily, her bosom broke his fall. She stared up at him.

"Did you say Shillelagh Hills?"

Alex stood and pulled her to her feet with one smooth tug. "Molly said he was high-strung."

"Oh, he's okay," she said, smoothing her skirt. "He just thinks he's living inside a mystery novel. That's Declan for you."

"Damn," said the short man, looking so sad that Danielle had to pat his head. "They really are perfect for each other."

"Back off, jimmy," Declan yelled; "you ain't sending me to the meat house!"

"Jimmy?" said Alex.

"A short—no offense—steel bar used to force entry," said Danielle, and shook her head. "I've been pouring Declan's drinks for too long. Don't know 'meat house.'"

"Morgue," said Alex. "Been married to Molly seven years."

The bathroom door flew open; and Declan, wild-eyed, dashed out with his pistol in front of him, waving long arcs that caused those back on their feet to dive behind pool tables or headfirst over the bar. Alex put his hands up. Declan grabbed Danielle's arm and yanked her toward the door. "We've gotta blow, right now!"

She twisted her arm and dug in her heels. "I'm working!"

"We're going to Mexico, baby."

"My purse! My tip jar!"

Declan covered the room (you never knew where goons might be lurking) while she skittered to the bar for her things. On the way back she stopped and kissed Alex on the cheek. "Nice to meetcha," she said. "You're a cutie."

Outside, they jogged down the sidewalk and around the corner to where Declan's XK sat gleaming in front of his apartment building. Molly was just arriving, an overnight bag on one shoulder and a grocery sack crooked in her arm. "Stay back!" he roared, and leveled the pistol at her. She rolled her eyes.

"Declan, what the hell are you doing? Put that away." Then she noticed Danielle, and her eyes narrowed. "And drop the bartender."

Declan shoved Danielle into the convertible, keeping his eyes on Molly. "What's in the bag, glamour puss? Arsenic? A garrote?"

"A nice Pinot Noir; *His Kind of Woman*, with Mitchum and Burr; and some handcuffs. Don't piss me off, Declan."

"We're long gone, whistle bait. Scram city I can't see the con yet, but I know it's there, and I'm nobody's fall guy." He moved around to the driver's side.

"You sap. Wherever you go, I am mister I can find you."

"Well, we'll just have to keep moving, zazz girl," he said from over the gun barrel.

"You'd look more hip-hop if you held it sideways," said Danielle.

Alex came jogging up the sidewalk as Declan vaulted into the convertible's driver's seat, his jacket flapping behind him. "Declan, you moron, don't do this," he said, touching Molly's shoulder. "She *loves* you. You're *made* for each other."

"She'll never take me alive!"

Danielle looked at Molly. "I'm sorry about all this...." Then her head flew back because Declan goosed it, laying down rubber, accelerating around the corner and off into the night. The last he saw of that beautiful, deadly woman she was standing on the curb crying, and Alex was handing her a handkerchief.

"They seemed like nice people," Danielle said.

Declan spoke from the side of his mouth: "Don't kid yourself, cupcake. We barely escaped with our lives."

Postscript

Molly and Alex continued with their divorce—their marriage was over.

Megan was informed by the home office that if she wanted Declan's old job, she needed to take some adult-education accounting courses. There she met a really cute, really short math professor who was going through a divorce and seemed lost without a strong woman in his life. When she asked him out, he wanted to know whether or not she read mysteries. "Hell, no," she answered. She currently enjoys living in Shillelagh Hills.

Alex discovered that in his haste to move his belongings out of Molly's mansion, he accidentally took some of her jewelry, which had been inside his wardrobe. He sent it to her immediately.

Molly, lonely and despondent, opened her door the next day to the tallest, cutest, hunkiest example of a deliveryman she'd ever seen. She interrupted her plans for the tracking and destruction of Declan to find out if this guy *really* delivered. She wasn't disappointed. Today she is a best-selling romance author, and even though all her plots seem to involve a heroine jilted by her true love but rescued at the end by a primal hunk of manhood, her fans don't seem to mind.

Kevin quit his job at UPS and moved in with Molly. Today he works several sort-of-grueling hours per year posing for her mass-market covers. He has never once considered fleeing from her in terror.

Declan and Danielle crossed the border into Mexico on a dark, dusty night and kept the Jaguar convertible pointed south. No one at the bar or at Declan's old job ever heard from them again.

Their whereabouts remain a mystery.

JOHN JASPER OWENS lives in the South, where he blogs for T2N, a diabetes magazine, and continues to offer fiction and humor at low, low prices. You'll also find him lurking in the terminal at TQRstories.com, on Twitter under @JJasperO, and at the various ports of call to be found when you Google his full name.

Want to read more by John? You'll find a second story in this book *Strange Attraction* on page 80, or you can check out these links.

Humor: yankeepotroast.org/archives/2008/05/on_a_deadline_t.html

Literary: everydayfiction.com/alice-after-the-mall-by-john-jasper-owens

Speculative: acappellazoo.com/fall095

Third Place

Who Let the Cats Out?

Faye Rapoport DesPres

THERE ARE two things I've never told anyone. But first I should tell you the story from the beginning. Then maybe there's a chance you'll believe me. Let me back up a few months so I can start with what happened the day after the fire.

I was standing alone in the old Victorian house that had once belonged to Jane S. Dooley. It was hard to remember what the living room had looked like before the fire engulfed it the previous night. The morning sun was streaming in through the bay window, which looked out over the front yard and the neatly trimmed bushes that separated the yard from the sidewalk. But everything inside—the mantel above the fireplace, the wallpaper with its delicate floral pattern, the wood floors, the furniture, the shattered flower vase—were charred and stained, blackened and peeling, covered with ashes.

I had no idea if I would be able to recover the key, and for reasons I couldn't have understood at the time, this thought inspired a feeling of panic. The floor-to-ceiling bookcase had fallen over during the fire and cracked into several pieces. Dozens of books, soaked from the hoses of the firefighters, were scattered across the floor. Some had lost their covers and were partially burned; others had singed pages that curled toward their bindings.

I spotted one edge of an old hardcover beneath what remained of the wooden coffee table. The cover of the book had been a prominent red, making it easy to spot in the sunlight. I knelt on the floor, pulled the book from underneath one of the table's legs, and brushed a light layer of ash off the cover. The book was the only thing in the room that had been mine: *Crime and Punishment* by Fyodor Dostoyevsky. I opened it and saw that the key was still there, taped inside the front cover. I sighed with relief. Then I loosened the tape, removed the key, and slipped it into my pocket.

"Adalyn?"

Slamming the book shut, I stood up so quickly that I slipped on the debris that covered the damp floor. My assistant, Billy, stepped through the doorway and caught my arm before I fell. Embarrassed, I thanked him, clutching the book to my chest with one hand while I used the other to wipe the soot off the knees of my cargo pants.

"It's a mess, isn't it?" I said, looking up at Billy, who was eight inches taller than me.

Billy smiled sadly. The apartment had been his home for nearly a year, since he'd accepted the job of assistant director of the Jane S. Dooley Cat Shelter. This rent-free apartment came with the job. The shelter's office was at the other end of a hallway outside the living-room door, and three upstairs rooms served as living space for ten cats waiting for homes with local families. Another twenty cats, the ones who got along well in a larger group, were housed cage-free inside a spacious cement Cat House that had been built behind the old Victorian at the end of the driveway.

Loose jeans and a black t-shirt hung on Billy's slim frame; and his short hair, dyed jet-black, was messy or spiked with some kind of hair product, I could never tell which. One of his eyebrows was pierced, and he had somehow found the time—even on a morning like this—to apply the touch of dark eyeliner that always made his blue eyes stand out. When people first met Billy, especially people living in our small Vermont town, they usually raised their eyebrows and assumed all the wrong things. They never suspected that Billy had a heart of gold and was also a musical genius. He could play Mozart as well as he belted out the grunge rock tunes he performed with his band, Black Buzzard, on Friday and Saturday nights. The job at the shelter was just a way for Billy to make money and have a free place to live while he finished his master's thesis on music education.

Now that free place to live, the apartment inside the house that Jane S. Dooley had left to Pineville as a cat shelter a hundred and fifty years before, had been torched.

Billy glanced around the room. I knew that he'd weathered worse than this; his mother had died when Billy was young, leaving his father to raise Billy and run their horse ranch on his own. It was one of the things Billy and I had in common even though, at thirty-four, I was ten years older. We both had been raised by single fathers. I had returned to town two years ago to be with my dad before he died, thinking I'd only stay long enough after he was gone to close up the house and sell it. My life had been at a crossroads at the time; I'd been living in Colorado, and the software company I worked for as an office manager had been sold to a larger company. When the director of the Jane S. Dooley Cat Shelter announced that she was getting married and moving out of town, I decided to stay and apply for the job.

"You're taking this pretty well," I told Billy, trying to convince myself that I also spoke for me. At exactly the same time, our eyes strayed toward the piano that Billy had moved into the apartment with the rest of his things. It had been a shiny brown upright with gleaming black and white keys, but now it was covered with soot. It had visible water damage, and a large dark spot was burned into the side that stood closest to the window. A flaming rag soaked in gasoline had landed next to the piano when it crashed through the window, which the firemen had temporarily boarded up.

"It's insured," Billy said with a shrug. "I'm safe; the cats are safe; Michelle is safe. That's all that matters." Michelle, a local nursing student whose smile lit up the shelter whenever she came by, was Billy's girlfriend.

It's not as if we didn't know that a certain element in town had been grumbling about the shelter. That element consisted mostly of Doris Nelson, the woman who had moved into the house next door five years before. She was joined in her disapproval by the town's mayor, Henry Carbunkle. Mayor Henry—as I call him because he hated what he referred to as my "unbelievable impertinence"—had, over the previous year, made it his personal mission to shut down the shelter. I had no idea why; Henry, who is in his midforties, has lived in Pineville all his life and has been mayor for the last ten years. He'd never had a problem with the shelter before. We suspected that it had something to do with Doris, who complained about everything from Billy's piano playing, which she claimed she could hear from inside her house, to what time we rolled the garbage bins out to the curb every Sunday and whether or not our driveway was plowed in the winter. She had installed a tall wooden fence between her driveway and the shelter's, and that was fine with us. The less we saw of Doris Nelson, the better.

Unfortunately for Doris and Mayor Henry, most of Pineville's small population love and support the shelter. Many local families have found their beloved pets at Dooley, or turn to us for help when an elderly relative passes away and leaves a cat in need, or when someone finds a hungry stray by the side of the road.

"Should you be in here, Addy?"

Billy and I both turned at the sound of the familiar voice. Mayor Henry was standing in the doorway between the hall and the living room. I wondered why he felt he had the right just to walk into my office, never mind down the hall to Billy's apartment.

"Tom said we could come in," I said, referring to the local fire chief. I stood up a little straighter and made sure my voice was firm. "Why are *you* here?" I asked.

He ignored my question. "I imagine this place is a goner," he said, raising his eyebrows as he looked around the room. He was six foot four and, in my opinion, an overgrown bully. He wore a cowboy hat and boots as if he lived in Texas and was a sheriff instead of mayor.

"Actually," I said, "this was the only room damaged by the fire. There's just water damage in the kitchen and bedroom. The office is fine, and the upstairs is fine." He shrugged. Getting angry, I added, "And I'm sure you'll be happy to hear that Billy saved all the cats who live upstairs. You do realize that Billy was in here last night when someone threw that flaming rag soaked in gasoline through the window. He could have been killed."

I noticed a flash of surprise in the mayor's eyes. "I thought you played with your band on Saturday nights," he said.

"Oh, did you?" I asked, suddenly suspicious. I took a step toward the mayor, and Billy put a cautioning hand on my arm. "Why would you keep track of Billy's nights out, Mayor Henry?"

I might stand five foot two and weigh all of 115 pounds, and my mane of brown curls might make me appear somewhat childish, but everyone in Pineville knows I'm no pushover. Once, in the tenth grade, I punched a kid in the face when he made a snide remark about a boy who didn't have a lot of friends. My father promised the principal I would be punished, but when we got in the car to drive home, he held up a hand and gave me a high five.

"I'm only saying I had no idea Billy was home last night," the mayor said, involuntarily taking a step backward. He had recovered from his surprise and was on the offensive. "Had I known, I would have asked if he was okay."

"Right, just like you asked about the cats," I said. "Whoever did this, even if they thought they were doing it when Billy was out, must have known they were going to kill ten innocent cats."

The mayor's face turned to stone. "Well, 'whoever did this' might not have even known this place is a cat shelter," he replied smoothly.

"And where were you last night, Mayor Henry?" I asked. "Your life's mission for the past year has been to shut down the shelter."

"You have to be kidding," he said, furious now. "I'm the mayor of this town, and I have better things to do than try to burn down someone's house or a cat shelter. I spent the evening with my wife, in fact, at Buddy's Grill and the cinema center in Layton."

"Will the police be able to find out who did this?" Billy asked, interrupting our heated exchange. He gestured toward the piano. "There's been a lot of damage; and the truth is, sir, that I *could* have been killed, and the cats could have been too."

The mayor shrugged again. "It was probably some teenager on a dare," he said. "I'm sure Sam will do his best to find out." Sam Reynolds was the local police chief. Sam and Henry were thick as thieves; I had no doubt that if Henry Carbunkle was behind this fire, his buddy Sam wouldn't do anything about it.

"Well, good luck to you," Mayor Henry said before turning on his boot heel. He walked back down the hall and out of the house. The office door slammed.

Billy turned to look at me. "Look, Addy," he said, his voice sounding tired, "I appreciate the invitation to stay at your house while this gets sorted out, but I'm perfectly happy to sleep on the floor of the office."

"No way," I said. "I'm going to sleep in that office tonight and every night until they find out who did this, and until we get the apartment back in shape."

Billy nodded and walked toward the entrance to the bedroom so he could pack up some clothes to take to my house. But before he left the living room, he stopped and turned toward me.

"Addy," he said, "there's something I should tell you."

"What?" I asked.

"Last night, before the fire, something woke me up."

"What?" I asked again. "Did you hear people talking, or a car outside the house?"

Billy hesitated. "No, it was the piano. Someone was playing the piano."

"What?" I asked for the third time. "Who?"

"I don't know. But I heard the piano, just a few notes. The sound woke me out of a deep sleep, and then I heard it again. I got up and came in here to see who it was, thinking maybe Michelle had come over. But when I got here, there was no one. The piano was just sitting there. And then a few seconds later I heard a crash, and that burning rag came flying through the window." He shook his head as if he still couldn't believe what had happened.

"The flames moved so fast," he said apologetically. "The curtains caught fire. I tried to pull them down and stomp on them, but it didn't work. The fire just kept spreading. I ran into the kitchen and grabbed the fire extinguisher; but by the time I got back, half the room was up in flames, so I grabbed my cell and called 911 while I ran upstairs to get the cats."

Billy hesitated again before continuing. "And it was weird, Addy; someone had opened all the doors upstairs and let the cats out of their rooms. All ten of them were in the hall near their carriers. I think that's why I was able to save them all."

We were both silent for a moment, remembering the hours that had followed that call: the sirens, the chaos, the worry about the animals locked in the Cat House. The terrible fear that comes with loss.

I was still holding my copy of *Crime and Punishment*. I patted my pocket subtly, feeling for the key. It was there.

"That's strange," I said. "Maybe some jokester sneaked into the house before lighting the place on fire. It doesn't really make sense. But if he—or she—comes back, I'll be waiting."

• • •

THE JANE S. Dooley Cat Shelter was established in 1863 by an elderly Pineville resident who had inherited her father's fortune and had no close relatives on whom to bequeath it. She had been married as a young woman, but her husband died of a terrible fever, and she never remarried or had children. According to local legend, Jane used to stroll up and down Main Street on warm summer days, delighting the town's children by handing out candy. She started a women's book club at the tiny town library and gave generously to neighbors in need. But her passion was animals, especially cats. And when she died at the ripe old age of ninety-seven, she left her entire fortune, including the large Victorian house she had called home all her life, in a trust for the establishment of a sheltering home for cats.

The residents of Pineville, mourning their elderly neighbor, founded the cat shelter that Jane had envisioned. And no one had ever had a problem with the arrangement until Doris Nelson moved next door and began her insidious campaign to close down the shelter. Of course Doris had been the first person I wanted to blame as flames threatened to devour Jane Dooley's house. I had demanded that Dave Miller, a local policeman who was keeping neighbors away from the fire and whom I knew I could trust, knock on Doris' door to find out if she was home. But Doris, it turned out, had been visiting relatives in Boston. She couldn't have started the fire.

The alarm clock I had placed on the floor of the office glowed in the darkness. 1:04 A.M. The office was cold, and I was huddled on the floor in my sleeping bag, wide-awake. October nights can be frigid in Vermont, but I didn't like to turn up the heat. I was dressed in a sweatshirt and sweat pants inside the sleeping bag.

I had spent the evening working in the office, sorting through the paper-work required to file a claim with the shelter's insurance company. At 10:30 P.M. I had attempted to turn in because my eyes were hurting and I could no longer concentrate. I pulled on my jacket and went outside to do a final check of the Cat House. All nineteen residents were sleeping in cat beds on the specially designed windowsills, nibbling at the kibble that had been left out in bowls, or chasing one another around the floor in the dark. When I left I made sure the door was locked, and then I paused next to the shed that backed up to the fence just outside the entrance. The moon was almost full, and the back of the shed was in shadow. It was there, behind the shed, that I had found Jocko on that terrible night.

Jocko. He had been a handsome, scarred, gray-and-white tom when he'd appeared in the driveway a few days after I'd started my job at the shelter. He was huge—twenty pounds—and tough, judging by his ears, which were all chewed up, and by the scar on his upper lip that turned his expression into a permanent scowl. It was clear that he had been living on the street for a long time. But he must have decided that he'd had enough, because he had marched straight up to the office door and strolled inside that day. He proceeded, over the next two years, to become the shelter mascot and the most beloved feline on the property. He spent his days lounging in the office and his evenings sleeping peacefully on Billy's bed after I had convinced the Board of Directors to let me hire Billy and moved him into the apartment.

Jocko was protective of the cats who arrived at the office hungry, scared, and in search of a new home. He nudged and groomed young kittens if they cried. Every morning when I arrived at work, Jocko left Billy's apartment, jumped up and unlatched the door from the hallway, sauntered into the office, and sat down in front of me, hoping to be petted.

Jocko had been wearing a collar with a tag when he showed up, but no one in town claimed ownership, even though neighbors reported spotting the big cat roaming the streets near the shelter for years. The tag he'd worn was fancier than normal cat tags: thick and heart shaped and made of silver. I was sure he must have belonged to someone. But whenever I tried to remove the collar so I could look more closely at the tag, Jocko hissed, bared his teeth, and unsheathed his claws—behavior he never exhibited at any other time. So the collar remained around Jocko's neck until the tragic events of July 4.

It had been 6:30 A.M. and raining when Jocko had raced past my legs and out the door as I arrived at the office to do some work I had planned to finish on the holiday. He ran down the driveway and behind the shed, and before I could get to him, I'd heard something that sounded like a terrified dog yelping. The next thing I knew I was frozen in horror, because a coyote had emerged from behind the shed. The animal ran right past me up the driveway toward the street, and I raced behind the shed, calling Jocko's name. I found him lying on his side in the dirt behind the shed with blood seeping from his neck. Next to him was a tiny white kitten, not more than a few weeks old, cowering against the shed, untouched. I realized in an instant what had happened: Jocko had attacked the coyote to save the kitten. I fell to my knees and begged Jocko to hold on so I could get him to the emergency vet. But he took a few last breaths, heaved a sigh, and died right there in my arms.

The death of any cat breaks my heart, but I had never taken a loss as badly as I took Jocko's. Billy had found me sobbing with the cat in my arms, and we buried him later that day in the yard in front of the Cat House. Before we laid him in his grave inside his favorite bed, I took off the collar that he'd never let me touch. As I fingered the tag, I noticed that it had a seam and might even open like a locket; but in my grief I didn't have the heart to look more closely. The next day I bought a small gold box and locked the collar inside it. I never told anyone about the box, which I placed in the bottom drawer of my desk at the office, or about the key taped inside the cover of one of my favorite books, *Crime and Punishment*. I stored the book on the bookshelf in Billy's apartment so I would have access to the key if I ever decided to open the box.

After the fire I realized how close I had come to never being able to find out what was inside the cat tag. So after Billy went to my house, I removed the key from my pocket, pulled the box from the drawer, and opened it.

The box was empty.

Sleep continued to elude me. I couldn't stop thinking about the fire, or the fact that Billy could have been killed, the cats who had been helpless upstairs, and Mayor Henry's visit. I went over and over our conversation with the mayor in my head, trying to pick out anything that would indicate that he was responsible. And finally, when my thoughts had raced in circles for so long that they had to land somewhere, I thought about Jocko's empty box, which was now sitting on the floor next to the alarm clock. Twenty minutes had passed since I'd last looked at the clock.

And that's when I heard it.

Plink, plink, plink.

At first it was one note, then two, then a slow crescendo as someone ran his or her fingers up the piano keys. I grabbed the flashlight and struggled up and out of my sleeping bag. Trying to control my ragged breath, I crept on tiptoes through the door that led to the hallway and made my way toward the apartment. The door to the living room was open, even though I was certain I had closed it after Billy had left. I clicked off the flashlight and moved quietly toward the doorway, guided by a sliver of moonlight shining through it. Peeking into the room, I looked toward the piano, but no one was there. The piano sat silent in the empty room, which was cast in a bluish light by the moon. I walked into the apartment and over to the bay window, listening for footsteps or any other sound and keeping my flashlight off. Nothing. No one. Confused, I stared out the window.

Something moved behind the bushes near the street, and suddenly I saw what looked like a human being running down the street, away from the house. I dashed into the foyer, unbolted the front door, and raced down the walkway to the sidewalk, forgetting that it was freezing outside and that my feet were bare. Staring in the direction in which I had seen the person running, I saw nothing but darkness past the streetlamp on the corner.

Whoever it was had disappeared.

• • •

TWO WEEKS later on a Thursday night, the meeting of the town council was a mob scene. Every seat in the town hall meeting room was taken; and men, women, and children were lined up along the walls and milling around the hallway just outside the double doors. Mayor Henry rapped his wooden gavel hard against the podium in a vain attempt to quiet the angry crowd. His wife, Anne, was sitting in the front row with their two children, twelve-year-old Ricky and ten-year-old Janine. She stared straight ahead, and the children hung their heads and looked at the floor.

The mayor had just announced that the Jane Dooley house had been condemned. The insurance company had mysteriously turned down our claim, saying they suspected that the fire had been a ploy to get money for the shelter by collecting on the policy. I was outraged at this implication, which in any case made no sense. But to make matters worse, the mayor had decided that because there were no other locations in town suitable for a cat shelter, the shelter would have to be shut down. Rumors had been circulating for days that this was his plan, and supporters of the shelter had vowed to pack the meeting and make their feelings known.

"What about the cats?" someone yelled from the middle of the crowd.

"They'll be sent to shelters in nearby towns," the mayor said, "and if any are left without a place to go, they'll have to be put down."

There was an angry roar from the crowd. I was shaking with rage; and Billy and Joanne Watkins, two of our most loyal volunteers, each pulled at one of my arms as I stood at a microphone stand that had been placed in front of the audience, shouting.

"What do you mean, condemned?" I shouted. "One room has smoke and fire damage. The rest of the building is sound. What are you talking about? You'll harm one hair on one cat over my dead body!"

"According to the town inspector—" the mayor began, but his comments were drowned out by more shouts from the crowd.

Billy dragged me back to my seat at the end of the seventh row, where I collapsed onto my chair, uncertain if I would be able to stop the angry tears that were springing to my eyes. I couldn't believe what was happening.

"Who set the fire?" someone yelled from the crowd, and the question was echoed by a chorus of other voices. "They need to be held responsible!"

"And who got into the house and let the cats out from their upstairs rooms?" someone shouted from the back of the room. "Who knew that the fire was going to be set?"

The mayor banged his gavel on the podium again until the noise had subsided just enough for him to say, "The police have not found a suspect in the fire. It is the assumption of the insurance company that someone involved with the shelter did the deed to make money, which would explain why the cats were let out." Anything he said after that was drowned out by angry objections.

Back at the shelter an hour after the meeting, at least twenty volunteers gathered under the outside light that hung above the door of the Cat House. They were wrapped in jackets, and wore gloves and hats. Everyone was still angry.

"There's no way we're going to let this happen," Joanne said.

"It's crazy, anyway," said Emily Leblanc, owner of the local breakfast spot, Toffee Coffee, and a long-time volunteer at the shelter. "Why shut the whole place down even if the house is condemned? The Cat House is still fine, and we could always rebuild."

"There's absolutely no reason to condemn that house," said Eric Horner, a local handyman who did repairs at the shelter and who had recently built an outdoor enclosure for the cats. "The structure is fine. Heck, most of the house is perfectly fine. This is a conspiracy if I ever saw one, and when we find out who started this and who set that fire, there's going to be hell to pay."

I had been sitting in the office, exhausted from my fury, trying to figure out what to say to everyone. When I finally joined the group, Joanne turned to me and said, "If the insurance company won't pay, we can fix the house ourselves."

"There's no way we could raise enough money," I said. The last few hours had drained my fighting spirit, and the reality of what we were facing had kicked in. "Our operating budget doesn't include a line item for repairs, and this is a major job. The shelter is barely making ends meet as it is."

"I'll give up my salary," Billy said. He was shivering, and his hands were stuffed in his pockets. Michelle put her arms around him and leaned her head against his chest.

"That's sweet of you, Billy," I said, and I was surprised that my voice cracked when I said it. My throat felt tight, and I forced myself to take a deep breath. "But I would never let you do that, and it wouldn't be enough, anyway. Believe me, I would give up my salary too."

A young girl standing next to her mother in the group started to cry. Her mom, Audrey Benson, leaned down and gave her daughter a hug. "It's okay, honey," she said. "Let's go into the Cat House and visit Pepper."

The girl sniffed but looked up hopefully. "Can we take Pepper home now, Mom?" she asked.

Audrey looked at me, and I smiled weakly. I knew that her family already had three cats. "Yes, sweetie, I think so," Audry said. "I think it's time for Pepper to come home."

I nodded at Billy. He unlocked the door of the Cat House and followed them inside.

After everyone had left, I climbed once again into my sleeping bag in the office and finally let myself cry. Occasionally I heard the swish of a car as it passed by the house on the street. As always, I'd closed all the window blinds. There was no moon that night, and the room would have been pitch-black if not for the red neon numbers on the alarm clock. The first time I looked over at them it was midnight. By 1:00 A.M. I had exhausted myself by crying, and my tears had dried. By 2:00 A.M. I was falling asleep.

Plink, plink, plink.

Three notes on the piano. My eyes flew open.

Plink, plink. Two more.

I was out of my sleeping bag in seconds, the flashlight in my hand. I crept down the hall toward the living room and again was surprised that the apartment door was open. When I reached it, I swung the door open and stepped right into the room, sweeping the beam of my flashlight from one wall to the other. Finally, I pointed it toward the keys on the piano.

Nothing. No one. But then I heard something: footsteps from somewhere past the foyer. I sighed with relief, thinking Billy must have decided to sleep in his room one last time. I crossed the room and entered the foyer.

The front door to the house was wide-open. I must have forgotten to bolt it shut that morning when I'd been arguing with the fire inspector in front of the house. Suddenly on guard, I looked toward Billy's bedroom on the opposite end of the foyer and saw what looked like a hooded figure moving around in the shadows. I held my breath, hoping whoever it was hadn't seen or heard me. Then I heard a quiet click and saw a small flame burst to life, illuminating a man who was standing near the bed. It looked like he was holding a rag in one hand.

"Hey! Stop that!" I yelled, turning on my flashlight; and the man dropped the rag and took a few steps out of the room toward me, trying to shade his eyes against the light.

I stared in surprise. The man in the hood—a hooded sweatshirt, it turned out—wasn't a man at all. He was a twelve-year-old boy named Jimmy Carbunkle.

"Jimmy?" I said in surprise. The boy dropped the lighter and dashed toward the front door; but I caught him by his hood, and he slid and fell backward.

"What are you doing in here?" I asked while he struggled to break free. "Are you here to... Are you the one who... Did your father put you up to this? Did you come back to finish the job?"

"Let me go!" Jimmy sobbed as he tried to wriggle out of his sweatshirt.

A police siren had started wailing and was getting closer to the house; and by the time Jimmy got the sweatshirt off and broke free from my grasp, a squad car with revolving lights had pulled to the curb. Dave Miller, illuminated by the streetlamp on the corner, leaped out of the car and raced up the walkway. He stopped short when he saw Jimmy standing at the front door.

"I parked at the end of the street after the meeting," Dave said when he saw the confused look on my face. "I was worried there would be trouble. I thought I saw some movement a few minutes ago, so I drove a little closer; and when I saw the flashlight go on inside the house, I put on the siren and pulled up." He looked at Jimmy. "So who do we have here? Jimmy Carbunkle?"

The boy, who was shaking now, continued to sob. Dave stopped me with a gentle hand when I reached down to pick up the lighter that Jimmy had dropped. "Evidence," he said, and I left it where it was.

"As for you, young man, it looks like I'll be giving you a ride down to the station."

Jimmy wiped his eyes with one arm and started to hiccup.

"Wait," I said. "Before you go..." I turned toward Jimmy, who refused to look at me. "Jimmy, tell me why you did this. Why would you want to hurt the shelter and the cats we keep here? I know your father doesn't like Dooley very much, but why would you get involved?"

Jimmy sniffed and stared at the floor. Dave and I waited. Finally the boy said, "Mom and Dad keep arguing about this place. Dad says he wants to get rid of it because that new lady, Miss Davis, promised to help him get reelected if he did. My mom was really upset. She said she was tired of my dad pan...pan..."

"Pandering," I said softly.

Jimmy hiccupped again. "Yes, pandering to people who he likes and who can help him, or something like that. She said she knew that my dad was in love with Miss Davis, and she was sick of it all and was going to leave him. She's said she would leave him before, but this time I think she meant it."

"But why would you try to burn down the shelter?" I asked.

"Dad said some bad things about Billy, about how he was a poor role model for the kids in the town anyway and how he played with some kind of crazy band on the weekends. He made jokes about his hair and his makeup and stuff. I just wanted it all to go away. I wanted it to stop, for everything to go back to the way it was before Miss Davis and Billy moved here. I figured since Billy was out of the house on the weekends I could just...just..." His voice faded.

"I think you'd better save the rest until your father comes to the station," Dave said. "Let's go."

He led Jimmy down the walkway toward his patrol car. Just before they reached the sidewalk, Jimmy turned back to look at me.

"I didn't know there were cats in the house," he said. "I thought they were all out back. I didn't know. I never meant to hurt them. I'm sorry!" And he started to cry again.

Dave put a firm hand on his shoulder and opened the back door of the squad car before ushering Jimmy inside. They drove off into the night.

It wasn't until after they were gone that it occurred to me: If Jimmy hadn't known there were cats upstairs, he hadn't been the one who had let them out of their rooms.

· · ·

A WEEK had passed since Jimmy had made a full confession. Ann Carbunkle had packed her bags and left her husband, who had been keeping a very low profile. The local paper printed at least twenty letters to the editor calling for the mayor's resignation—not because his son had been implicated in a crime or even because of the whispers that he had been having an affair, but because an investigation had unearthed a conspiracy between the mayor and the town's police chief and fire inspector to close down the shelter.

Still, our problems weren't over. The insurance company had agreed to review our claim, but the appeal process was going to take months. We had to repair the main building so that Billy could move back in and there could be twenty-four-hour supervision at the shelter, a town requirement. Our volunteers had put up donation boxes in every store they could think of and were brainstorming about organizing fund-raising events. But I couldn't think of any way we could get the money we needed in the short time we had to save the building and the shelter.

I had continued to sleep on the floor of the office so we would be complying with the town's twenty-four-hour requirement. I just didn't feel right making Billy do it. But my back was beginning to hurt, winter was getting closer, and I knew I couldn't sleep there forever. I lay awake in my sleeping bag late almost every night, trying to come up with a solution. But as the days wore on and no answer presented itself, I began, in my exhaustion, to consider whether it might be best to focus my energies on finding homes for our remaining cats and preparing to close down, at least temporarily.

Late one night I was running through the names of the cats in my mind as the light of the returning moon peeked through the blinds. "Dave might take Midget," I was saying to myself. "Joanne might open her home to one more. I know she loves little Simba."

And then I heard it again.

Plink, plink, plink.

I thought I might be dreaming in my half-asleep state, but this time the notes kept coming. *Plink, plink, plink, plink, plink*—up the piano keyboard and down again. It was 3:00 A.M. I crawled out of my sleeping bag, picked up my flashlight, and walked through the office into the hallway and toward the apartment.

The door was open again.

I closed my eyes, shook my head a few times, and looked again. Yes, it was open. And this time I could still hear the piano. *Plink, plink, plink,* faster and faster.

"Billy?" I called out. Silence.

"Is this some kind of joke?" I asked in a loud voice as I pushed the door open and walked hesitantly into the room. The music stopped, and it took a moment for the beam of my flashlight to find the piano. I thought I saw something move. Was it a shadow from the branch of a tree outside? Or was it the flick of a tail? I walked over to the piano, but the window was closed and no one was there. Then I stopped dead in my tracks. Something was lying across the piano keys.

Jocko's collar.

I stood motionless for a moment, barely able to breathe. Finally I moved forward and picked up the collar. It was time. I opened the locket, and something small and shiny glinted in the beam of light.

• • •

IT WASN'T until the diamond was appraised two days later that I was able to announce that the Jane S. Dooley Cat Shelter had been saved.

• • •

HERE ARE the two things I've never told anyone. The first one is this: Before I placed *Crime and Punishment* on the new bookshelf Eric built when the apartment was fully renovated, something fell from the pages onto the floor. It was an old photograph of Jane S. Dooley. When I looked closely at the picture, I noticed she was wearing something around her neck. It was a thick, heart-shaped locket, probably silver.

The second thing is this: When I left the apartment on the night I found the diamond, I paused at the door and locked back into the room. I swept the beam of my flashlight from one wall to the other, letting it rest first on the piano and then on the floor. And there, for the first time, I saw something in the soot that I had never noticed before. There were paw prints leading from the door to the piano and back.

And then I recalled that on the night of the fire I had also seen paw prints on the staircase leading to the upstairs rooms.

Both times, the paw prints were gone by the next morning.

FAYE RAPOPORT DESPRES earned her MFA from the Solstice Creative Writing Program at Pine Manor College. Her debut book, *Message From a Blue Jay: Love, Loss, and a Writer's Journey Home*, will be published by Buddhapuss Ink in Spring 2014. Her essays, fiction, poetry, interviews, and reviews have appeared in a variety of literary journals and magazines. She lives in the Boston area with her husband, Jean-Paul, and four cats. Faye is @FayeRapoDesPres on Twitter, and her website is fayerapoportdespres.com.

Negotiate in Good Faith

Cyndy E. Lively

AS THE top hostage negotiator at Lindstrom Security, Emma Lindstrom was used to middle-of-the-night journeys to countries where kidnapping was a business pursuit. A small town in New Hampshire wasn't a place she'd ever imagined her skills would be needed. At four o'clock on a crisp September morning, she flung the bag she kept packed for just such emergencies into the passenger seat of her BMW roadster and headed for Teterboro Airport. The insurance company might wince at the cost of the emergency charter, but it was the only hope Emma had of arriving at the client's home in time.

Like many executives who travel abroad, William Titcomb carried kidnap-and-ransom insurance. The policy stipulated that in the event of an incident, Lindstrom Security must be notified in order for coverage to remain in effect. Titcomb was CEO of one of the largest wood product firms in New Hampshire. His son, Nathan, had received a call just after midnight from someone claiming to have Titcomb imprisoned at a remote location in White Mountain National Forest. A ransom hadn't been demanded during the initial conversation, but a dazed Titcomb had pleaded with his son to stay the hell away from the FBI.

The Titcomb family estate occupied several hundred wooded acres on the outskirts of Plymouth. Sunrise was still almost an hour away when Emma drove the rental SUV through an open gateway onto a narrow ribbon of asphalt. Tree limbs brushed the vehicle's windows, forcing her to slow to a crawl. She was all too aware of time slipping quickly away.

Trees gave way to a manicured lawn. The drive widened to a generous car park. Floodlights illuminated the front of a white colonial saltbox that Emma was sure belonged on the historic registry.

Nathan Titcomb greeted her at the front door with a moist handshake and alcohol on his breath. Approaching forty, the man had the look of a college athlete gone to seed. The condition of his pupils had her wondering what other substances besides alcohol he'd ingested over the last several hours.

"Have you had any further contact with the kidnapper?" Emma asked as she followed him through rooms furnished with antiques as old as the house.

"Not since the first call."

Their final destination was a kitchen filled with sleek stainless steel appliances that clashed with the period table where her host collapsed onto a chair. A nearly empty bottle of Macallan rested beside a full tumbler. He raised the glass, drained it, and returned it to the table.

Emma scanned the room. "Where's the telephone, Mr. Titcomb? I need to set up my equipment before the kidnapper calls again."

Bleary eyes squinted up at her. "You're going to trace the call? The guy said I'd better not try anything, or he'd kill my father."

"I'm going to record our conversations." She spotted a cordless phone partially buried under a pile of junk mail on the kitchen counter and went in search of the charging station. "As I told you when we talked, Lindstrom Security doesn't have the capabilities of a law enforcement agency. We strongly recommend bringing in the FBI."

"You can't do that." Even in his alcohol-induced haze, the man appeared truly terrified.

Emma located the phone connection and pulled the recording device from her bag. "Then let me do my job."

• • •

THE VOICE echoed from the speakerphone, distorted by a mechanical device. So much for obtaining a voiceprint they could use if they managed to catch this guy. Emma repeated her demand to speak with William Titcomb. Hostage Negotiation 101: Always confirm the well-being of the client. While paying a ransom for a dead body was certainly considered poor form, so was allowing a client to suffer if it could be prevented.

"The man's chained to a tree. I'm not babysitting him."

"Mr. Titcomb needs food and water. Call me back when you go to him." Emma had explained her involvement as a security operative at Titcomb Industries, taking the call because the son was too distraught to speak to the kidnapper.

"A dead man doesn't need to eat and drink, and that's what he'll be if Nathan doesn't do exactly what I say. Put him on the phone."

"Nathan's not in any condition to speak with you right now." Stalling was one of the tools in a negotiator's repertoire; so was making the kidnapper believe the negotiator was on his side. "I'm trying to help here. Give him time to recover from the shock."

"You mean give him time to sober up. Twenty-two years and nothing's changed; the bastard's still looking for courage in a bottle. Tell him he's got until noon, then the clock starts ticking."

The sky—visible through the lace-paneled curtains on the kitchen windows—had lightened from pitch-black to pewter. Noon was less than five hours away. "I'll do the best I can, but I have to speak with Mr. Titcomb. At his age, the stress could be too much. He needs to hear that we'll do what it takes to insure his release."

The silence that followed had Emma worried that the kidnapper had disconnected. Then she heard a crackle of static that could have been a sigh. "I'll call back at noon. You can talk to Titcomb then. Tell Nathan, if he wants to see dear old dad again, he'd better be ready to follow instructions."

• • •

EMMA'S ASSERTION that Nathan wasn't up to talking to the kidnapper hadn't *just* been a stalling tactic. After four cups of strong coffee and more than an hour of questioning, she'd gotten little more than a string of grunts in reply.

"How the hell would I know who it is?" Nathan sat at the kitchen table, head cradled on his arms. "The voice sounded like something out of a horror movie."

Emma shoved the man's shoulders against the back of the chair and held him in place, barely controlling the urge to throttle him. "We don't have time for this, Nathan. I need to know what's going on here. The kidnapper hasn't mentioned a word about a ransom, and obviously it's someone you know."

He pushed her hands away and regarded her with a glare. "No one I know would have any reason to kidnap my father."

At least he'd sobered up enough to feel an emotion besides the self-pity she'd dealt with since her arrival. "Twenty-two years. Someone from the past?" Before the man shifted his gaze from hers, Emma saw the horror in his eyes. "You have to talk to me, Nathan. Your father's life depends on making this person believe that keeping him safe will achieve the desired result. That's how this works."

• • •

THE CALL came precisely at noon. The kidnapper kept his promise and put Titcomb on the phone.

"This is Emma Lindstrom, head of security at the Laconia plant." She hoped Titcomb had the presence of mind not to dispute her assertion that she worked for him.

"Tell him we'll pay whatever it takes." In spite of his age—Titcomb was nearing seventy—his voice was steady and had the tone of a man used to being in command.

"Are you all right, Mr. Titcomb?"

"I'm chained to a tree like a dog. Do you call that all right?"

"Have you been given something to eat and drink?"

"Do a couple of candy bars and a bottle of water count?"

"Are you warm enough?" The overnight low had been in the forties. Emma had no idea what the man was wearing.

"What the hell does that have to do with getting me out of here? Everybody's got a price. Find out what this bastard's is and pay it."

One of the ways a negotiator worked to insure the safety of a hostage was to encourage a positive relationship with the kidnapper. Titcomb wasn't making Emma's job any easier. "There hasn't been a ransom demand. Has he told you what he wants?"

Titcomb's voice was replaced by the eerie screech of the kidnapper. "That's enough; now it's my turn. Put Nathan on the line."

Emma handed the phone to the man sitting beside her and listened with mounting alarm to the kidnapper's demands.

• • •

"WHY THE hell didn't you tell me hours ago? You must have at least suspected James Elliott was the kidnapper."

Emma wrestled the bottle of Scotch from Nathan's hands while he regarded her with the petulant frown of a two-year-old.

"How was I supposed to know he'd gotten out of prison?"

"Is Elliott telling the truth?"

"The guy's a convicted murderer. No one's going to believe a word he says."

"That isn't what I asked, Nathan."

"Your job's to pay the ransom and get my father back."

"He isn't asking for money. I can't negotiate for something Elliott doesn't want."

"What's that supposed to mean?"

"It means you either do what he says, or we come up with something the man's willing to take in its place. If he's telling the truth, I don't have any idea what that might be."

Emma left the stunned man slumped in an armchair in the great room and stepped out onto the lush lawn in front of the house. The warmth of the afternoon sun did little to erase the chill that gripped her. The fewer people who knew about the negotiations the better, but she didn't have time to stumble around in the dark. Pressing the speed-dial number for the CEO of Lindstrom Security's private line, she willed her grandfather to answer.

"Nils Lindstrom."

"It's Emma. I need your help."

He listened in silence while she spoke, then ticked off the pertinent points: "Police reports on the murder of a young woman named Sarah Coburn in Grafton County, New Hampshire, twenty-two years ago; trial testimony in the conviction of James Elliott for her murder; and anything I can dig up on the client's son, Nathan Titcomb."

"There's not much time. Elliott's given Nathan until noon tomorrow to contact the Grafton County Attorney and confess to the murder. He's threatened to kill William Titcomb and bury the body at a remote location in White Mountain National Forest if his demands aren't met. I'm not getting any cooperation from Nathan."

"You believe Elliott will carry out the threat?"

"I don't have any reason to believe he won't. He served twenty-two years in prison for a crime he says Nathan committed." Elliott acted like a man who didn't believe he had a future. In Emma's experience, they made the most dangerous kidnappers.

"I'll get back to you when I have something."

· · ·

IT WAS close to midnight and going on twenty-four hours since Emma had been awakened by the emergency call. She pressed the cell phone to her ear with one hand and scribbled notes with the other. The Concord, New Hampshire, investigator her grandfather had contacted had managed to obtain copies of the records before closing time and fax them to Lindstrom Security headquarters in New York. It had taken hours to glean the information Nils considered pertinent.

"Sarah Coburn was sixteen and a sophomore at Plymouth Regional High School at the time of her death. Her body was found on the bank of the Pemigewasset River, in a wooded area south of Plymouth, the morning after the junior-senior prom. She'd been strangled, no evidence of sexual activity. Police reports indicate suspicion fell on James Elliott—then a senior—early in the investigation. The girl left the dance with Elliott, even though she'd originally been Nathan Titcomb's date.

"William Titcomb alibied his son for the early-morning hours when the girl was judged to have been killed. He reported that Nathan arrived home around midnight, miserable because Sarah had dumped him for Elliott, and didn't leave the house until after the girl's body was found the next day. Two of Titcomb's employees were at the house playing poker and corroborated his account, at least until sometime around four in the morning.

"The police didn't have much to go on, except reports that Sarah was last seen alive in Elliott's company. He maintained his innocence. Claimed he dropped the girl off at her home just in time for a one-o'clock curfew. Her parents swore the last time they laid eyes on her alive was when Nathan picked her up for the dance."

"Any physical evidence linking Elliott to the crime?" Emma asked.

"Some forensic evidence—fingerprints, several hairs, and a lipstick belonging to Sarah—in Elliott's car, but he never claimed she hadn't been in the car. Nothing at the location of her death."

"No DNA?"

"This happened in 1986. The first DNA evidence wasn't used in a trial until 1988."

"That's all they had: He was the last person to see her alive?"

"The Grafton County Sheriff's Department picked Elliott up shortly after Sarah's body was identified. The boy was unable to provide any kind of verifiable alibi for the time of the girl's death. At the trial, the County Attorney made much of the fact that Elliott gave conflicting statements during his interrogation. An interrogation that apparently lasted for more than twenty-four hours without benefit of counsel."

"What motive did Elliott have for killing her?" Emma knew that plenty of murder convictions were obtained with circumstantial evidence alone, but this case seemed pretty thin.

"The prosecution theorized about any number of possible motives. The defense argued he had absolutely no reason to kill her. In the end, the jury convicted him. As the County Attorney put it, 'Who else had any reason to harm the girl?'"

A young man made to look like a fool in front of his classmates and alibied by a pillar of the community. Titcomb had enough money either to coerce or buy the cooperation of men who relied on him for their livelihood. Emma was beginning to believe her client's son was a murderer.

"Anything of interest on Nathan?"

"A string of DUIs starting in his early twenties, all pleaded down to lesser violations. Two assaults on a female, both dismissed."

"Titcomb spreading money around to protect his son?"

"It's possible. Nathan's a VP at Titcomb Industries. Company scuttlebutt says it's an empty title; the man rarely bothers to show his face at work."

"Thanks for all your help."

"Not sure I've been of any help. What are you going to do?"

"I wish I knew."

• • •

EMMA DRAGGED Nathan from his bed shortly after dawn, refusing to acknowledge his indignant protests. Seated at the kitchen table with cups of coffee in front of them, she shared what she'd learned from her grandfather.

"The only way to keep your father safe is to negotiate in good faith. Elliott has to believe I'm trustworthy, that I'll hold up my end of the agreement. Understanding his point of view can go a long way toward gaining his trust. If he's innocent and your father allowed him to go to prison in order to protect you, he may feel justified in what he's doing."

Nathan avoided her gaze as he gripped the mug with trembling hands. "You're supposed to be on our side, not the guy who has my father chained to a tree."

"You're not listening to me, Nathan. If his grudge against your family is real, he's not going to accept money as a substitute for clearing his name, and he's more likely to carry out his threats if we don't meet his demands. Did you kill Sarah Coburn and let James Elliott take the blame?"

If she'd had any respect for the man sitting across the table from her, it was erased by his wide-eyed appeal. "You can't really expect me to confess to murder?"

• • •

ELLIOTT HAD abandoned the effort to disguise his voice. It made it possible for Emma to hear the nuances necessary to judge emotional tone but meant the man was no longer concerned with the consequences of being recorded. "I told you what would happen if Nathan refused."

The nightmare that haunted every negotiator was the knowledge that failure meant a dead hostage. Emma's success rate in obtaining a safe release was among the highest, but no one's record was perfect. No matter what Titcomb had done, she was responsible for his safety. Unable to meet Elliott's demands, all she could do was stall for time and hope the man could be convinced to accept an alternative she was capable of providing.

"Let me talk to Mr. Titcomb."

"What's the point; he's a dead man. Tell Nathan he's next. If I'm going to hell, I might as well take him with me."

"There's no need for anyone to die. We can work this out." Sweat beaded on her upper lip. Struggling to keep her tone calm, Emma resisted the urge to scream her frustration into the phone.

"What's there to work out? Nathan's too much of a coward to save his own father. This whole thing was a stupid, crazy idea."

"You're right; kidnapping Titcomb was a crazy thing to do. Killing him would be stupid. Murdering a kidnap victim is one of the few offenses that will get you the death penalty in New Hampshire. You have a lot of good years ahead of you. Don't waste them on the likes of these men."

"I've got nothing ahead of me."

"Take Titcomb's money. Nothing can make up for the years you've spent in prison, but at least you can start a new life."

"You don't understand; my father's dying of cancer. He'll go to his grave with the whole town believing his son is a murderer. I want him to be able to hold his head up at the end."

"Killing Titcomb will only convince them they were right all along. You weren't a murderer twenty-two years ago, and you're not one now."

"Twenty-two years in prison makes a man into a lot of things he'd never thought he'd be."

How much of what Elliott felt was regret rather than bitterness and self-loathing Emma couldn't tell. But she knew defeat when she heard it. She was negotiating with the wrong man.

"Put Titcomb on."

"You're just wasting time."

"What have you got to lose?"

There were several moments of silence while the phone changed hands, then a tentative "Are you there?" Titcomb had lost the brash confidence evident the day before.

"Mr. Titcomb, we don't have much time. Elliott's not going to accept a monetary ransom."

"I don't understand. I was assured your firm was one of the best. That's why the insurance company has you on retainer."

In this man's world, it all came down to money. Experience had taught him he could buy whatever and whomever he wanted. Emma couldn't afford to let her contempt for the man come through in her voice if she wanted to convince him otherwise.

"Negotiating a ransom isn't always about money. Elliott insists Nathan tell the truth about Sarah Coburn. He isn't going to be bought off with cash like the men you paid to help alibi your son. Either you agree to his demands, or I'm afraid he'll carry out his threats against both you and your son."

"What does Nathan say?"

The fear in Titcomb's voice signaled progress. Maybe the father could succeed where she'd failed. "I want you to talk to him."

• • •

THE GRAFTON County Attorney was housed in a complex of redbrick buildings surrounded by woods and carefully tended fields just outside North Haverhill. The man who currently held the office had been in middle school when Elliott was convicted of Sarah Coburn's murder.

William Stratford didn't bother to conceal his astonishment as he sat behind his desk listening to Nathan Titcomb confess to a twenty-two-year-old crime. "Let me get this straight: You strangled a young woman to death in a fit of rage because she dumped you on prom night for an older guy. Then you stood by while the guy was convicted and sent to prison."

Nathan sat in a chair next to Emma, shoulders hunched, eyes glued to his lap. "I'd been drinking. I didn't mean to kill her. I guess I just lost it. When Elliott was arrested, I thought they'd let him go when they figured out he didn't do it."

"I don't mean to belittle your act of contrition here, Mr. Titcomb, but why confess now? The man's already served his sentence."

They'd rehearsed several answers to this question, and Emma had been the one to come up with the explanation. Nathan remained silent long enough to have her worried he intended to back out of the bargain they'd made.

"I'm in a twelve-step program. I'm making amends."

Now, sitting in the attorney's office, even to Emma's ears it sounded lame. "Mr. Titcomb knows he can never make up for the injury Mr. Elliott has suffered. But vacating the conviction will allow the man to make a fresh start without the stigma of being labeled a murderer."

Stratford didn't look entirely convinced. "You're prepared to make a statement under oath?"

Nathan's eyes rose to meet Emma's gaze. Whatever he saw must've been enough to convince him there was no backing out. "I am."

• • •

EMMA CLIMBED the steps to the front porch of a log building that served as park headquarters for Crawford Notch in White Mountain National Forest. William Titcomb rose from a wooden bench, tired and disheveled but otherwise unharmed. "Call the police; Elliott can't be more than a couple of miles down the road."

"Nathan made a full confession under oath. The County Attorney's going to petition the court to vacate Elliott's conviction in the morning."

"A confession coerced by his father's kidnapper."

Emma wondered if this had been Titcomb's plan when he begged his son to confess. Had she missed some subtle communication between the two of them that let Nathan know his father would come to his rescue?

"A very convenient story. Almost as convenient as the alibi you provided your son for the night Sarah Coburn was killed."

"It'll be your word as well as mine."

"Like the two employees who backed your version of events?"

"You can't mean to let Elliott get away with this."

"I negotiated in good faith, Mr. Titcomb. Mr. Elliott kept his part of the bargain."

"For God's sake, the man's a kidnapper. You don't owe him anything."

"No, but you do. As far as he's concerned, Nathan's confession settles your debt. It's a cheap price to pay, considering what the man's suffered."

• • •

IF IT hadn't been for her passenger, Emma would've savored the drive through the forest. Trees hugged the road, the splendor of their leaves reminding her that she needed to get out of the city more often.

Titcomb tried bribing her. When she showed no interest in his offers, he moved on to threats. She finally shut him up with a threat of her own: Lindstrom Security employed some of the best operatives in the business. Was Titcomb convinced his business practices could stand the scrutiny of a no-holds-barred investigation?

Fatigue muted the satisfaction she felt when she dropped her client safely at his door and headed to the airport. Emma dialed the number, hoping to get an answer in spite of her instructions.

"I told you to get rid of the phone."

"What's the point; you recorded every word I said." Elliott sounded as tired as she felt.

"It's seems there was a mechanical problem with my equipment."

"Who the hell are you, anyway? And don't give me that bullshit about working for Titcomb."

"I'm a hostage negotiator employed by Titcomb's insurance company."

"Has the old man called the sheriff yet?"

"Mr. Titcomb is satisfied with the deal as it stands."

The laugh held more bitterness than mirth. "That's the second time you've lied to me."

He was right; she'd violated a cardinal rule of negotiation: Don't lie unless absolutely necessary, and never get caught. "He may not be happy, but he's agreed to keep his part of the bargain."

"Why are you doing this?"

The explanation she'd given Titcomb was true, but if she was honest with herself, only partly. A negotiator walked a fine line. Building rapport required a degree of empathy with the kidnapper. For the first time in the years since she'd freed her first hostage, Emma knew she'd stepped over that line.

CYNDY E. LIVELY is a retired physician living in Winston-Salem, North Carolina. While she has been pursuing her dream of becoming a published novelist, her short fiction has appeared in *Jupiter* magazine, *Leading Edge*, and two short story anthologies. You can find her on Facebook at Cyndy Lively or contact her at celivel@triad.rr.com.

My Grandmother's Attic

Selaine Henriksen

IT WAS raining again, and it was cold out too; and there was nothing to do.

"Watch TV," my grandmother said.

"Done that to death," I muttered.

"Read a book," she suggested.

"There's nothing here," I snapped.

She glanced up from her book and gave me a hard look over her bifocals. "Well, well, April May." My name is April, but everyone calls me April May as a nickname, only it isn't shorter. "You're looking for something new to do." She carefully placed the bookmark I'd made her in kindergarten, the one with a big, lopsided, purple-colored heart on it—I'd first made it blue and then had to go over it in red to make it right—and set her book down on the side table. "Have you ever been up in the attic of this old house?" she asked.

I shook my head, beaming at her. I knew she'd come through; Gran always does.

She led me up the stairs. There were three bedrooms opening off a square hallway: my gran and gramps' room; the guest room, which was mostly mine because I was the only one who ever stayed there; and a tiny third room that Gran used as a closet. We made space by pushing boxes and piles of books out of the way, and Gran pointed to a rectangular cutout in the ceiling. "A lot of times in these old houses the attics are just a space with no floor, so they can't be used. But Walt finished the floor ages ago because we needed the extra storage." Walt was my gramps. Gran was hunting around amid the boxes, and behind some old coats she found it: a step ladder.

"You ever throw anything out, Gran?" I asked.

Gran laughed. "Listen to you. Don't you sound like your mom. Yes, dear, I've thrown lots out, but when you get as old as me, there's that much more you want to keep too. Here now." She set up the ladder and carefully climbed the rungs, with me holding on to the ladder and keeping a hand out in case she fell, although what that was supposed to do if she did, I don't know. Gran's a big woman but not stiff. "These old limbs are still limber," she'd say, patting her big leg, and my mom would always roll her eyes.

A cloud of dust fell through the hole when she pushed the trapdoor aside. We both coughed and waved our hands about. "It's been a long time since anyone's been up here," she said. "I don't even remember what's here." She climbed back down. "You can be a big help to me, dear, if you'd take a pen and paper with you and write down what you find. With Walt gone now I might just take it all to a flea market."

She found a pen and paper in the top drawer of an old desk shoved into one corner and piled high with books. She had a gleam in her eye as she handed them to me. "That should keep you busy for a while. I'll be down-stairs if you need me."

The attic was like the rest of my grandmother's house, both in size and clutter. I could stand once I'd pulled myself up through the trapdoor but could only turn and look at the piles of boxes and various bits of furniture. The roof sloped from a peak in the middle, where I was, right down to the floor. It was hard to know where to start, so I picked right in front of me. There was a beat-up dresser with only one drawer, and the space where the other drawer was supposed to be was filled with papers. I pulled open the top drawer and found photo albums stacked inside. I sat with them on my lap and flipped through. Mostly they were full of people I didn't recognize until the third album, where there were lots of pictures of a chubby little baby that suddenly turned into me, except I was hanging on to the wrong parents. I'm always told I look like my mother, and I guess I roll my eyes because I didn't know they meant I look like mother when she was my age. Me and the girl in the pictures could be twins. Weird.

My mom didn't have any brothers or sisters. "Not for lack of trying." My grandmother would laugh, shaking her belly; and my mother would glare hard at her, whispering "Shhh," and her face would go all red. Anyway, there were a lot of pictures of my mom. I especially liked looking at the ones of her all dressed up for Halloween.

I guess she knew what she wanted to be when she was real young, because she's an art restorer now and works at the university. Gran told me Mom's the first in the family to graduate university. She says I'm to be the second. I don't know about that. I want to be a writer and can't see how university would help me. The How To Be a Writer sites online all say I need to read a lot. So that's what I do, and write too, of course. Only I don't tell my gran that; she has her heart set on me going to university.

One picture of Mom showed her sitting in front of a large frame with brown paper in it that she was painting on. She was about seven and looked just like I did a couple of years ago. She was facing the painting holding a homemade palette and a brush, wearing a smock, with a French-style beret set on her head. She was looking back over her shoulder at the camera with a big grin.

The papers stuffed into the bottom of the dresser turned out to be my mom's old paintings and drawings from school. She seemed to like writing her name real big on her work. I wrote down as neatly as I could: "dresser; photo albums, paintings."

I started to shove them back into their spot when I noticed one painting was on thicker paper, like a real canvas. I know about those things 'cause of my mom's job. I unrolled it and was surprised to see that it was a picture of a beautiful little dog with big black eyes and the cutest little bell on his collar. My mom's name wasn't on this one, I couldn't make out whose name it was, but it started with an R and looked like it ended with a z. At my school we don't learn cursive writing anymore. We print or else sign stuff with a picture made of our initials. Like, I use a small *a* with a big *S* around it to look like a flower with petals. I had to show this painting to Gran. We'd both been working on Mom—Gran and I—trying to get Mom to get me a puppy. Mom always said no; she had enough work as a single parent.

"Look, Gran," I called, clambering back down the ladder. "Gran!" I shouted, running down the stairs.

She was back in her chair, with her book open in her lap, but I know she was sleeping because she jerked her head up and snorted real loud.

I had to shout a couple more times till Gran woke up a bit and got what I was saying. She looked at the painting and sat up and pulled it closer and looked again, frowning. She put on her glasses and looked at the picture over the lenses, through the lenses, and every which way.

"What is it, Gran?" I asked.

She shook her head. "I'd forgotten about this; I really had. And it's very important."

She looked at me thoughtfully for a long time. Then she stood up and headed into the kitchen. She put on the kettle for herself, though she always asks me if I want a cup. She set a big bag of cookies on the table and pulled out the whole tray. She watched me eat one, then poured me a glass of milk. I ate a whole row of the tray before the kettle boiled. I'd eaten a few more before Gran sat back down with her tea. But I hadn't forgotten her reaction to the picture. I think maybe she thought I would.

"So?"

"So what?"

"Gran." I sighed. "You said that picture was really important. Why?"

She looked at me over her teacup. "I guess I'll tell you, April May, because

I think you're old enough and smart enough to understand. Lord knows your mom won't agree and would tear a strip off me for telling you this, but she doesn't know anything 'bout it either, so you just need to keep quiet, okay?"

Gran had never spoken to me like this before. I brushed the crumbs from my mouth and nodded seriously.

She set the picture on the table between us and tapped it with her finger. "This picture is important because it tells me who killed your grandfather, Walter, may he rest in peace."

I stared at her, waiting for her to give a big belly laugh like she does, but she just looked at me and nodded. "The problem," she continued, "is that I don't know how I can use this information. It tells me *who* done it, but it's not proof." She tapped the picture some more, frowning as she thought.

Since I want to be a writer when I grow up, I knew she was dragging out the story on purpose. I waited, but she was thinking. Finally the suspense was killing me. "Gran, you've got to tell me what happened!"

"All right, I said I would." She poured me some more milk and herself another cup of tea.

"You know Walter was a carpenter and handyman?" At my nod she continued. "One of his clients was Mrs. Braithwaite. She was an old lady, living in a big house all by herself. She had children in town, but they weren't much help to her, so Walter did all the work around the house. She paid well or else he wouldn't have gone near her." Gran chuckled. "He used to complain about how she'd treat him, the terrible things she'd say; but worst of all for Walt was, she always put down his work. She was paranoid that everyone was out to steal her money and take advantage of her. Now, Walt, I don't know how much you remember him, dear, but he would never take advantage of a little old lady, even if he hated her; and anyways, I always made him go help her out.

"So one day she calls and says the tap in her bathtub is leaking again, the one Walter had fixed the year before. She starts in on him about how she doesn't see why he has to fix it again if he'd done it right the first time.

"'It's an old house, Mrs. B., needs a lot of care,' Walt told her. That's what he always called her, Mrs. B.

"'And you get to charge me twice for the same job,' she said. 'Everyone thinks because I live in this big house I must be rich, and they can take advantage.'

"'Who's everyone, Mrs. B.? Are you telling me I'm not your only handyman?'

"Walter was only joking with her, but humor was lost on that woman.

"'I always have someone check your work, Walter,' she told him, and Walt insisted she cackled so hard she had a coughing fit.

"What did you say?' Mrs. B. demanded sharply when her fit had passed. 'Don't swear, Walter.'

"Now, when Walt told me that I laughed so hard that he even laughed a bit too, even though he didn't really think it was funny."

Gran started to laugh at the memory, shaking her head and jiggling her belly. I felt a strange feeling in my heart, kind of sad and kind of mad at the same time. Tears pricked my eyes. "Grandma, why are you laughing when you're talking about Gramps? He's dead!"

Gran looked surprised. Then she pulled my chair toward her and put her arms around me. "I remember and miss him every day. But part of remembering is thinking about all the times—good, bad, and funny—that we shared. That's how I keep Gramps alive, in here." She pointed to her heart. "And telling you stories about Walt will keep him alive in here too." She pointed to my heart. "It's not disrespecting Gramps to laugh remembering him. Do you want me to go on?"

I nodded.

"Walter was upset, and he wrenched the faucet off the old tub with unnecessary force.

"'You've got a problem, Mrs. B.,' Walter said with a perplexed frown.

"'Oh yes, it's my heart. Those kids of mine…'

"'No, ma'am, I mean over here.' Walter pointed to the tap. 'You know I just took that off, but I'd forgot to shut off the main. There should be water pouring outta here. When's the last time you used this tub?'

"'Look at me. Do I look like I can use this tub? I'm too old to get in that big thing. I had a shower put in downstairs six months ago.'

"'Not by me,' Walter snapped. Walter stared at the decapitated, nonleaking pipes and wondered why he was even here. He thought about walking out right then, but he knew I would be upset some with him for leaving an old lady's pipes like that.

"'Something strange is going on around here,' the old lady muttered, 'and it's not just taps. I'm not senile yet, you know, and they're trying to drive me crazy.'

"Still examining the nonfunctional taps, Walter mouthed 'Yeah, yeah' as the usual rant about her kids began. She'd start on workers next.

"'…then there was a chimney sweep—there's three fireplaces, you know; and in the same day a roofer was by to reshingle a patch at the back, so he says, but I didn't see anything wrong. Then the next day a man came to clean the furnace and ducts, and someone came to clean out the hot-water heater. I've never even heard of that. Walter, are you listening to me?'

"A surprised Walter glanced over his shoulder and saw her frowning at him. He automatically hitched up his jeans…"

"Gran!" I grinned.

She winked at me. "Well, it's true. Anyway, then he heard what she'd been saying.

> "'Did you say someone was here to clean your hot-water tank?'
> "'She scowled at him. 'It's fishy, isn't it? I knew it.'
> "'Well, now, it's unusual. Probably explains why the water isn't running here.'

"At his request, Mrs. B. led him down to the furnace room. Walter was surprised by the condition of the room. There was an open bag of garbage spilling dust, and a bucket full of water sat beside the hot-water tank, which had layers of pink insulation lying all around it.

> "'New tanks don't need that,' Walter told her. Naturally, she thought he was trying to talk her into buying a new tank.
> "'Did he actually empty the tank and clean it?' he interrupted.
> "'He started to, but I came down and demanded to know who had ever heard of a tank getting cleaned. Did he think I was senile, I said. I'm not, I said, and told him no one was going to take advantage of me. I'm no one's fool, I said.'
> "'And he ran out screaming,' Walter said under his breath.
> "'What was that, Walter?'
> "'Tell me about all these workers again, Mrs. B.' And she was happy to oblige in detail."

Gran sat back and ticked them off on her fingers. "There was the roofer—for the shed, mind you—a chimney sweep, a furnace and duct cleaner, and the hot-water tank cleaner; and all of them came by within a couple of days. Mrs. B. was surprised by all the workers in her house. What does that make you think of, April May?"

Another cookie helped me think. "I've never heard of a hot-water tank cleaner." I raised my eyebrows at Gran, and she nodded. "And if she didn't call for the workers, then it looks like someone was trying to get into her house?"

"Smart girl." Gran smiled.

"Casing the joint," I added eagerly.

"Kinda. What I got out of it was those were all places where someone might have hidden something. So I sent Walter back the next day and told him to tell Mrs. B. he thought she was right, and there was something fishy about all these workers, and he was going to check it out for her. And I told him to check all the places she said the workers had been and especially the hot-water tank, because she'd interrupted his work." Gran took a sip of tea.

"And?"

"He found that." She pointed to the painting of the dog. "Rolled up inside the insulation that was still wrapped around the water tank. He showed it to Mrs. B. and told her he thought the 'workers' were looking for this. Mrs. B. told Walt to take it home with him, that he could have it and that should stop her from being bothered by those people." Gran had a faraway look in her eye.

"What, Gran?"

"I was just thinking of how Mrs. B. never seemed to worry about who was sending all those workers to look around her house. She must have known who it was."

"So who killed Walt, I mean Gramps?" I asked.

"Do you remember when Grandad died?" At my nod, she continued. "We had gone to your house for supper, and your mom wanted to borrow a circular saw from Walt 'cause she was planning to lay new wood flooring. Walt had forgotten, and he came back home to get the saw. He didn't come back for the longest time, so we got worried and rushed home, only to find him lying dead on the kitchen floor. Heart attack, they said."

"You don't think it was a heart attack?" My heart was pounding just thinking of it.

"Oh, it was. But I always had a feeling something wasn't right that night. I found that things had been moved and just had a feeling someone had been going through the house. Nothing was stolen though, so what could I do? And what with the funeral and missing Walt…" Gran took a deep breath and let it out slowly. "I forgot about it. Until you showed me this picture. I remember that Mrs. B.'s youngest son had been by to tell us that Mrs. B. had died, and when the funeral was, and that she had left some money to Walt. He asked me if his mother had ever given Walt anything, like a painting. Now, how we came by that painting was strange enough, so I said no."

"And you think he came back and killed Grandad to get the painting." I gasped.

"Not exactly. He may have just been looking for it and surprised Walt so's he had a heart attack, or maybe he confronted him and caused it." Gran shrugged. She sat back, staring at the ceiling and sipping her tea.

I waited as long as I could. "So, let's call the police!" I finally shouted out.

Gran shook her head. "Like I said, it ain't proof. I wonder what's so important about this painting? It's just a picture of a dog."

"It's a cute dog, really cute," I said.

"You don't break into a man's house for cute," Gran mused.

"Let's Google it," I suggested.

"Do what now?"

"On the computer. Jeesh, Gran."

"Language, dear. I have a TV, and that's enough for me."

I knew she meant it. She still had an old phone too, the kind you had to stick your finger in and roll the disk. It took forever to call anyone. Gran said it worked fine, and why should she replace it when it worked fine?

My big Christmas present this year was a cellphone. My mom thought I was too young when I asked for it. I told her all the kids in my class had one, and I was left out of the texting. She started on the whole "If everyone jumped off a bridge, would you too?" I said having a phone wouldn't make me stupid. She said, "Watch your tone, young lady; you sound just like Gran." I said it's a safety thing, I could call or text her whenever I needed her, like if someone tried to get me to help find their lost puppy, for instance. That swayed her, the safety thing.

So I laid out the painting, with books to hold the corners down, and took a picture with my phone. Gran had asked me not to mention it to my mom, so I didn't show her the picture when she picked me up after work. I should have, probably. It would have saved me and Gran a lot of trouble.

Instead I Googled "dog's head painting" on my laptop at home. Turns out it was a famous painting by a famous painter, Renoir. I thought maybe it had been stolen, because why else hide it in an old lady's house? And then I thought, why steal a famous painting, anyway? It's not like you can hang it on your wall for everyone to see. You know how Google is. You ask this or that and get links to all sorts of things; and next thing you know, Mom is yelling at you to turn off that darn thing and go to bed or she'll take it away for a week.

I found out people don't steal famous paintings to sell or to hang in their houses. They steal them to make copies and sell those. I lay awake in bed a long time, thinking. It bothered me that my grandad maybe died over a stupid painting; I don't care how famous it was.

• • •

IT BOTHERED me all the next day at school too. Mr. Grant, my teacher, said he had to be extra patient with me. Just because I couldn't find my math homework and he had to wait while I checked in my backpack and desk before I remembered I had left it on the kitchen table.

And it weighed on me still when I got off the school bus at Gran's house after school. Gran had the usual cookies and tea set out on the table. I asked for a glass of milk, like always. "You know I don't drink tea, Gran," I muttered.

Gran raised an eyebrow. "Cranky today?"

"How can you act like normal? Knowing maybe Grandad was killed? Over a stupid painting?" I burst out.

"Oh dear." Gran sat down with her tea. "I shouldn't have told you any of that. That's just an old woman's foolish rambling. I didn't mean to upset you, April May. There's nothing to that silly story." She reached over and patted my hand, looking worried. I could tell she was thinking I'd say something to Mom and get Gran in big trouble.

What she said didn't make me feel better, even though maybe she was right. Dectective stories are my favorite. The heroes always lure the perp somehow and catch him. I had an idea how I could draw out Gramps' "maybe-killer." I opened my mouth to tell Gran then shut it again. There's no way she'd go along with my plan. So I'd just do it myself.

• • •

AFTER MOM picked me up, I went straight to my laptop and used Paint to make a poster. I blew up the picture of the dog's-head painting and wrote YARD SALE in white block letters across the top, with Gran's address underneath. I put Saturday's date on it. I honestly thought the perp would wait till Saturday. And that's why nine-year-olds shouldn't play detective, which is what my mom said afterward.

I told Mom I was going out to see Pam, my friend who lives just down the street. She said it was good for me to get off the computer and to be back when the streetlights came on. I knew where the old Braithwaite house was, so I ran all the way over and stuck the posters around on the telephone poles. If Mrs. B.'s kids were still around, they'd see them for sure.

The streetlights were just blinking on when I got home. I slept better that night feeling like I was doing something about Gramps' death.

• • •

PAM'S MOM was working late the next day, so Pam was coming to Gran's house after school with me. I told her about the painting and what Gran had said. Pam wanted to see it because we'd been talking about what kind of puppies we would get if we were ever allowed. I told her too what I had done to draw out the perp.

"My mom tells me what you read or see on TV isn't real, except the news, maybe. You read too much," Pam said.

"There's no reading too much," I said.

Gran wasn't waiting when we stepped off the school bus. Pam and I were talking puppies again, so I didn't notice. That is to say, I noticed but it didn't exactly click in my mind.

Gran never used her front door. It opened right into the living room, and she liked to keep her living room pristine. Mom always said Gran would cover the living room all in plastic if she could. Gran lived in the kitchen, where it was okay to make a mess, and the door we used was up a stoop on the side of the house. The door was open a little, and that's when it clicked.

I set down my backpack and crept up to look in. The kitchen was empty. A cup of tea sat on the table steaming alongside a bag of cookies. Two glasses, ready for milk.

"Hello," Pam called.

I whirled around, pressing my fingers to my lips to shush her. A crash from the living room shook the floor. Pam's eyes got wide.

"Go," I shouted, giving her a push back out the door. "Call 911."

Gran stumbled into the kitchen. A man charged in behind her. Gran was holding the rolled-up painting. She threw it toward me and I caught it. "Run" she yelled.

The man gave her a shove and she fell. As she fell, she pulled a kitchen chair down in his way. Then she started crawling toward the stove, reaching for the drawer at the bottom.

When she fell, I automatically ran to her. When she said to run, I turned and tried to run back out, but the man had come around the table and grabbed my arm. He gave me a shake to make me drop the painting, but I held on. My other arm fell onto the counter, and there was the phone. I grabbed it by the space in the back, spun, and beaned him in the head as hard as I could. One thing you can say about those old phones is, they are heavy.

The man staggered back, his hand on his forehead. Blood spilled between his fingers. By now Gran had got her frying pan out of the drawer of the stove, and she reared up and clocked him from the other side. He went down, all limp. Soon the sweet sound of sirens was singing down the street.

My gran's a toughy. We stood over the guy, her with her frying pan and me with the phone, ready to pop him again if he moved.

"Is he one of Mrs. B.'s kids?" I asked.

"The youngest," Gran said.

"Why didn't you just give the painting to him, Gran?"

"Huh," she said. " He didn't ask nicely."

"I should call Mom." Gran and I looked at each other. She sighed.

"Guess you'd better."

• • •

MOM HAD lots to say. She was real nice to the police officers who came to drag the thief away, but as soon as they were gone, she started in on Gran first. Then I said it was all my idea to lure out the perp, and she started in on me. Mostly along the lines of "Just what were you thinking? Gran could have been hurt—Pam too. And you." She clutched me to her bosom.

The waterworks were going to start, so I interrupted her by showing her the painting. "Is it the real one?"

Mom pulled herself together and looked it over. She shook her head. Told me about colors and what was available at the time and such. "It's a good copy," she said. "There's been a rumor around about a group that produces high-quality knockoffs like this, but I never thought it was true. It takes a lot of knowledge, not to mention skill, to make a copy this good."

"It's too bad he was a bad egg," said Gran.

While Mom was expounding on the merits of the painting, Pam had been looking it over. "That is a really cute dog," she whispered to me.

"Right?" I whispered back. I didn't think we were any closer to getting puppies; Pam's mom was likely going to be pretty po'd too.

What I did think was that Gran and I, we made a good team. I wondered what else she had up in her attic.

SELAINE HENRIKSEN has supported her writing habit by working a variety of jobs over the years, from bookstore clerk to research technologist. Currently a fitness instructor and mom to two editors-in-training, she lives in Ottawa, Ontario, where she is a member of Capital Crime Writers. She has eclectic reading tastes, as well as writing, but is a firm believer that at the heart of every good story is a mystery. She blogs at miss-selaine-ious.jesande.com.

Strange Attraction

John Jasper Owens

THE FIRST time I saw the cat it worried me—this isn't a cat-friendly neighborhood, which is why my own two beasts are strictly indoors. I assumed it belonged to Marlene, the new girl who moved in across the street a few houses down, and thought maybe I should warn her. The few outdoor cats we've had over the years haven't lasted long, replaced in no time by sad little lost-pet posters.

Marlene and I had chatted already. She was a looker but comfortably about a third my age, so we could pause on the street and pass the time without any of that opposite-sex foolishness that might get in the way if I was in my twenties or she in her sixties.

"Don't worry about Tabitha," Marlene said over the phone. "She only goes out once in a while, and she's very cautious." She laughed. "Kinda like me."

I assumed this was a reference to one Skip Tyler, whose daddy owned Tyler Realty, which, in turn, owned half the rental units in our neighborhood—including both mine and Marlene's. Skip was the kind of boy to make you pissed off at God or Darwin, depending on which way you bent—he was tall, strong, handsome, and smart, like a checklist for attracting women. He was also what we called, back in the service, a complete dickhead.

I'd often noticed his red Escalade parked at the curb outside Marlene's house. I asked him about that when I was up at the rental office.

"Just checking on the new tenant, Pops," he'd said, and winked. "Addressing her *every need* in a timely manner." He winked again.

What an ass.

"Oh, I can handle Skippy-boy, Mr. Edelman," Marlene told me, still on the phone. "He just doesn't have any experience taking no for an answer. He'll learn."

I hoped so. When I first moved here, Skip had been the star pitcher on the high school team. There were rumors that his daddy had to bury some nasty allegations from one of the local girls under a big pile of hush money. But those were just rumors, and I don't spread rumors.

• • •

THE SECOND time I saw Marlene's cat it was the same as the first time— about four in the morning. Thirty years of doing the hands-on work of overnight shipping permanently reset my circadian rhythms. I'll never be peppy at 10 A.M. again.

I was sipping tea and listening to my radio out on the porch, just watching the night go by, when Tabitha came stalking up the other side of the street. When I whistle-*tck-tck*ed to her (force of habit—I love cats) she sauntered right over.

Either Marlene didn't know her own cat very well, or she and I had two different definitions of the word *cautious*.

Tabitha let herself be scratched and petted, then jumped up on the porch table. I noticed she didn't have a collar and made a note to give Marlene an old-man's lecture on responsibility.

My photo album was open on the table, as it usually is that time of night when I'm most likely to feel alone in the world. Living too much in the past. There was my wife, back in the seventies and in full disco mode, ready to Hustle. On the opposite side we were with our oldest, after a baseball game. Chuck went two-for-five that night, with a triple.

I turned the page, and Tabitha caught it with a paw. I scratched behind her ears.

Next were more pictures of the kids, all three of them, then Betsy again, posing at the beach, just being goofy. Beside that was one of Betsy's behind—she was bent over a clothes hamper. I caught hell for snapping that one.

I still miss her so much.

Betsy died of pneumonia at the cruel age of fifty-four.

I turned the page, and Tabitha pawed at it again.

After a while I'd sold the big house in the city and moved out to the suburbs, to these tidy little townhomes. With the house money and my retirement, I'll be comfortable until they take me out of here feetfirst, and there'll still be something left over for the grandkids.

I heard a rustle across the street, and the cat froze.

Up the hill, about twenty yards away, a rabbit broke from cover, and the cat took off after it in a blur of orange and white.

"Good luck," I yelled after it.

There's a reason rabbits survive in suburbs—they're more nimble than dogs, cats, even squirrels. With those hind legs they can turn a right angle at full speed, and they don't stray far from their holes. The only way rabbits get caught is when they're old, like me, or a cat manages to catch one unaware. That rabbit was well aware and had a twenty-yard head start on Tabitha.

There was no way. I just hoped the cat enjoyed the chase.

I went inside and watched the early news.

When I got up the next day—afternoon, as usual—there was an eviscerated rabbit waiting for me on my front porch.

● ● ●

THE NEXT night Marlene knocked on my door unannounced, carrying a grocery bag. "Hey, Mr. E.!" she said. Her voice went to a stage whisper: "Skippy-boy's on the prowl." Then back to normal. "Let's drink wine and watch movies."

"I've only been up about six hours," I said, "but what the hell. I'm retired."

Marlene turned out to be good company, even if her taste in film (horror) wasn't my cup of tea. I sat in my captain's chair, and she curled up on the couch, normally the cats' domain. They hopped up and immediately began walking all over her, which was unusual. Normally a person taking over their couch would elicit a running commentary of indignation.

We chatted through the first movie, joking about the huge amounts of red-dyed corn syrup being splattered across the screen. At one point her cell rang. She glanced at it, turned it off, and dropped it in her purse.

"Bad news?" I asked.

She sighed. "My faucet was leaking, so I called the agency," she said. "I guess Skip got wind of it, because he rushed right over. Of course. By the time he got there the faucet had stopped leaking, so I guess he thinks I called just to lure him over or something." She rolled her eyes. "And what's worse, I'm walking around in my home-alone clothes, which means a halter and underwear. Not much left to the imagination. Not that Skippy-boy has any imagination."

On-screen, the last two teenagers left were clawing their way up a mud bank.

I chose my words carefully: "He's got quite a reputation, you know."

Marlene waved me off. "I can handle Skippy-boy."

She did seem like a capable girl (and forgive me for using *girl* and *boy* to describe Marlene and Skip, but they weren't much older than my grandchildren). She was a skin-over-muscle type, into hiking and rock climbing—the sort of stuff I left off of as soon as they let me out of the army. But that girl was no match for Skip. He was a natural athlete, a foot taller and almost a hundred pounds heavier than Marlene.

After the first movie ended, I ordered a pizza (my half veggie, her's double meat), and she opened another DVD, a brand-new one. I watched her run one long, pinky nail around the shrink-wrap and peel it away.

"All veggie?" she said. "That's no meal for a growing boy."

I took the DVD and went for the television. "You just wait," I said. "That metabolism of yours won't last forever. You'll be eating salads before you know it."

"Never!" She gave me a huge smile. I've mentioned Marlene was a beautiful girl; but truthfully, even if we'd been closer in age, she wasn't really my type. Too hard-body for me. I've always liked my women with some wiggle, some "junk in the trunk," as my grandson would say.

Va-voom girls. Pin-up types.

Like my wife was.

The second movie was psychological horror—smarter and more intense than the gore fest we watched first—and our conversation petered out. This was a good one to watch late at night; we really got into it. Near the end came a fascinating scene in which the man who may or may not be the serial killer stood outside in the snow, staring through the window at the woman who may or may not be the killer's next victim. The music rose, and I leaned forward. The actress on-screen turned and gasped.

I heard a snort and a soft snore from over on the couch. Marlene was fast asleep, empty wine glass on the floor in front of her, with Jinks, my tabby, dozing on her hip and Vagabond, my gray longhair, draped over her ankles, munching a stolen pepperoni.

Too cute.

Marlene's right arm was tucked under her head, and her hand hung limp over the edge of the couch. I happened to notice her fingernails. They were buffed close, the fingernails of a girl into rock climbing. But I distinctly remembered how she'd opened the DVD, holding it in one hand and turning it with her thumb and three of her fingers while her long pinky nail sliced the wrap. Neat trick—very dexterous.

Weird. I must've just imagined it was long.

Then I had a most unkind thought about my new young friend.

Why would you be walking around your house half naked if you knew someone was coming to fix the faucet? Even if Skip didn't come, they'd almost certainly send a man. And how could you not expect Skip to show up? He never misses a chance to come to your house. You know that.

Truthfully, Marlene's "Skippy-boy" talk had a little "the lady doth protest too much" quality to it. I looked at her and shook my head. Marlene certainly wouldn't be the first woman who had a soft spot for bad boys. Or the first to be embarrassed to admit it. It was none of my business, but I still hated it. I hate to see people like Skip win at anything, and I hate to see someone as smart and funny as Marlene fall for a man like that.

Maybe I was just a little jealous.

I turned back to the television. On-screen, the man in the snow couldn't break into the house fast enough, and the actress took a meat cleaver right through the throat.

• • •

THE THIRD, and last, time I saw Marlene's cat was about a week later.

It was a steady rain, not that any sort of night weather had ever stopped me from sitting on my porch, staring out into it. Not since Betsy died. I noticed Tabitha (her shape, really) walking up the other side of the road. I whistled, and her ears pricked. There was a car coming, so she didn't just hop over to me. Smart cat.

I'd been thinking about Marlene, how we hadn't spoken much since she'd flopped on my couch. But I'd seen her three nights ago talking to Skip Tyler out on the curb beside her house. Must've been going on two in the morning. And yesterday I did my grocery shopping at the gourmet store across town, getting the cats some chicken livers, and I saw Marlene and Skip walking across the parking lot together. She didn't even look at me.

But the cat was looking at me, waiting for the car to pass so she could come over and be adored.

Then it happened.

The car came into my view from the left, and I knew immediately it was Skip's Escalade. It looked as if it would speed past, but at the last second the driver jerked the wheel, and the SUV hopped the ditch, heading straight for Tabitha.

That's when I knew why outdoor cats in our neighborhood always went missing.

Tabitha bolted—that cat was *quick*. Even caught off guard like that, she should've easily dodged Skippy-boy's SUV—the cat cleared two bounds in less than a second.

Then she hit some bad luck.

It had been raining off and on for days, so the earth was soft, and her right hind leg must've slipped under a wandering root.

For a moment she couldn't yank free.

The SUV turned a bit more, and its front left tire ran over the cat.

I came off my porch screaming, running in my pajamas out into the rain.

The SUV gunned it, and I saw Tabitha's body hit the underside of the car before getting caught by the rear tire, down into the ground and up in a floppy, lifeless arc.

By the time I made it uphill to the road, the car's back lights were pinpoints, taking the curve that leads to the highway.

What do I do? My slippers were already soaked through, and the rain was beating on my shoulders.

I ran back inside and called Marlene. No answer. I called again. And again.

I jogged back off my porch and across the road. I wanted to collect Tabitha's body, put her in a box, and get her out of the rain.

But when I got back outside and fixed on where Tabitha's body should be, I saw a cat sitting up.

In the dark, in the rain, the cat staggered around a bit drunkenly, then sat down again. I whistled, and it turned its head to look straight at me.

When I walked toward it, the cat limped off slowly, favoring its right side. It headed toward Marlene's house, and even at quarter speed it was faster than me in my sodden slippers.

I went back inside and called Marlene again. No answer.

Screw this, I thought, and got dressed. Tabitha may still be alive, by what miracle I couldn't imagine, but she needed the emergency vet right now. She had to have internal injuries, broken bones, maybe a fractured skull; and if Marlene couldn't pay for it, well, that's what friends (and retirement accounts) were for.

It was useless trying to track the cat through this mess; I just hoped she'd had the good sense to run home. I followed a path through the yards, the way I thought the cat would've gone, in case she'd collapsed on the way.

Marlene's car was in her drive, and there was a light on around back, so I ducked around to the little covered patio. The screen door was closed, but the back door was slightly ajar. I rapped and pushed it open.

"Marlene?"

The living room was empty, and I glanced into the kitchen. No Marlene. But I saw little wet paw prints on the carpet—a good sign. They ended at the stairs, so upstairs I went. Marlene must be out, the door cracked for the cat, although I had no idea how she'd worked the screen. But cats can learn all sorts of tricks. I just didn't know why any sane woman would go out and leave her house standing open.

At the top of the stairs the wet paw prints resumed, and I followed them to the bedroom, which was softly lit in candlelight. Marlene was there after all, stretched out on top of the bed, sort of zoned-out in the way sick people sometimes get.

She was also stark naked.

"Mr. Edelman!"

I slammed my eyes shut and slapped a palm over them for good measure. But I sure saw enough in that half second. "Sorry! Sorry-sorry-sorry." I started babbling about the cat, the car, the phone calls; and I think I was about ten seconds away from dropping dead of embarrassment when I realized she was laughing at me.

"You can open your eyes."

Marlene was covered in a blanket up to her neck, a thick LSU job with a brilliant gold tiger on the center. "I was asleep," she said. "I didn't hear the phone. I have an ulcer, and sometimes it gets pretty bad, so I stay in bed and take a pill to rest."

I backed up to the beginning about Tabitha, but Marlene raised a palm to stop me.

"The cat's fine."

"But—"

"She's fine, Mr. E. I checked her out right before you got here—the accident must've looked worse than it really was. She's hiding under the bed right now."

"It wasn't an accident," I said. I told her about the Escalade and reminded her about cats going missing in the neighborhood; but even when I went into all the brutal details about her cat, I could tell I was losing her. She kept glancing away, her head dipping toward the pillow.

"You can't know it was Skippy-boy's gas-guzzler," she said. "It's dark out."

I couldn't believe it.

"It's dark out, Marlene, but it's not black. I know Skip Tyler's car."

Weakly, she propped herself on her elbow. "I'll ask him about it."

I guess that's the best I was going to get. "Fine. Then I'll go home, leave you alone. Do you need anything?"

"Yeah, actually, if you don't mind. Could you get me some milk? It really helps my stomach. Big glass."

I hoofed downstairs and into the kitchen. Her refrigerator was covered in a lot of cute girly magnets ("Give the Bitch Her Chocolate!") and four or five photos of Marlene in various places out in the wilderness: forest trails, rock canyons. The girl liked to hike and camp.

I wondered who took the pictures.

The inside of her fridge was like a butcher shop. Stacks of roasts and hamburger, whole chickens—the good stuff too from the gourmet store. Way too much for one young woman.

After I poured the milk, I was leaving the kitchen when I noticed something—more accurately, a lack of something. I scanned the counters and out of curiosity checked the cabinets.

No cat food.

Come to think of it, no cat bowls either.

Some indulgent owners feed their cats fresh meat all the time, and maybe she was one of them; but that sort of diet is bad for their kidneys. They need their kibble. Marlene should know that; she told me she was a zoology grad student down at the city school.

That's why she moved here.

Back upstairs, she took the big glass of milk in two hands and drank down the whole thing like medicine. "Thanks, Mr. E."

"You'll be all right?"

"Oh, yeah. I just need some rest. I've been worse than this." Then, almost to herself: "A lot worse, actually."

She looked so small and frail in the candlelight, I wanted to reach out and stroke her hair. Of course I didn't do that. I left the glass in the sink and locked the door behind me on the way out.

• • •

WHEN I was a young buck back in the army, I'd believed in material things: my rifle; my bunk; my best girl, Betsy, the woman I was going to marry. I didn't have any patience for people who said they'd seen a ghost, or strange lights in the sky. Wood-knockers and rosary-kissers. Believers. But an entire adult life keeping vampire hours has changed me. The night, with its starry sky of infinite possibilities, with its unexplained knocks and whispers, has settled on my skin.

I believe in weird things.

I watched a healthy, vibrant woman's lungs fill up with fluid over the course of nine days, and there wasn't a damned thing any doctor could do about it.

I believe in the unexplained.

It was a long walk home.

I kept reliving the flash of Marlene's naked body I saw when I walked into her bedroom. Yes, it was candlelight, and yes, my eyes aren't what they used to be; but in that split second before slamming my eyes shut, I knew what I saw.

That the girl, from shoulder to knees, was covered in bruises—the deep, painful kind.

That her toenails, all ten, were white and crescent shaped, three inches long to sharp points.

And I knew, I just knew, that if I were to turn around and march back up to Marlene's bed, she'd poke her feet out from under the blanket and wiggle her toes at me, and each nail would be close trimmed, smooth, and polished. And if I were to yank back that blanket, she'd still be bruised, but even now the bruises would be lighter, already fading to nothing; and by dawn (maybe an hour off) she'd be perfectly healthy again.

"I just need some rest. I've been worse than this."

Back home, and soaked through, I poured a big slug of Scotch and drank it down like medicine, just like Marlene. I found some dry pajamas and settled down at my computer. I was no expert on all things Marlene, but I knew her name, phone number, address, car make, and tag. That and fifty bucks are enough to get an Internet detective working.

Jinks walked in to see what was up. He loves it when I put my hands on either side of him and scratch back and forth really fast, so I did, and he spun around and grabbed my hand. Such a sweetie. But one thing I never forget about cats is their dual nature. His favorite toy, a jingle ball, was under my chair. When I rolled it out my office door, he watched it a moment, tail twitching, then leaped to kill it.

• • •

THREE DAYS later, on a stunning, sunny afternoon, Marlene showed up at my door holding a Frisbee in one hand and a picnic basket—the old-fashioned kind, like Yogi Bear used to covet—in the other.

"Come on, Mr. E. Let's get you outside."

"Marlene. I just got up."

She poked my arm and grinned. "That's why there's coffee in the car."

I assumed we were headed for the local park, but Marlene had more ambitious plans. She had me drive her car twenty minutes up the interstate to Red Tail Falls, a state preserve with all sorts of camping and recreational lures. I sipped my coffee, which was rich and delicious, and tried to pry out the truth about her and Skip Tyler.

"He says his little brother was driving his car that night. He offered to beat him up for me."

"How gallant."

She looked out the window at a bare ridge passing by. "It could be true."

"Marlene, make me understand. It's driving me bonkers. What is the deal with you and Skip? It's a small subdivision, you know—I see you two together a lot. He dropped you off at your house last night. Tried to kiss you, but you dodged at the last second. Nice move, by the way."

"Thanks. He's someone to do things with, Mr. E., the things I like to do. Yesterday I got Skippy-boy to hike the reservoir gorge with me. You're the only friend I have in this town; and please don't be offended, but you could never make that hike. That's a tough fourteen miles for someone his size, and he was barely winded. He's in fantastic shape."

"I'm not offended. Even back when I could make that hike, I wouldn't have done it. Who the heck wants to walk around a gorge all day?"

She laughed. "This girl, that's who."

"So what's Skippy-boy getting out of all this?"

Marlene stopped laughing. For the first time since I'd known her, she looked a little embarrassed. "Well, he wants to get me in bed, obviously."

"And you're leading him on. Skip hasn't figured that out yet?"

I glanced over again, and the girl was positively beet red.

"W-e-e-e-lll, you give a little to get a little. Don't look at me like that, Mr. E. I really want to climb Witch Rock this weekend, and that's not a one-person climb."

Very true. Witch Rock was a semipro ascent, a local legend. Every few years someone died trying to do it. But at this point I had no doubt Marlene could climb it alone, if she wanted.

She could probably do it backward.

"And rest assured, Mr. E.," she went on, "I am not going all the way with Skip Tyler."

That cracked me up. "'Going all the way'? Are you in junior high?"

She punched my arm.

"Be careful at the prom. He might spike the punch bowl."

"I don't like foul language, Mr. E. I happen to have sensitive ears."

I bet you do.

I thought about the detective's report I had back home in my desk drawer. Marlene Amanda Clark, aka Marlene Ann Clarke, aka Marlene Amanda Clarkson. Seven changes of address in the last twelve years, and all big moves. Before she lived down the street from me, she'd lived in Deliho, Arizona. Two years before that, Subsequata City, Alaska. I loved the summation at the end of the report:

> *"Subject carries identification listing her age as twenty-three, although she lists the same age in identification carried twelve years earlier. Subject moves frequently and has access to three financial accounts, though possesses no visible means of support. This is strongly suggestive of illicit activity, although subject has no criminal record. It is the opinion of this detective that subject is a con artist."*

The opinion of this retiree was somewhat different.

I declined the online agency's offer of a more complete background check for a few hundred dollars. I could do all the sleuthing I wanted myself with newspaper archives, and maybe I'd find information I didn't want to share.

I have to admit, we had a great time at Red Tail Falls.

I jogged around and got the ol' ticker pumping, working up a sweat while Marlene, of course, was a complete acrobatic showoff. She leaped and dove, making spinning midair catches and shooting the disk right back to me before her feet touched grass. She was so graceful, so beautiful in the wind and late, slanting sunshine.

Six months ago, a month before Marlene had showed up here, a lone hiker had been killed and eaten by a mountain lion on the outskirts of Deliho, Arizona. There had been no witnesses.

I threw the Frisbee, and Marlene did a spectacular tumbling catch, ending with her flipping over on one hand and landing in a crouch. That got her a round of applause from an extended family over at the picnic tables. Marlene took a bow.

During her two years in Subsequata City, there had been four deaths by wild animal reported: a couple mauled to death and eaten as they camped by a river, about five months after she arrived; and a man and his dog (Marlene, how could you?) so completely mutilated that the attack had been attributed to a grizzly, about three weeks before she moved away.

The family at the picnic tables waved us over. They were multigenerational, so I got to sit and chat with folks close to my own age while Marlene flirted with the middle group and played with the children. They invited us to dinner, so we spread out our picnic goodies and joined them. Marlene charmed everyone.

I watched her bounce a little boy on her knee while she dug into a fat, juicy burger.

Six years ago, approximately five months after Marlene had arrived in Jacob's Corners, South Dakota, a family of four had been slaughtered while hiking a trail twelve miles north of town. Again, no witnesses; but authorities theorized two mountain lions had been involved, because it was mating season and because of the sheer amount of human flesh that had been consumed.

I watched Marlene feed the boy a French fry, a dollop of ketchup bright red on its tip. She touched his nose with it, and he squealed.

In the report back in my desk drawer (which had been a good value for fifty bucks), the detective wonders how a woman could keep up the façade of being twenty-three for at least a dozen years and probably longer. But I had no problem with that.

I had a feeling Marlene was much, much older than twenty-three.

Eventually the shadows lengthened into night and the party broke up, but not before every male present managed to hug Marlene. When we left the park, Marlene pulled a pillow out of the backseat. She slept like a rock all the way to her driveway.

We'd barely pulled in when headlights came up the road behind us and Skippy-boy's gas-guzzler parked at the curb. Skip had been drinking—he wasn't drunk—but we could smell it on him. He wanted to take her out, and she wanted to change first; and during that back and forth he wrapped her in his arms and tried to give her a big kiss, which Marlene managed to turn into a short peck before wiggling away. She led him inside by the hand, laughing out loud at some internal joke that Skip was never going to get.

• • •

MY WIFE always told me that my biggest strength, and my biggest failing, was my soft heart. It made me the man she fell in love with—a defender of the weak, a champion of strays of all species—but it also clouds my judgment, making me a fat target for unrepaid loans, a walking ATM for bums on the street.

I wondered what Betsy would say if I could ask her advice now.

The day after I saw Marlene lead Skip into her house, I stopped by the agency building to collect a check I was owed for paying to fix my own gutters. And who should be there, ordering the poor staff around like some hungover potentate?

I felt a big arm sling over my shoulder.

"Pops! Let's talk."

I let him lead me to a shabby little office.

"I hear you've been hanging with my girlfriend," he said, coming through the doorway.

"I hope not."

"No worries, Pops, I'm not gonna…" Then he got it. "Oh yeah. You mean you hope she's not my girlfriend. Funny guy."

I took my seat, and he went around his pasteboard desk to his swivel chair. The room was wood paneling and cheap carpeting, featuring a shelf of athletic trophies. When he settled his impressive frame in his seat, I looked into his face for the first time since I walked in.

Skippy-boy had a hell of a shiner.

He saw me notice, and one hand went up to his eye.

"Bitch nailed me, man. Oh yeah. Never saw it coming, and she's *strong*. We're on the couch, right? Things are going okay—I'm just trying to get some action. I know she wants it. They *all* want it. Okay, maybe I got a little pushy. But God *damn*, give it up already." He shook his head. "Next thing I know it's lights out. I come to flat on my back and Marlene's standing over me, handing me a raw steak."

Eleven years ago, in a suburb outside White Plains, a burglar had broken into the house of one Marlene Ann Clarke and somehow managed to get his arm caught in the garbage disposal—all the way up to the elbow. He bled to death, probably in considerable agony. The "victim" was not home at the time.

But I bet the cat was.

"You know, Skip, maybe you should forget about Marlene and find yourself another young lady."

He cut his eyes at me (his good one, anyway), like maybe I was up to something, but then turned and stared out the window at the hedges and the little office park beyond.

He shook his head. "She's under my skin, man."

Skip reached down to a mini-fridge, took out two beers, and plopped one down on the desk in front of me.

Lovely.

"You know we hiked the gorge the other day, right?" I nodded. "There's this waterfall about halfway in, a straight-drop eight footer. Doesn't get much traffic 'cause it's so far out. Really nice. I've gotten so much tail out there, man. Get a girl out there with the flowers and the waterfall? Panties fly right off."

"I've seen pictures," I said. "Of Faithful Falls, I mean, not the flying panties."

"So anyway, we get out there, and Marlene freaks out on account of it's so pretty and shit. Says she just has to take a shower. And she strips naked right there, man. Goes and stands under the waterfall. I'm thinking, Hot damn! Finally." He winked at me. "You remember, right?"

"I recall sex, yes."

"Get you some of those blue pills, Pops; go up to the retirement home. You just know those old biddies are raging for a boner."

This was never going to end.

"So I get naked, right? And I head into the waterfall, and those rocks are slippery, Pops. I barely made it across. But when I get there, I can't get a hand on her. It was unreal—I could barely keep my feet under me, and she's dancing around like some sort of circus act. Then I fall on my ass. By the time I get up, I look out, and Marlene's already back on land getting dressed." He leaned forward. "So answer me this. What the fuck *was* that? I know women, Pops. They don't get naked like that unless they plan to give it up. Fucking little cocktease. She knew what she was doing."

If I wore a watch, I would've glanced at it.

"Anyway, Pops. What I want, since you two hang out and shit, is talk to her about me. Okay? Give a report back, like mano to mano. See if she's really interested, you know. If I'm even on her menu."

I burst out laughing.

Skip laughed with me, even though he didn't know why. We laughed until finally he caught himself and asked, "What's so funny?"

I stopped laughing too.

If what I suspected was true, it really wasn't funny.

I hated Skip Tyler. I hated every boorish, cocky centimeter of Skip Tyler. And I adored Marlene. She was my friend. My only friend, really. My children were scattered around the country, and my last real buddy had died a few years back. It was just me and the cats until Marlene came along. Now I even had the phone number of one of the gals from back at the picnic site, a trim and sixty-ish woman who wanted to catch a show with me sometime. Marlene was responsible for all my recent happiness.

And my cats loved her.

But Skip Tyler was still a human being, and my soft heart went out to him. Marlene had to be stopped.

And I was the only one who could stop her.

• • •

THE CONCEPT of the werecat exists on five continents, from the were-jaguar in South America to the were-tiger in Asia. The belief that a human can shape-shift into a common cat is the oldest lycanthrope legend of them all. It predates the werewolf by at least a thousand years.

It originated in ancient Egypt, in the era of the Sphinx, the land of Ra and Set.

The fear that somewhere out there lurks a creature that can assume multiple feline forms is strictly North American, however. This includes the monster that can be half cat, half human. All were-creatures seemed to share one common trait: an aversion to silver.

Marlene didn't own any silver.

I turned off my computer and rubbed my tired eyes.

Why would I do anything to help Skip?

How could I hurt Marlene?

I imagined Betsy's voice, as I sometimes do when I have to make a difficult decision. "You'll do the right thing," she told me. "You always do."

Marlene and Skip were going to climb Witch Rock on Saturday morning. They planned to go up Friday night and camp at the base, where the lake spreads out smooth and glassy to the cabins far on the other side. It's a beautiful, isolated spot. I didn't think Marlene would kill Skip that night. For one, I really believed she wanted to scale Witch Rock; and for another, I think she knew I'd be suspicious if she went out into the wilderness with Skip and came back without him, no matter what panther-attack story she came up with. No, I think Skippy-boy was "on Marlene's menu" for some-time next week, some impromptu thing where she swung by and picked him up from work and headed for the hills.

Something she wouldn't tell me about.

There was a single constant in every town in which Marlene had lived over the last dozen years. An animal attack about five months after she arrived (and she'd been here about five months), then a long stretch, sometimes two years, followed by a second attack. Then she moved, often within weeks. It made sense. One attack, well, these things happen occasionally in the wilderness. A second and the locals got up in arms. Time to beat the bush, find that creature. Kill it.

I thought about Skip and Marlene's campsite, how they would pitch it near the lake, with Witch Rock looming above.

I wasn't going to get a better chance.

I sighed.

I was going to need special bullets.

That's all right though. I learned how to pack my own ammo back in the service, when I was PFC Edelman, later Sergeant Edelman. Infantry and expert marksman.

• • •

THE NEXT day I stayed at home doing chores, "Livin' La Vida Local," as my son calls it. By the time four in the morning crept up, I was sitting on the porch sipping my tea with the radio turned low.

Marlene came walking up the opposite side of the road, taking the same path Tabitha used to take. I whistled to her. She crossed over, down the hill, and plopped into the chair beside me as if she owned the place.

"Can't sleep," she said.

"Take one of your pills," I said.

She looked at me blankly. "Oh! My sleeping pills, for my ulcer—I'm out."

"That's a shame. Guess you'll have to be a creature of the night, like me."

"There are worse fates." She arched her back and stretched out her arms. "I don't know why I'm so restless tonight."

"You know what we should do? Drive up to Red Tail and watch the sun come up. Betsy and I used to do that every once in a while. If you've never seen dawn break over the ridge up there, you're missing out."

"Why, Mr. Edelman. Are you suggesting an unmarried woman such as myself and a distinguished older gentleman such as yourself undertake a wilderness excursion unchaperoned? At night?"

"What would the neighbors think?"

"We could always ask each other, then we'd both know." She nudged my leg with her foot. "You aren't afraid I might take advantage of you?"

"Nope." I looked in her eyes. "I trust you."

She smiled. "I can tell."

• • •

THERE WASN'T even the slightest gray in the east when we arrived at the preserve, but dawn was coming. Call it pre-predawn. After all my nights wide-awake, I can sense it.

The best place to watch the sunrise required us to cut a shallow path through the woods, and I led Marlene by the hand, stumbling over roots and dodging branches. I wondered if she was laughing at me back there, since I knew she could see just fine.

We broke from the copse, and I spread the blanket on the hill as the slightest lightning appeared over the ridge. We laid back, really more of a recline because of the angle, and waited. The first part of the show takes a few moments: The sun burns off the cold dew on the other side of the ridge, and vapor rises among the trees, which are just coming into silhouette.

"Ooooh," said Marlene. "Ghostly."

We were alone as far as I could tell, maybe the only people within miles.

"You'll love this. I wanted to find some way of thanking you for all you've done these last few weeks. You've made me realize I still have a little gas left in the tank, after all. I think I'm going to try some ballroom dancing with Clara—the woman from the picnic?"

Marlene put her head on my chest like a daughter might. "Watch out for her, Mr. E. I think she set her cap for you as soon as you sat down."

The sky on the ridge lightened, and the vapor was rolling up like steam through a grate. The breeze whisked it around in eddies.

"I knew you were a good person as soon as I met Vagabond and Jinks," said Marlene. "Cats are picky. If your cats love you, you can't be all bad."

"I've probably had a dozen over the years. The three great loves of my life: Betsy, cats, and the night. Cats are great. Beautiful, smart, independent, companionable, and playful when they want. It's easy to forget they're basically little killing machines."

I felt her nod against my chest. "Dual natured, they are." Her hair smelled like strawberry shampoo, the crown of her head just below my chin.

Her mouth a half foot from my throat.

The sun broke over the ridge. Deep gold and feathery pink washed over me, Marlene, the hill, everything.

"Wow," she whispered.

About fifteen yards away, a rabbit hopped out of the grass and toward the ridge. It wasn't in any particular hurry as rabbits go. It hadn't noticed us. I had a flashback of the rabbit I saw that first night that Tabitha had come to visit.

Marlene's body twitched against me.

The rabbit froze, looking back at us, its fur streaked gold and red in the sunrise.

I felt four long fingernails against my shirt, poking at my shoulder.

Marlene's stomach rumbled.

Marlene sat up abruptly, then stood, smoothing her jeans with her palms. She watched the rabbit hightail it off into the distance. "Come on, Mr. E.! I'm thinking breakfast."

"Right now? There's a lot more sunrise left."

"Yeah, now, I think." She turned and helped me up with one smooth pull of her arm. "I see a big plate of sausage and bacon in my future." She turned and headed back toward the parking lot, pulling me along by the hand like an eager kid.

"There's a breakfast place right at the bottom of the drive," I said.

She laughed out loud, like an explosion of relief. "That's good news, Mr. E. I'm *starving*."

• • •

I HOPED I'd only need one bullet, but I broke apart and refilled a dozen. I'd need some for target practice since the lighter weight of the ammo was going to throw off the sight and range, and some more for my back-up plan in case I was seen before I fired: just point the rifle and start pulling the trigger.

I decided to go with a .22 short—an assassin's rifle—since I wasn't concerned about stopping power. And a .22 short will take a silencer.

On Friday, the day Marlene and Skip were heading up to Witch Rock, I went to the target range, fired some rounds, and adjusted my sight.

I needed to be at the lake before them, settled in downwind and under the cover of darkness. I called Marlene and fed her the oldest lie in the book.

"I'm going to visit a friend in the hospital; do you think you could drop by and feed the cats dinner? Around five?"

"No prob, Mr. E. That's about when me and Skip are heading out, anyway."

Nice to know. But I needed some insurance, so on my way out of town I stopped by the rental office, strolled by Skip's Escalade, and slipped my jackknife into the sides of both front tires. He wouldn't notice until he left work, and that should hold them up an hour, at the least.

Then I rented a car, on the wild chance Skip or Marlene might notice my own parked up around the mountain, and I made the ninety-minute run west to Witch Rock.

I hadn't been up there in about twelve years; it was the last time Betsy and I had rented one of these places. Not much had changed: cabins on one side of the lake, the mountain face rising near vertical on the other. I made it around the long trail to the mountain, huffing and puffing, and stopping twice to rest, about the time I figured Skip was staring at two flat tires, cursing out loud.

Plenty of places to camp over here, in theory, but I was betting on the place where a sandy beach led down to the lakeshore. If I knew Skip, a suggestion of skinny-dipping was on the agenda; and if I knew Marlene, she'd be up for it.

I scanned the low foothills at the rock's base until I found the best spot—not too far away, good brush cover.

I pulled a protein bar and a thermos of coffee out of my pack, and waited.

• • •

I HEARD them before I saw them. There's not much but rock and water out here, so sound carries. A female voice was chirping along, and a deeper voice sounded at intervals. Then two flashlight beams began sweeping the ground a hundred yards away, at the bend in the trail. They came closer, and I knew the beams were searching out this narrow strip of beach.

They stopped to pitch their tent close enough to where I thought they would. I didn't have to move.

The night wasn't very dark—a bowl of stars above the lake and moonlight bobbing on the water—but I had to wait until they built their campfire. My eyes aren't what they used to be. I was just glad things had quieted down on the cabin side of the lake. Just two hours earlier I could still hear raised voices and boat motors, but now there was only the still water and the cabin windows, little stars of yellow light.

I had a bad moment when they started gathering brush; but there was no reason for them to come up to where I was, and they didn't.

The campfire crackled and rose, and I finally started to get a decent visual. Marlene danced around the flames, and Skip trotted behind her. She let him get his arms around her—a kiss, a grab on the behind—then she was off, laughing about it.

I steadied my rifle.

Hold still, people.

The fire finally roared up. Marlene circled Skip, pulled off her shirt, gave a yank, and stepped out of her shorts. Naked as the day she was born. Whenever that was.

Skip and I both paused in admiration.

Marlene watched him, her weight on the balls of her feet. She licked her lips. I was sure when Skippy-boy lunged she would sprint off into the lake. But at that moment they both stood still.

I settled my sights.

Sorry, Marlene.

I squeezed the trigger and put a bullet into Skip Tyler's chest. Marlene yelped and jumped back from the blood spray. The special half-powder ammo I'd packed had a subsonic muzzle velocity, so coupled with the silencer, the sound that carried over the lake, to the cabins, was less than a finger snap.

If it even carried that far, which I really doubted.

No reason anyone would investigate.

Skippy-boy dropped like a fat sack of obnoxious flour. I aimed and put another in his head.

Marlene watched me come out from my cover and down the hill, hands on her hips, just like Betsy used to do when she was peeved at me.

"*Dang*, Mr. E. For someone who's not my mate, you sure do see me naked a lot." She looked down and nudged Skip with her foot—he was still gurgling and twitching.

"I hope the gunshot doesn't show up on the autopsy," I said.

"Don't worry," said Marlene. "There's not gonna be a whole lot of Skip left to autopsy."

"I apologize."

She shrugged. "That's okay. The fresh meat's more important than the kill. Although I do enjoy the kill."

Then she glanced off at the cabins across the lake, the dots of glowing windows. Licked her lips.

"Marlene!"

"It's okay, Mr. E. I'm fine for now." She reached down, came up with a palm full of blood, and lapped it, closing her eyes in delight.

When she opened them, they were bright yellow and split vertically, like a cat's.

"I'd take off now if I were you. Once I start, I have a bit of an impulse control problem."

"See you tomorrow night?"

"Absolutely! Wine and movies. I'll bring a roast."

I turned and walked off down the trail. I'd gone maybe a dozen steps when she called after me.

"Mr. E? Why'd you do it?"

"Because I know cats, and I have a soft heart. I just couldn't stand it anymore." I looked at Skip's body. "You keeping that poor thing alive just so you could play with it."

AUTHOR

JOHN JASPER OWENS lives in the South, where he blogs for T2N, a diabetes magazine, and continues to offer fiction and humor at low, low prices. You'll also find him lurking in the terminal at TQRstories.com, on Twitter under @JJasperO, and at the various ports of call to be found when you Google his full name.

When Your Thieving Days Are Over

Wendy Sparrow

HE'D TIMED it so he'd be there when the mail carrier opened the large block of postboxes. Houston, as he was calling himself these days, had raised casual to an art form. He leaned against the wall opposite and fiddled with his mobile. He could have been checking his e-mail, playing a game… or taking a picture of the post slots that he could consult later.

No doubt in his mind—there was at least two days' worth of post in number 42's box. She lived alone, didn't buy much, and rarely had visitors; and when she'd collected her post on other occasions, when he'd been standing right beside her, subtly inhaling the perfume she wore, she'd only ever had a couple envelopes.

Something was wrong. Decidedly wrong.

Bloody hell.

Unfortunately, he didn't have time to investigate. He was late for group.

Later.

Later, he'd break into the flat above him and find out what had happened to the short, sweet brunette. Though he shouldn't…because he didn't do that anymore.

• • •

IT WAS difficult to find a support group for Houston's niche. Few people were trying to recover from successful careers as up-market thieves. More than anything, he wanted to experience some sort of remorse. He wanted to *want* to recover.

A good person, a righteous person, *would* feel remorseful.

He'd committed felony after felony. He'd violated the eighth commandment time and again. He should desire to do penance—even if he wouldn't actually follow through. There should be that desire.

Instead there was pride, pride that he'd gotten out at the top of his game and retired in his thirties. Most of his compatriots were caught because they became greedy or sloppy, or the game and the rush drew them back in. They couldn't remain retired.

He'd stolen enough for his needs. Sloppiness wasn't in his makeup. And Houston was too methodical for it to be a game, and there'd never been a rush.

What was a chap to do when he stopped coveting as his needs were met and had never been punished for his sins? What should a sinner do?

Houston went to a support group for shoplifters, and he was on time because punctuality was a long-forgotten virtue.

Sitting down in his regular spot in the circle, Houston nodded at the group's moderator, Katya Dodger. Dodger wasn't her real last name. It didn't feel right for a person not to have a surname, so he'd made up last names for all of them. You couldn't trust a person who didn't have a surname. Not that he trusted any of them; they stole things.

"There's refreshments in the back," she told those filing in. She'd written a sign that said: "Help yourself! You don't have to steal!"

Well, no, not anymore he didn't, but mostly because he'd helped himself.

Conrad Stickyhands sat down on his right—as Conrad always did.

They always sat in certain spots, and their sharing went in a clockwise direction, not anticlockwise. There'd been a group in L.A. that went anticlockwise. Starkers. He couldn't move there. You *always* went clockwise. His world was a world of order. Situations should make sense. People should be where they belong.

Unless there wasn't a support group for them, in which case you took what you could get.

He *should* want to reform. What sort of person didn't feel guilty about nicking what didn't belong to him or her? Everyone else at these meetings was here in order to recover from an *addiction*.

"How are you, Houston?" Katya asked.

Not one of them ever told the truth either—which is how he could look her in the eyes and say, "Can't complain. Life's been good. How have you been?" All while thinking, *When was the last time Melody walked across her floor... Tuesday, Wednesday? Here it is early Thursday night, so it might have been two days. She might have been missing for two days.*

A good person would call the police.

Well, a good person with no skills to speak of and a conscience that prevented him from using any such skills.

Not using his skills when he could was a sin, a crime. Possibly.

"I'm fine," Katya said with a warm smile. She'd invited him out for a cup of coffee after the last meeting, but he'd told her he'd recently cut out of a long-term relationship and wasn't ready to move on.

He'd been a thief since he was sixteen. Twenty years devoted to that was longer than most marriages. It didn't feel right to date when he wasn't sure he had a heart to give.

Of course if it'd been Melody asking, they'd have had coffee, dinner, breakfast, lunch, brunch, elevenses—endless meals—because he was a heartless bastard, a sinner, a thief. He'd nick every moment he could get with her and not even think of reforming. It'd be worse than a relapse—it'd be true addiction.

Houston slapped Conrad's hand without looking. There wasn't a support group for bad pickpockets either, so Conrad was a man without a country as well. They had to stick together. To band as brothers, to reform. To that end, the pocket Conrad always tried to swipe from was full of broken glass. Eventually he'd find that out...when he managed a respectable level of subterfuge. Right now his piss-poor attempts couldn't outwit Houston's instincts against letting another chap reach into his pocket.

"Well, let's get started," Katya said, clapping her hands together.

The others had all been late. Punctuality truly was a forgotten virtue.

Houston only gave the meeting half his attention. It was impolite. He nodded and said names and tried to attend to their trivial problems.

Amy Manhands had nearly slipped and stolen from her husband's boss during a work party.

Gemma Babbles told some rubbish about a little black dress and a bounced check. It was difficult to care that she'd gone back to nick the dress when you were cheering for her to get it over with. Pinch the dress already! Let us get on with our bleeding lives!

He slapped Conrad's hand before rubbing both his hands down his face. These tedious people with their silly, sad-sack problems.

He'd rung Melody's place of work and asked for her, but she telecommuted a portion of the week, so she didn't go in to the office. She should be at home in her flat, typing away on her computer. *Where are you, Melody?*

And all around him, the group spilled story after story.

Joseph Wartface had a stereo in his car; he didn't know where it came from. Right, mate. Sure. It'd appeared. Out of nowhere. He claimed his kleptomania was involuntary. But he also liked the attention. It was tempting to involuntarily trip him.

Gary Nochin was doing much better. Good for him. Of course, Gary being here was court ordered, so he was motivated to improve. He shouldn't get full marks if he was being coerced. Not that it was Houston's place to judge. Judge not that ye be not judged.

He did give Lana Rack all of his attention because some people sincerely needed more support, and several of her shoplifting stories included indecent-exposure sidebars, and those were always good for a laugh.

Houston slapped Conrad's hand again.

Jake Darkalley, on the other hand, was a liar about being a thief. He'd sit there in the tippy orange plastic chairs and stare at them with hot eyes. Jake was a killer. There was always a pause—a telling pause in his speech. "This week, my neighbor left her car unlocked, and I resisted the urge to…take something from it." Or hide in it and slit her throat. The way he looked at the women in the group—well, good thing the parking lot outside the church where they met was well lit and visible, not a dark alley.

Jake was one opportunity away from a nasty regression.

Men without consciences recognized other men without consciences, and Jake *should* catch fire every time he set foot in this church. Unfortunately, there didn't seem to be a support group for serial killers either. This shoplifting support group was a bit of a catchall when you got right down to it.

One of these days Houston would follow Jake home and break into his house and prove what he suspected. But he didn't do that anymore—breaking and entering. He still followed people. All the time. A sort of recreational surveillance, if you will.

He slapped Conrad's hand again.

Conrad's turn. He rubbed his hand as he said, "Hello, my name is Conrad."

"Hello, Conrad," they all murmured. The monotone chant always made Houston's left eye twitch. Some repetition he appreciated, even approved of, but not the monotone greeting. He still did it—it'd be rude not to—but he loathed it.

"I've been making some real progress," Conrad said. "I haven't stolen anything for two months." Not for lack of trying, of course.

He should give the bloke lessons in proper thieving. How could you reform from something you'd botched to hell?

But the fact that Houston considered that was another sign he was without conscience, a sinner of the worst kind: a sinner who celebrated sin and wanted a few mates to join the party.

A minute later it was his turn.

"Hello, my name is Houston." Still not his real name.

"Hello, Houston."

"It's been six months since my last theft." A whale's bungalow in Vegas. The two vases were the last buffer he'd needed to keep him comfortable for the rest of his life. Comfortable—but not excessively so. Greed was a vice.

Katya leaned forward. She always did when he spoke. It was a classic sign of attraction. Lana crossed her legs and aimed them in his direction—and made pointed eye contact.

From an objective standpoint he *was* the most attractive man here, but it was Houston's next words that were the true draw to their attention. "It doesn't matter. I could do it again tomorrow and not recognize it as an offense."

He slapped Conrad's hand.

Women were attracted to men without principles. It ignited a desire to save them, to fix them, to let themselves be broken. Both Katya and Lana were attracted to Jake as well—and that prat needed a bath more than Conrad *didn't* need a handful of broken glass.

"Houston, I think it's important that you recognize the people you've hurt by stealing." Katya always spoke to him as if they were the only ones in the room. Her eyes locked on his. Her voice was hushed and heated.

After slapping Conrad's hand again, Houston held out his hands. "That's just the problem. I haven't hurt anyone."

"Your family," Katya said.

"I have none."

"No parents?"

Houston shook his head. It was another lie, but Tom and Valerie of Liverpool deserved better than a son without a moral compass.

"No girlfriend or wife?"

He raised his eyebrows. Technically, she wasn't to ask that. He could volunteer it, sure, but she wasn't supposed to ask him for personal information. He shook his head regardless.

She smiled. Unprofessional. He expected more of someone entrusted with moderating this rabble. You'd think she'd at least bring *that* to the group.

Out of the corner of his eye he saw Lana sit up just a bit straighter. Yes, well, Lana was...Lana.

Making her face blank, Katya asked, "Well, what about those you stole from?"

"They could always afford it, and besides, an attachment to material wealth is often acknowledged to be a sin as well."

"Yeah, but they don't throw you in jail for having a flat screen," Joseph said.

Everyone laughed. And it was funny. Why shouldn't they? Most of them were far more concerned about the legal repercussions of their acts. *Morality* and *sin* were words that tasted old-fashioned and outdated. They embraced the terms *legal* and *illegal* and let the government dictate and replace their consciences.

"Well, how would you feel if someone stole from you?" Conrad asked.

Houston sat back with a sigh. How would he feel? If it was all gone tomorrow, perhaps he'd need to get a real job and make something of himself. Find something he did well, something rewarding. The thief might even be doing him a favor. "There's nothing I have that I couldn't do without." Still, he slapped Conrad's hand again. Conrad would momentarily realize he could do without a handful of broken glass.

"Nothing?" Jake asked.

Houston shrugged. They pitied him. It was in their eyes, their body language. Who wouldn't want things? Feel comforted by things? How would it be not to miss a car or a laptop or a what-have-you?

But they were merely items, property he didn't have ten years ago. Things he hadn't earned for the most part—unless you considered a well-planned and flawlessly executed robbery a worthy venture, in which case he deserved every last penny. In the grand scheme though, possessions came in and out of his life and didn't possess him.

"The first step is to recognize you have a problem and you aren't in control," Katya said.

"I've quit of my own volition because I was done. Does that mean there's no need for recovery?" It would seem to mean that. This *was* an addiction recovery group, after all. He'd never been addicted. It'd been similar to a hobby he'd quit when the price of supplies got too high. When he had enough means for his needs, he needed to stay out of jail to enjoy it. Voilà. Retirement.

"No, that means you're full of it," Jake said. "We've all said we can stop any day; but we don't, unless someone, or something, stops us from… stealing."

Houston looked around at the others to see if they'd noticed Jake's pause. The git had as good as admitted what he was; but, no, they were all nodding and staring at Houston.

He was the freak here. Hell, maybe even Jake wanted to quit. Doubtful but possible.

Then there was Houston. He was conscienceless. He couldn't make it past the first step in the program. That ruddy first step.

"One step at a time," Conrad said, patting him on the back and trying a swipe with his other hand.

Houston blocked him—because he genuinely appreciated the gesture. Conrad was, at heart, a good person…and a shite thief.

Katya motioned for the woman at his side, Harriet Housewife, to take her turn when Houston held up a hand. She nodded at him.

"What about a relapse in an emergency?"

"An emergency?" she asked.

"What if…nicking something was more moral than not?" Or breaking and entering was the only way to find out what had happened to his upstairs neighbor. He'd sworn he wouldn't do it again six months ago. The vases were the last time.

Plus, technically, the crime he was committing would be against Melody. He only committed crimes against people who were worse than he was—not far, far better than he.

If he wasn't amoral he'd consider this a moral conundrum. Since he was unscrupulous, it was simply a conundrum.

"How could that *ever* be more moral?" Ned Nosefiend asked. The twit lacked imagination—and should be in a narcotics support group. Stealing was the least of his worries.

"You mean like stealing medicine for someone dying?" Lana asked. She wanted him to be a good person so much…or at least moderately redeemable. Her legs crossed in his direction, and the softening lilt in her voice spoke volumes.

"Sure," he said. It was as good a scenario as any. "Is there ever a time when a righteous person would commit a crime and it *would* be morally justified?" Should he feel bad he was about to relapse? Because he didn't. He was intending to do it the instant he got home.

"Maybe that's just rationalization," Katya said.

He shrugged again. "Or maybe I'm just not a righteous person." Houston stood up. "If you'll excuse me, I apologize, but I have somewhere I need to be." He leaned down and made eye contact with Conrad. "You, my friend, will find that what you think you want is not what you want. Stealing from a thief can be a bleeding pain."

And he left with all their thieving, guilty eyes following him.

• • •

THE LOCKS on the postboxes were a sin. A crime. A felony against all theft protection. Twist a pin—and as neat as that you're in. Of course, there was the matter of postal fraud being such a big deal among the law abiding, but it wouldn't keep him up at night. Nothing kept him up at night. He slept better than a newborn babe.

He sorted through Melody's post.

"Oh, hey, Dallas," his idiot neighbor, Chad, said.

"It's Houston," he said, though it was still not his name.

"That's right. Houston, we have a problem!"

More forethought would be put into his next given name, providing he did change. The righteous probably seldom changed their names and identities.

Chad chuckled to himself while pulling his own post from the box right beside where Houston was reaching in. A brighter chap would have noticed that Houston was blatantly searching through someone else's postbox. Chad was no such person, and thus Houston's current apparent sloppiness was truly a versed awareness of the intuition of the average person. In Houston's opinion. He hadn't gotten shoddy because he was worried about Melody.

Conscienceless bastards didn't worry—they were intrigued. They sometimes felt compelled to solve a mystery. This was a one-off though. One last hurrah and then he was once again retired.

They both turned from the postboxes, and Houston used the lock pick to close Melody's box. He'd known Chad wouldn't notice—he'd *known* that.

"So, how come your name is Houston, but you're from England?" Chad asked as they climbed the stairs while Houston was still opening Melody's post.

She was paying too bleeding much for Internet. Highway robbery right there.

"My grandparents were British."

"Oh, and you lived with them?"

"No, but they were, and you can't contest your DNA."

"But you have a British accent," Chad said.

Melody was due to have her teeth cleaned as well, a tooth figure on a postcard insisted.

"I have from birth. They say it's like that sometimes."

The git was at least bright enough to give him a quizzical look, so he might be of some use after all.

"Have you seen the brunette who lives in number 42 recently?" Houston asked him.

Chad grinned. "I saw her a few days ago. She had on this tight black shirt and whatever girls call those shorts that aren't shorts but they're not pants."

"Capris?" Luckily even dimwits could be of use. So Chad hadn't seen her for a few days.

"Yeah. Those. I was going to ask her out or something, but she's been acting funny the last week. Avoiding me and everything."

So it hadn't just been Houston she'd avoided.

Houston and Melody had been pushing closer to doing more than nodding and chatting whenever they bumped into each other. And they'd been bumping into each other more and more. It was getting more blatant. More…bumping.

They used every excuse, no matter how flimsy, to touch each other. He was purposefully demonstrating to her he was open to a relationship—she was most likely doing it instinctively. Courtship body language was Human

Nature 101. Procreative presentation was how even fools such as Chad outwitted Darwin.

If Houston had any principles, he'd leave Melody alone.

She deserved a partner of strong moral fiber.

On the other hand, he didn't have a conscience preventing him from wanting her, so he'd been planning on asking her out as well.

Melody and Chad—would have been a sin, a crime against nature. Houston would have been saving her from that.

Maybe he was a good person.

The past week, for the most part, he hadn't seen her—and he'd *tried* to see her. She'd been purposefully avoiding him. Sweet, sweet Melody had even ducked into a ladies' lavatory to avoid him.

It'd hurt. He might not have a conscience, but that didn't mean he didn't have a heart.

Then, in a sudden contradiction, on Monday she'd chased him down on the pavement and walked beside him for several blocks, talking about nothing: a film she'd been to. It'd been as if she was trying to prove she wasn't avoiding him.

"You like her, don't you?" Chad asked, stopping beside his door.

Houston was going through her post, reliving every moment they'd spent together, and about to break into her flat; but he shrugged.

Chad grinned. "You do! Well, I'd like to tell you I'll back off and let you have her, but I'm not that great a guy."

It was too easy. The verbal setup was too obvious. Still…"I'm sure you're not."

Grinning inanely, Chad shut the door.

Tucking the post into his inside pocket, Houston headed for the roof.

• • •

HOUSTON WAS born without a fear of heights. He could've stood on the Tower of Babel and only noticed the wind on his face—and what a view—before God knocked it down on its sinful architects.

He'd often told people that he climbed out of his cot at four months. It was a lie—how would he remember that? But he told people that. He never gave anyone *true* personal information. It was like what some cultures believed of mirrors. If someone knew the truth about you, they'd steal your soul. And despite what he said in group, thieves didn't appreciate being stolen from.

They all lied in group though—so that wasn't a sin.

Rappelling the side of the building, Houston dropped onto Melody's balcony. If they were together, he'd have insisted on updating the locks on any external door. Instead, he popped it open and went inside.

Her flat smelled empty. To a burglar's nose, the place had been vacant for two days.

When he'd first moved in five months ago, she'd been dating some bastard who wore white socks with black pants. She'd dumped him…which spoke to her good taste. Her ex had been around a few times since then. Once he'd hammered on her door, plastered after a bender—so drunk she'd threatened to call the police. When she'd gone to the phone, Houston had escorted the sot out of the building and onto the pavement. The ex wasn't in the picture . . . or, indeed, any of the pictures around the flat.

All the pictures were of people who resembled Melody—obviously family. She'd mentioned a sister once when they'd talked. You didn't tell single members of the opposite sex about your family if you weren't attracted to them.

Her counter was free of clutter. Everything was sorted out to its proper spot. No dishes in the sink—perhaps this was a planned trip. Houston opened her fridge. An unopened quart of milk and leftover Chinese food. She wasn't wasteful, and she wouldn't be on holiday and not hold her post. Not Melody.

Perhaps an unplanned trip? An emergency had come up. The place seemed too tidy for her to have rushed out.

Still, no stone left unturned.

An organized soul, like himself, would keep things they might need in practical locations. Her address book was next to her phone. Admirable. Exactly where it should be. He flipped it open and skipped to "Mom" and dialed on his burner mobile.

"Hello?" Her mum sounded like Melody would in twenty years.

"May I please speak with Melody?" He dropped his accent. It was too memorable. Too soul stealing.

"My daughter?"

"Yes, this is a coworker of hers, and I have something she needs, and you're listed as a contact."

"She's not here. Have you tried her cell phone?"

Repeatedly. That's why he'd started using a burner. If something untoward had happened, he didn't want the police wasting precious time chasing him down. "No, I haven't. The number we have on file is wrong."

"Oh, she changed it a few months back. An ex-boyfriend was stalking her."

"That's horrible." A good person, a decent person, would recognize that he was fundamentally doing the same thing.

"Here's her cell phone number." She rattled off the number he'd been ringing.

"I'll try that then. Thank you." As soon as he hung up, the home phone beside him rang. Melody's mum was a good sort. Of course, she'd try to get hold of her daughter now. She wouldn't have any more luck than he'd had most likely. At the very least, he wasn't planning on answering Melody's home phone.

He moved on to Melody's bedroom. She made her bed. Like he did. That was commendable. If he hadn't already fancied himself in love with her, the knife-edge of her turned-down sheet would have done it.

Sitting on the bed, he opened her nightstand. Reading glasses. He knew she had them, of course. Once when she'd left her flat, the indents had still been there, faintly, on the sides of her nose. It had unleashed a subset of fantasies for him.

Underneath the glasses was a manila envelope. He should feel bad about pulling it out and opening it, but he didn't.

Then he grew a conscience. Quite suddenly. Immediately. It bloomed like a late rose inside him.

Ruddy hell.

No wonder she'd been avoiding him. He wasn't a good person, but whoever had sent her a photo of Houston and her talking on the pavement that had been torn in half with "You don't belong with him!" scrawled across was a truly deplorable person. He sighed and dropped the pieces of the photo on the nightstand. Having a conscience was bloody awful.

• • •

THE PHONE hadn't stopped ringing in her flat—and it wouldn't. Her mum was decent, kind, caring; she'd raised Melody, and Melody was all those things.

Meanwhile, he was in his own flat. The sun had gone down, and he'd wanted her place to appear vacant. His conscience was weighing him down—so much so that he was lying on his back on the floor while throwing a racquetball against the ceiling. He only did this when Melody was gone. And she was definitely gone.

Someone had taken her.

The photo had been torn to separate him from Melody. He'd taped the two pieces back together. It made sense, and it eased the pangs from his newly born soul somewhat as well.

Who could have taken her?

Someone who wanted the sweet charmer for himself—for him alone. That queue of suspects included any man who'd ever met beautiful, delicate, sweet Melody, but especially that ex. Bloody hell, even Chad made the list.

No, it wasn't him. Chad was too daft. He'd believe it was Melody's mum before he'd believe it was that git. Bugger, he'd believe it was himself before Chad.

The other option was that they didn't want her seeing Houston. Specifically. Which made his brand-new conscience sting in his chest.

Either scenario explained why she'd stayed away from him, as well as why she'd then decided—because she was as fierce as she was sweet—that no one was going to tell her what to do, so she'd chatted with him on Monday.

Fierce, sweet, beautiful…and someone had stolen her away from him.

Setting the ball beside him, he picked up the photo again. From the angle it must have been taken from above and likely from a building down the block. He pushed up off the floor and collected his kit—the kit he'd sworn was as retired as he was. He'd always dressed in dark colors. Tonight was no different. This wasn't a complete relapse. Not until he took something. Until he nicked something he was a man in dark clothes, stumbling into a door with lock picks outstretched. Implausibly accidental.

Twice in one night, Houston. Twice in one night. This was no longer a one-off.

But his new conscience didn't keep him in his flat.

Syracuse was nice this time of year. If you *had* to relocate to a city that had a support group for thieves, you could do worse.

He glanced from the building to the pavement behind him and back at the building. The picture had definitely been taken from one of four flats' balconies. Bugger all. Four balconies to check? This was beginning to reek of a relapse.

Twice. Thrice. He blinked. What did one call breaking out of retirement four and five times over? Frice? Fice? Quarce? Quince? Damn, he didn't even know. When had the world ceased to make sense?

This was what came of crowding your mind with scruples. Houston *had* to go and grow a conscience at a bleeding inconvenient time.

On the other hand, group was a success. Well, not entirely. He'd met some interesting people, and perhaps they'd help him wrestle this conscience he'd developed into behaving.

But he *did* think someone stealing Melody from him was wrong. He'd made that first step. He was there. Stealing could *be* reprehensible. Whoever had stolen her would be feeling the full force of the consequences. There'd be penance.

Houston took his bag of tricks up the fire escape and rappelled down. He always rappelled down rather than climbing up. He lost a rope now and again that way when he couldn't take the time to get it before leaving; but, by and large, it just made sense.

The telly was flashing inside the flat as he looked over the balcony and pulled out the picture and squared it up with his view. Not quite. But it had to be the balcony beneath this one. He didn't need his rope this time as he hopped over, hung, swung, and dropped. Good thing he'd kept in shape—even if he hadn't planned on doing this anymore.

Holding up the photo again, he compared the angle. This was it. Turning around, he scanned the door—then pulled out his lock picks. People in this area were too trusting. A quick flick later he was in, and it'd been empty far longer than Melody's flat. He inhaled, exhaled. At *least* a week, but he'd guess more like two weeks. Whoever owned this place hadn't been on the premises in a while—during which this place had been vacant and asking for someone to use the balcony for a reconnaissance, someone accustomed to breaking into places he shouldn't. He pulled out his penlight.

Fourteen lace doilies, two glass containers of ribbon candy, eighteen photos of grandchildren, and a fine layer of dust on the floor later, he knew three things: He was dealing with someone else who wasn't rehabilitating effectively either, he'd either scaled or rappelled the outside of the building, and it wasn't someone who wanted Melody for himself. He just wanted to steal her from him.

And you don't steal from a thief.

He pulled out the photo again and squinted. Oh for crap's sake, he *was* getting sloppy. It was just as well this was his new last job.

• • •

"SIX MONTHS gone…just like that," she said, setting down the glass of wine. She folded her hands in her lap. As prim and proper as royalty. He should have paid a lot more attention to her legs. She had a climber's legs.

Houston put his lock picks away. "You should have updated your security system. That's child's play. So it appears I'm not the only one off the wagon."

She rolled her eyes. "Have I ever claimed I was on the wagon?" Another thing he should have noticed.

"Sounds like rationalizing to me." He tilted his head and folded his arms. "Where's Melody?"

*Tsk*ing, she pouted. "Starving in my basement. I left her near a faucet and a toilet because I'm not a monster."

That was debatable.

Then, smiling, she shrugged. "Actually, I just didn't want to clean up a mess."

That was more like it. She had the sharp teeth and talons of a predator. On some level he'd recognized that—or he was just getting sloppy, and it was just as well he was retired. Again.

"I'm going to retrieve her, and then we're leaving."

"Oh, c'mon now, Houston. I put in all this effort, and you're just going to steal what I've stolen and be gone? I know you're at least interested enough that you found out where I live."

"I know where *all* of you live. I wouldn't join an anonymous support group if I didn't know all of your identities. I followed you all home six months ago before I even relocated here." It was still a lot more fun to make up last names for them. People's real surnames weren't very descriptive. Well, his was, but that was an odd coincidence.

She narrowed her eyes. "You've completely missed the point of both *anonymous* and *recovering*…and you're *not* a shoplifter."

"Yes, well, you made me develop a conscience." He wrinkled his nose. "Somewhat. For the first time, I genuinely understand *why* it's wrong to steal."

"Well, that's something, I suppose. So, how did you know it was me?" she asked. "What gave me away?"

He pulled out the picture. "Exclamation marks. Your writing is filthy with them. Though your observation point narrowed my choices down significantly." There were only four members of their group who could use that balcony without entering through the door. "I'm actually *glad* it was you."

Her victorious grin made his left eye twitch.

"But not because of that. Now, you've taken something that I'd like to belong to me, so I'll be reclaiming Melody and leaving." He strode through her house to the door down to the basement. If anything had happened to Melody, he would feel a lot less guilt, eventually, about what was likely to happen here.

She flipped around on the couch. "Houston! Houston! Don't you dare leave me alone like this! I went to all this trouble to get your attention. You should have just gone out for coffee with me." She snorted a laugh. "You know what? Scurry off then. We both know this isn't the end. If I was willing to kill your girlfriend…" She let it trail off as she arched her eyebrows.

The doorbell rang.

Luckily there was an outside door into the basement, so Houston's involvement in this situation was at an end.

"I'm not leaving you alone, Katya. You remember Jake from group? I think you two will really hit it off. I call him Jake Darkalley, but his last name is actually Christiansen. I gave him your address. He's anxious to spend a lot of time with you. Hours if you're lucky." He lifted a hand in farewell. "No need to get up. I told him where you keep your spare key." Houston smiled. "Remember, I warned you I wasn't righteous." He shut the door and locked it as he heard the front door open.

Not that he'd ever call Jake virtuous, but he could be punctual when it pleased him, apparently.

• • •

THE POUNDING started immediately. Hoarse screaming. "Please help me!"

When he opened the loo's door, Melody jerked away from him and pressed herself against the wall. Her wrist was raw from the handcuff that was linked to a bolt near the toilet. His conscience pricked and bled. She'd been here two days because of him. He'd have to make that up to her.

"I'm here to help you." He approached her slowly, pulling his lock picks from his pocket.

"She said it's your fault I'm here." Her voice was croaky from screaming. It made his fist clench at his side.

"Sort of. I wouldn't go out for coffee with her."

"No?" She watched him make quick work of the cuffs.

"I'm more of a tea connoisseur."

She laughed, and it sounded beautiful and awful both at once. The cuffs clicked open and fell against the bolt. "You can open handcuffs?"

"I can open anything. Well, not some of the new stuff. It's partly why I retired." She'd been chained in a loo for two days. If anyone deserved a bit of truth, it was Melody.

She rubbed her wrist, wincing at the tears in the skin.

"Right. How about we get out of here? Your mum is probably out of her mind with worry."

She nodded.

"Can you walk?"

She didn't stop him when he picked her up. Instead, she put her arms around his neck. It felt nice. His heart beat faster and harder, and his conscience didn't feel too bad either.

"I knew you were one of the good guys, Houston," she said with a pathetic breath of a sigh.

"At the very least, by comparison I am."

She laughed.

"And my name is Arthur. Arthur Steele," he said, opening the door to the outside. It was dark, so he'd felt comfortable parking fairly close. A quick getaway was always vital to any operation. Even your final one.

"Then why have you let me call you Houston all this time?"

Because that's what he'd told her. He had no idea that he'd grow a conscience and decide he'd finally met someone who deserved to know the truth. Well, some of the truth. Well, the truth was relative. "I sort of fancied the name."

"I like Arthur better." She looked over his shoulder back at the house. "What happens to her?"

"We'll take you to the hospital—get you checked out. You'll call your mum to tell her you're okay. Then we'll call the police, and you'll give them this address."

If Katya was lucky, Jake wasn't in a rush, but her manky treatment of Melody didn't dispose him to care. Melody was likely to end up in her own group. Hopefully there was one for kidnap victims, because the shoplifters group was turning out to be a rubbish bin of psychopaths. That bolt in Katya's toilet *hadn't* been newly installed.

"What if she escapes?"

"She won't escape. I've somewhat killed two birds with one stone here." He should probably feel guilty. Shouldn't he feel guilty? Maybe gaining a conscience was a twelve-step program in itself. You didn't have to tackle it all at once. He'd learned stealing was wrong today. Maybe tomorrow he'd work on something else—work his way through the commandments.

"Thank you for coming to my rescue," Melody said as he set her gently on the passenger seat of his car. She looked shattered; it left him gutted, utterly gutted. Having a conscience was no easy thing.

He crouched beside the car. "I'm sorry she took you. I thought there was nothing I'd miss if it was taken from me, but I was wrong."

She smiled—it was pathetic. Droopy. Shattered. And her eyes were half closed. But she did smile. "Maybe you should take better care of your things."

Leaning in, he buckled her seat belt. "Maybe I will."

Perhaps to be done, he'd needed to nick something priceless, and *now* he was retired. Again.

"Can you teach me how to pick the lock on handcuffs?" she asked as he started the car.

He shouldn't. He didn't do that anymore. On the other hand, some skills were only dubiously unlawful. "If you ask nicely."

One step at a time. One step at a time.

WENDY SPARROW writes for adult and young adult audiences with a focus on happily ever after. She reads far too late into the night and laughs at her own jokes. Wendy is an autism advocate and a cleaning procrastinator, and spends way too much time on Twitter @wendysparrow.

Martin Lenk

Tom Irish

MARTIN LENK felt a thrill of pain down his left arm a split second before his heart seized. The pain was enormous; it felt as if his torso had been electrified, as if all the muscles in his chest had contracted to minuscule proportions instantly and unanimously. He had been reclining in his chair; and even as his back arched and a weak, mournful cry escaped his lips, he could feel the fine, supple leather beneath his hands. He was dying; he knew it, but at least he had a chair as fine as this one to die in.

He had suffered another heart attack three years before, but that one had been minor. This one was different, a hundred times worse, and the pain was somehow different. Sharper. Crueler. There was some insidious difference between the two, and he knew it. They felt so different, and yet the *first* attack had *almost* killed him.

Deep in the recesses of his dying brain, someone or something whispered, "They finally got you."

The thought made no sense. He had lived a quiet life, a boring life even, and he had no enemies. No survivors either, and precious little inheritance to leave them even if he had. He would leave virtually no mark on the world; and here he was, spending his last few moments wondering who might have killed him, and it was ridiculous. No one wanted him dead, unless one counted idle threats. He had had a neighbor once, years ago, and they had had a sort of a feud over a tree. Surely that man, whose name Martin couldn't recall, wouldn't have the power, let alone the intelligence, to get back at him in such an elaborate fashion. And yet he had threatened Martin all those years ago. Who else was there?

The feud had started because the neighbor's ancestors had planted the tree that Martin had wanted cut down. Most of its leaves and seedpods wound up in Martin's yard, and he cleaned them up twice a year, every year for a decade. When the tree had started to die, he had simply wanted to do what made the most sense: cut it down to avoid the mess and eventual expense when the tree fell on someone's car (or worse, on his or his neighbor's roof). When he had called the man to suggest this idea, the man had screamed at Martin over the phone, calling him names and insulting his heritage. At the end of the call, he had said to Martin, "If you lay one red finger on that tree, I will knock down your house. Do you hear me? I'll make sure that you suffer. I will kill you, and no one will care."

In the end, Martin had called the city, and the tree was cut down. It was what he had always loved about America.

After that his life in the neighborhood had become decidedly uncomfortable. His gas tank was sugared three times over the next two years. His tires were repeatedly slashed, and once a baseball had crashed through his front window well *after* dusk. Not long after, he had woken to find dozens of profanities and a crude drawing of the USSR covered in skulls and crossbones scrawled on his driveway in pink chalk. He had finally called the police, who had insisted that all of these were likely just the pranks of some neighborhood children. When they left, Martin washed the driveway with the garden hose and installed outdoor lights.

He was transferred to another city, and he never saw that neighbor again. The whole episode was one of his most unpleasant memories of his life in this country, and he supposed he had blocked it out until now. Still, that neighbor surely wouldn't have been able to locate Martin all these years later, let alone have been capable of finding some way of inducing a heart attack without Martin ever knowing he was around. Yes, it was a foolish notion. Martin seemed to remember that the man had been a deliveryman of some sort. The thought of him as some diabolical villain was absurd.

Surely there was no one else. He could hardly remember any significant arguments at work, let alone anywhere else. He had no family, and he had never been in a life-threatening situation that he could recall, not even a car accident.

Martin jerked in the chair and was wracked by fresh pain. He thought of trying to stagger across the room to the telephone, but the pain was too immense. He was so distracted that he couldn't even remember the emergency number. No, this was the end; he knew it, and he tried to suck in a deep breath, to relax. Instead he began to cough. The fit lasted for what seemed like minutes. It felt as if someone had inserted a tree branch into his mouth and was pushing it into his throat and then pulling it back out, over and over. It felt like torture.

Martin *had* worked for a few years for the US government. That had been during the late fifties and early sixties, a tumultuous time, to say the least. The project he had been working on was incredibly benign though, and he couldn't imagine that it had anything to do with this. He had merely been translating textbooks, simple textbooks for children; and though they had to do with science, it was clear that these books in particular were easy for the US government to obtain and told them little. He had been a low-level functionary, nothing more.

Still, there was the time that he had been approached. At least he had believed that he had been approached. Perhaps, even after all this time, someone remembered him for working for the Americans or for turning down the offer from his former homeland. He had never felt completely comfortable with either group after his defection and as a result had always kept a low profile.

The day he had been approached he had been sitting in a bar, alone, watching a baseball game on the huge black-and-white on the wall. The television was immense, high technology in those days, and Martin had been fascinated. Still, when the man next to him spoke to Martin with a Russian accent, Martin almost fled without a second thought. The man had been there for nearly an hour, as Martin had; and if he had ordered his drinks with any hint of Martin's own accent, Martin thought later, he would have noticed, distractions aside.

The man had said, "I do not understand this game." That was all, and if he had said any more, Martin almost surely would have fled. Instead, both men just sat there, and after a time Martin had felt that not to reply would be rude. He was, after all, just a simple translator.

"There are two teams," Martin began hesitantly. "One is in the field. They are the ones with the gloves on their hands." The man didn't understand *gloves* so Martin explained, using his own hand. It had never occurred to him in those days to speak Russian in a public place, and the man near him undoubtedly felt the same, so they had gone on in their halting, self-conscious manner. Martin told the man about the bat, the ball, the bases, and how the teams switched from batting to the field, and back.

He began to relax, but only a little. He had been told by his American trainers what to look for and had seen none of the signs. Yet when he'd dropped the word *diamond* into his explanation, the man had grinned hugely and clapped his hands once before saying, "Diamonds! I should offer you diamonds for your valuable assistance, yes?" He clapped his hands once again, sharply.

Martin's guard had gone up in spite of the man's elation at his simple English pun. Martin began to pay careful, painstaking attention to each and every one of the man's words. At one point the stranger engaged Martin about the coaches and their hand signals, asking about the details of the *code*. Another time he had wondered aloud about the trading of valuable players and asked Martin if the players might be excused from playing against their former teams. At the end of their discussion, the man had repeatedly thanked Martin for his valuable "information" and had expressed his pleasure at finding "someone with whom to discuss, to practice English."

Martin had been sweating then, and scared. He knew how delicate his position was, minor though his job might be. To be seen with another Russian, even in so public a place...he suddenly wondered how he could have been so stupid. The bartender, usually friendly, had suddenly seemed to be watching Martin. The faces at the shadowy tables in the smoky corners of the bar all had seemed to be pointing toward them. The man next to him, the Russian, wore a small smirk, and his clothes seemed to bulge oddly. Martin had quickly paid his tab and stood up. The Russian man suddenly seemed shy. He said, "Again I thank you." He had hesitated and then gone on. "If you like more, more to discuss." He stopped again, and just as Martin had been about to turn, he finished. "I come here often. To this place. Perhaps I will see you again."

Martin had never gone back to that bar or to any bar within two miles of it. In fact, he didn't think that he had taken a single drink again, even in private, for more than a year. He had never seen that Russian man again either, and he had slowly convinced himself as time passed that the incident had been a coincidence, that the man had just been lonely and looking for some sort of companionship in a strange country. Still, as Martin's chest throbbed again and he felt himself begin to slide slowly downward in his recliner, he thought about that man, about the way that he had looked, the way that he had smirked, and how Martin himself had never noticed an accent until the man had begun to butcher American English in Martin's general direction. Yes, though Martin was never important, that man might have been. He would be old now but not necessarily *too* old. That man could be at the top of his field, an agent or a high-ranking official of some kind. Yes, it was just barely possible that Martin could be a loose end. He could be in this man's way without even knowing it. And government people knew how to kill without evidence.

Yes, it was possible. Just barely possible. The idea was somehow appealing to Martin. He didn't want to die, but that was beside the point now. And for someone to go to that much effort to kill him...it would be a worthy death. Martin closed his eyes and slid even farther down in the chair. He had lived a long, quiet life for the most part; and he realized that dying now, while not his preference, was acceptable. He closed his eyes and tried to relax, to breathe deeply; but his breath caught in his throat, and he began to cough again. The sharp, wrenching explosions tore from his chest and propelled him down even farther, until he was lying flat on his back on the seat of the recliner, wedged there momentarily by the tension of the muscles and tendons in his legs and feet.

He opened his eyes. He could feel himself about to topple, and he realized that he wanted to die in the chair, his comfortable symbol of the life he had built for himself. The chair had cost him nearly two months salary at his job as a restaurant manager, but he'd had enough in his savings and hadn't balked at purchasing it. He spent most of his day there, now that he was retired, and slept there often as well. There was a certain poetry to dying there and a certain romance to fighting for something during his last few seconds or minutes of life. He sucked as much air as he could into his lungs, bit his bottom lip, and began to push with his legs.

For a few seconds he didn't think anything was going to happen. The pain in his chest was constant; he felt confined by iron bands, and his legs felt weak and without strength. Still he pushed, past the pain, past the point where the hope of any result was gone. The massive effort was almost exhausted when he lost his grip on his breath and the air whooshed out of him like a cold Siberian wind. Slowly he began to rise. As the air left his chest, he pushed himself farther and farther up in the chair, face heating, legs aching, quivering with effort. It was as if the weight of the air in his lungs had held him down; and as long as he could exhale he would rise, rise until he was in a sitting position, then standing, then floating in the middle of his living room like an American superhero, like a pagan god of old. The bands on his chest felt looser, and for a second his impending death faltered and even retreated a step.

Then his breath ran out, and his ascent stopped. He griped the arms of the chair with the last bit of panicky strength in his body. He gasped, hoping to gulp in enough weight to hold him in position. He managed to remain there, trembling and moaning softly, but still his effort pleased him. He had exerted his will one final time; and clinging there in his slouched position, he knew that he would die just that way, fighting to remain upright. His breath was shallow, and his face felt like a furnace. The edges of his vision were beginning to go gray, and his arms and hands were trembling violently. He was dying, *really* dying.

And no one had done it. He knew that as well as he knew how much he had paid for the chair he was fighting so hard to die in. There were no conspiracies, no haunting figures from his past seeking revenge. He was, as he had always thought, a quiet man who had led a quiet life. And he was an *old* man, more than seventy, and heart attacks happen to people at that age.

His elbows almost gave out, and his mind went blank with the effort of holding himself up. Nothing else seemed to matter. He put all the strength he could into his arms and legs, and he clenched his butt for good measure.

There was a faint but sharp pain in his left cheek, just strong enough to notice (though it was nothing compared to the iron maiden closing around his chest), and he idly wondered what he had done to hurt himself. His mind drifted back over the last twenty-four hours, seeking the corners of furniture, the contraction of his own eyes and mouth. It took a second, and then he gave a violent start, almost losing his grip.

It had happened at the movies.

The night before he died, Martin had gone to his last movie. He had stood in line holding the cane he had carried since his first heart attack; and though he had recovered to the point that the thing was little more than an affectation, he had noticed some shortness of breath during the last few days.

He had dropped the cane at some point, a pure accident, and when he had bent to pick it up, he caught the profile of a woman several places ahead of him in line. Something about some part of her face seemed familiar when he was bent over, but as he straightened up, he lost his grip on the memory. He had finally dismissed her and hadn't even noticed what theater she went into.

But it had to have been her.

Years ago, in the USSR, there had been a woman. She had claimed that there was going to be a baby, but Martin hadn't believed her. He had been set to travel to the United States at the time, and the woman had something of a reputation. Martin had gone on his trip, and when he arrived, he decided to stay. He had forgotten about the woman, putting her out of his mind each time that she tried to enter it, like a grocer would put out a thieving urchin, gently but without remorse.

On the way out of the theater, among the flood of people, he had felt a sharp sting in his left buttock. He had no reason to suspect that it was anything but someone's keys or the sharp metal corner of a decoration on a woman's purse. He hadn't even looked behind him.

There had been a cloudy day in a park with the woman back in Russia. A picnic. There had been no one else around for miles as far as they knew. Martin had had his way fairly easily, and afterward he lay on the ground, his head propped up by a tree root, and watched her dress. She had done so with her back to him, turning her head slightly to murmur over her shoulder. She *had* been beautiful, in an ordinary way. He remembered appreciating the curve of her jaw and wishing away the lumpy, bulbous quality of her nose. Now, after conscious repression and the passage of more than fifty years, enough of the profile still remained lodged in his brain that he had recognized it, even twenty hours too late.

His vision seemed covered with a dark-gray film now, but still he tried to fight. Maybe, even if he died, he could still have some measure of revenge. He decided to put the last little bit of strength into propelling himself out of the chair and toward the telephone. He could at least report her before he died. Maybe, if he took another deep breath and pushed with every muscle in his body, he could propel himself onto his feet. Whether or not he could stay up he didn't know, but he thought he could make it. He took in air in a shuddering, wheezy gasp, filling his lungs as far as they would go. Then he tensed all the muscles in his entire body and began to push.

For a second he didn't move at all. Then he began to slide inexorably downward again. He tried to fight one last time, to catch himself, to throw himself in the right direction when he finally flopped forward onto his living-room floor; but it seemed that all of his reserves were gone.

He *was* being murdered; the ridiculous had suddenly become not just plausible but real, and his dying thought was that no one would ever know.

Martin Lenk died in the living room where he had spent a good deal of his quiet, boring adult life. He was finally found weeks later when a deliveryman peered through the window next to the door. The coroner had no reason to check for poison, and her verdict was death from natural causes, namely a heart attack.

TOM IRISH is a writer, teacher, and father who lives in Davenport, Iowa. He has been published in CALLIOPE magazine, The Mochila Review, and at thewritegallery.com.

Dear Courtney

Georgia Ruth

EIGHT YEARS ago I got married on a beach in Aruba. Lovely weather, very informal, no folks from the office. No chance to make a social blunder. This blond bride had no responsibility.

Marrying my boss was intimidating when I thought about it. Actually, I didn't think about much when I was with Archie except how long it had been since I'd felt loved, since my former boyfriend had moved up to the major leagues without me. I was happy to have a man to help me with my coat, with the door, with a menu order. With my future.

My matron of honor had warned, "Mara, when you marry a widower, you get his history and all the leftover characters. His daughter isn't much younger than you."

"That's okay. He's a good man. I'm sure he has a good history," I had assured her. "We have so much in common. We love to travel, and we like seventies' music. He buys me diamonds, and I like to wear them." Our laughter had been exuberant, a trademark of our years of friendship. But I wanted her approval. "Courtney and I don't have siblings, so she'll be more like a sister."

"That's my point. Archie became a father the year you started kindergarten."

"Yes, he's older. And a lot wiser than me."

"I hope he's wiser than his brother who tried to get me into bed last night."

"Norman is an actor. He's harmless."

"I want you to be happy. You've had a lifetime of heartache."

"Thanks for caring. I'll be fine." I hugged my roommate from junior college days. Both of us had dropped out. My parents died, and I ran out of money. She followed her baseball player to the other side of the country.

The first cloud appeared on my wedding night. Dear Courtney had stayed out past three and came in sloppy drunk. When Archie finally confronted her, at my insistence, she had a crying jag. She wanted to go home to "Daddy's house."

"You never loved me," she had sobbed as she sat with her father on her bed in our two-bedroom suite. "You were always mean to me and Mommy. Now you want a stranger to take over your house and all of Mommy's things. I hate Mara, and I hate you." She threw herself down to bury her nose in the pillow, shoulders heaving.

"Angel Face. That's not true." He rubbed her back. "You always come first with me. I took care of you when Mommy was sick. You remember that."

Courtney sat up and threw herself into his arms. Where I was supposed to be.

Instead, I was in the doorway, arms crossed over a beach shift that covered up my lace teddy. I focused on the size of my diamond wedding band compared to my mother's tiny cluster worn on my right hand.

"I'll always love you best. I promise." He had enveloped her in a bear hug, and Courtney had smiled smugly at me over his shoulder, dry-eyed.

In the privacy of our bedroom, Archie had assured me that Courtney's jealous feelings were normal. "Courtney is still getting over the loss of her mother. I don't want her to think she's losing her daddy too. When she gets a baby brother, she'll be fine." He tossed his white shirt on the floor, and his tan hairy chest distracted me. "C'mere." And I had obeyed enthusiastically.

• • •

COURTNEY WAS a sophomore in college and had her own apartment when Archie and I got married. Our log home was on a rural road, and our ten acres backed up to a national park. I thought I was the luckiest woman in the world. The community was old and the road narrow and winding, but I loved the mountain setting. Huge rhododendrons tangled along the front of our property to give a natural hedge under the hickories lining the road. The house sat perched on a slope, with a garden downhill behind it. A deck was covered and screened outside the kitchen but open as it wrapped around the dining room and continued in front of the soaring windows of the living area, library, and master bedroom on the other side. Landscape timber steps from the porch exited to a small terraced flower garden, a beautiful nook to temper headaches. The toolshed on the west side of the patio was edged with forsythia bushes that blocked the neighbor's view. I was willing to fight for my place in this fifty-year-old house, light-years away from the double-wide in Spartanburg where I was raised.

Courtney had her parents' master bedroom suite and leather sectional, and when she visited, her daddy gave her anything else she wanted. I didn't begrudge her taking whatnots and doodads that had belonged to her mother. Or clothes and jewelry. Or china and silver. But her frequent visits to "Daddy's house" became more like war maneuvers. Often at the dinner table where breaking bread should have been a peaceful experience, Courtney tried to pit us against each other.

"Remember the day we launched our boat after you painted my name on the bow?" Dear Courtney turned to converse with her father, swishing her long brown hair in my face.

"Yeah, you kept whining about how hot it was." Archie reached for his beer.

I glanced at my Movado, estimating how long I would have to endure our guest. I wished Archie wouldn't talk with his mouth full of food. It reminded me of my father.

"Daddy." She laughed. "You said you couldn't work unless I stood right next to you and held the paint rag."

"And you were in a hurry to swim in the lake. Like a ten-year-old." His dark eyes twinkled.

"I was ten! And then Mommy brought sandwiches, and we had a picnic in the boat." Courtney's glance flitted over to her new stepmother. "Those were the good ol' days."

As she flexed her claws, I smiled at this threat to my marital harmony. I never liked felines.

Projects at Archie's construction company took a downturn in the third year of our marriage. Interest rates escalated, and Archie's temper went up with them. Somewhere the future turned bleak. When I didn't get pregnant, Archie decided that I was unable to bear children, a serious defect to a man who wanted a male heir. The gentle man I had known now paced the floor like a beast, snarling about numbers and charts and graphs and unfaithful employees. I lost track of my college friend because I was embarrassed to admit her warning had been prophetic.

I found a job in an Asheville jewelry store and kept out of Archie's way. My salary was small, but customers who bought jewelry for special occasions were in good spirits, and the inventory was incredible. Work was fun.

I also found harmony on my knees in the flower beds behind our house. Archie's first wife must have spent a lot of time doing the same thing. The deck was bordered by hydrangea bushes that seemed to perform without help, as though they had been well trained years ago. Patches of thyme and oregano and mint had tried to take over at the edge of the patio. Diligent pruning got them under control, and I rescued some of the less-aggressive plants that had refused to give in to neglect.

Only two years later, Archie's business picked up again, but I enjoyed my independence too much to give it up. To keep the peace inside my home, I cut back my hours at the jewelry store. Archie was not appeased. One night he had pressured me to quit my book club.

"Darlin', don't you want to be home with me? I can't see why you have to be roamin' around at night. Our road is dangerous in the dark." He blocked the doorway to my walk-in closet.

"The bookstore is only halfway to the city. I don't have to drive far, and I cut back my hours at work to have more time for you." I patted his black beard as I maneuvered around him.

"Are you complainin' about the time you spend with me? You'll throw me a couple hours to show your Christian charity? Thank you, Queen Mara." His breath had been ragged and his nostrils wide. "I brought you out of poverty. I expect you to be more grateful."

I had seen his temper flare before, so I calmly tried to reason with him. I selected a sweater and came out again to face him. "If I'm working that day, honey, the meeting is on my way home." The look on his face had frightened me, and I stammered. "A get-together with other women once a month is fun. And you know I like to read." He stared at me, and I whimpered. "I can't see that I'm doing anything wrong."

Out of his thunderstorm flashed an accusation that had left me speechless. "You think I don't see other men lookin' at you?" He pointed his finger at me. "You like that, don'tcha." His face had been red and splotchy. "All right, go on then. Go out to your damn meeting." And he slammed the bedroom door behind him. Just like my daddy.

With teardrops trailing down my cheeks, I had called the hostess and left my feeble lie on voice mail. "I have a terrible sore throat. I'm so sorry I won't be able to make it tonight."

I never went to another book club meeting. It was easier. Mama would have done the same.

I had backed out of a Bible study group when Archie shoved me against the wall with his forearm tight against my neck, his eyes bulging, lips in a tight line. "You are nothing without me."

Once again I whined my excuse. "Ladies, I'm sorry. My schedule at work conflicts with the meeting time. But I'll be there in spirit."

I literally became a housewife, but I had been determined to keep my job even if it meant minimal part-time. I altered my personality to keep from provoking Archie, but his requirements for a peaceful marriage changed weekly. I was a paper doll Barbie.

I thanked God for my older neighbor who had lived next door for years. Our house was higher on the steep hill, but from her screened porch Louise could see the eastern portion of our garden where the pansies always flourished. Across from them, Fraser firs fringed our iron table and chairs sheltered from frequent winds and her scrutiny. Sometimes on afternoons when I wasn't working, I visited my friend.

"When I rescued my tomatoes that the 'coon forgot, I saw y'all were working the chrysanthemum bed. Hasn't been touched since Edith died." Louise offered me her herbal tea specialty.

"Archie told me how much Edith loved that garden."

"She did? I never saw her outside except to sit on a lounge chair like a pampered princess. Like Courtney," said Louise. "Archie was the one who puttered around with the wheelbarrow and garden tools. Probably therapy."

"Therapy? For what?" I nibbled a piece of sage oatcake.

"Maybe his business wasn't going well. Edith seemed real nervous right before her second miscarriage. I remember how our conversation stopped in midsentence once when she heard his truck climbing the hill. She jumped to her feet and ran for home."

"What did she say?"

"Somethin' about standin' by her man. Since I didn't have one, I wasn't sure if she was bragging or jealous." Louise flashed a smile. "Courtney was in middle school then, and it seemed she was involved in plenty of activities that kept her away from home. It was Archie and his brother that took her to Scouts or soccer or whatever. Edith hid behind closed castle curtains. Only when the weather was warm would I see her outside, strolling around the yard. Occasionally she would come over to visit like you do."

Louise poured me a refill. "Your sapphire pendant is beautiful. Is it new?"

"For my anniversary."

"You are so lucky."

"I bought it for myself."

"Oh, well." She offered me another oatcake. "Just listen to that blue jay scolding us. Go away. No cake for you." She flapped her hand at him. "I love to spend the afternoon rockin' on my porch. My Alabama roots, I guess. I cleared my view of the road so I could watch the world go by in slow motion from up here."

"Archie said Edith was a perfect wife." I trolled for clues, trying to understand the sad face in the photo on the mantel.

"Then he didn't mention her little ol' drinkin' problem."

"No, he didn't."

"Maybe I should keep my mouth shut, but it's like déjà vu. You and Edith are a lot alike. You even favor each other. I only knew her for five years, but it seemed to me she just wasted away."

"She must have loved her beautiful house."

"I rarely saw her leave it, but I really don't know how Edith felt."

"Maybe she felt like a prisoner," I murmured. I knew that feeling myself.

• • •

ONE LEISURELY Sunday afternoon my husband surprised me with an announcement. "I know what we need. A dog."

"Why?" I looked over the top of the newspaper. I had gone to church by myself again, but I had prayed for harmony, not a dog.

"To keep you company. Edith always wanted a dog because she was lonely."

How true. I had removed her photo, but her expression was etched in my memory.

So on Valentine's Day three years ago, a wriggly, warm fur ball with big ears showed up at our house. A cuddly black German shepherd. I crooned to that sweet, adorable puppy in baby talk. Archie mocked me.

But soon Archie fed him from the table, sometimes with a fork. "Here you go, Baloo. Who's your daddy?" It didn't take long for our baby to cross the eighty-pound line. "When I come home, my buddy comes a-runnin', don'tcha?" Archie cut his eyes at me while he scratched the dog's head.

Baloo humored him, watching me with chocolate-colored eyes until Archie grabbed his muzzle. "Look at me! Who's your daddy, big boy?" The mountain peak ears pointed directly at Archie, who suddenly had a snack in his hand. And Baloo would dog Archie's tracks in case there was another treat hidden in a pocket.

But Baloo loved me. I was the dependable parent who provided food and water at the same time every day. And walks every morning. When Archie was out of the house, I talked to my best friend. He embodied compassion, the omniscient priest who dispensed love with the wave of his bushy tail. Baloo absorbed my despair.

Last July Archie came home early with a bottle of wine, a box of chocolates, and an apology. "Look, I've been an ass. I know I don't deserve your forgiveness, but I'd like a chance to start over." He tilted my chin upward with his finger and kissed me tenderly. I had hope for a change.

His plan to take me to the Grove Park Inn for the weekend had been irresistible. I wore the diamond stud earrings that Archie had given me for my birthday before we were married. They usually stayed in the safety deposit box at the bank. We left Baloo at our house because Louise had agreed to care for him. I worried about him as though he were a child, but it had been a relaxing interim that continued when we returned home. Archie was very attentive, even cooking dinner for me several times a week on the days I worked. And I was charmed, again. Foolish. Again.

In late August we rented a cottage on the Outer Banks. While we were gone,

Archie's brother had come to dog sit. He was between plays and stayed with us for several weeks. The day after we had come home, Baloo and I walked to our neighbor's house.

"How was your trip to the beach?" Louise had her refreshment tray ready for business.

"Very nice. Archie was so thoughtful and treated me like a queen," I said. Her herbal tea was a thirst quencher in the summer heat. "Louise, we were going through a rough time, and he said some things—we both did—that we didn't mean." I helped myself to an oatmeal cookie.

"That's life, I guess." She shrugged. "It's so nice to see Archie's sweet brother again."

"While we were gone, he modernized the powder room with a granite-top vanity. If we ever have guests, I'll be proud to show it off."

"Edith used to say he did the repair work that Archie neglected. If I remember correctly, she died the year Norman planted the Fraser firs. I haven't seen him much since then, but he was always so friendly, a real gentleman." Her eyes seemed to glisten.

Soon after that I had started feeling very sluggish and sometimes found it hard to get out of bed. I went to the garden less and less, and before long the mint took over again.

One Saturday in September Archie volunteered to battle the advance of the flora. Norman had gone to the grocery, and I managed to get out of my pajamas to sit on the patio. My aching bones soaked up the warmth of the early-fall afternoon. Louise saw us and came over. She stopped to talk to Archie before sitting next to my chaise lounge in our equally old canvas lawn chair. Baloo sat on my other side. He had been my constant companion since we had returned from the beach.

"Archie said you've been sick. A little sun will do you good," said Louise. "Sugar, I can't get over how fragile you look. Have you been to a doctor?"

"Mostly it's just fatigue." I took a swallow of water and rejected the cake slice she brought for me.

"Do you have trouble keeping food down?"

"I don't eat much, because nothing tastes good. Archie's brother took over the kitchen. I can hardly make it to bed, I get so tired." My tongue felt swollen, and the words had dragged out. I took another sip and put the glass on the squatty lawn table. "I don't know what I would do without Norman. He does all the housework for me."

"He's a fine man." Louise patted my arm. "He really likes you." She gave me an appraising look through her thick glasses. "You're very lucky to have two handsome admirers. Some of us don't have one. A brown bear and a black bear. And you are Goldilocks." She pulled her graying braid over her shoulder and leaned back in her chair. "Déjà vu. Like Edith."

"I can't handle two. You can have one." I laughed uneasily.

"Really? I can have Norman?" Louise giggled. And stared at the garden. "Back in July when I was feeding Baloo, I peeked at the flower beds y'all were bringing back to life. I'm glad to see Archie still has the foxglove spikes I told him about years ago. They are so elegant and are just the right neighbor for the cheerful little pansies."

"Norman tried to rescue the landscaping while we were at the beach."

"I saw him puttin' up the split rail fence along our property line. I came over to tease him about workin' for me."

"He leaves tomorrow. But he'll be back."

"He said he'd seen the world with his touring theater company, and this is his favorite place. He hopes to retire here."

"That explains why he painted the guest room," I muttered.

"Look at the titmouse trying to get close to Baloo's water. They are too trusting for their own good." Louise reached for my hand, too thin for my wedding ring.

My mother's ring was on a chain around my neck, close to my heart.

"Are you still working?"

"Only a few hours a week. Archie wants me to quit, but I feel as though it's my lifeline. If I let go, I'll be smothered by this black curtain I dream about."

She gently squeezed my fingers. My eyes had filled with tears.

"It'll be okay," she said.

• • •

BY THE time the leaves turned in the fall, I had begun to feel stronger.

In late October Courtney had come over for a Sunday night dinner. I got home at six and set the kitchen table that was tucked into the corner next to the arched doorway to our formal dining room. I hadn't been in the mood to drag out the company china. The slow cooker roast and vegetables were ready, and I was hungry.

Dear Courtney strolled in and sat down at the table. "Why don't you fix dinner for Daddy every night? My mommy did."

"I work. Why don't you invite him to your house?" I said. "Do you want milk?"

Courtney's eyebrows went up. "No, a beer." She gave a kiss to the fluffy Shih Tzu that sat in her lap. "Is my little Cher hungry?"

While I put warm French bread in a basket, I told her to call her father to dinner. Without getting up, she hollered loudly, "Come and eat." And gave me a sassy look I wanted to slap off her face. Instead, I served their beer.

Our dinner conversation had been dominated by Archie's complaints about his lazy crews and his project manager's lack of intelligence. After a long, strained silence, dear Courtney opened a new topic.

"Daddy, when Uncle Norman comes back for Thanksgiving, tell him this floor needs to be replaced."

"Are you going to pay for it?" Archie leaned back in his chair and lit a cigarette, a revived bad habit. "I think your mother used to wax it every once in a while to make it shine. Mara, don't you do that too?"

"I did until recently. Courtney is right. It's a tired old floor that has seen better days."

Archie glowered. "Maybe you should clean it more often." He flicked his ashes onto his empty plate.

Courtney sneered at me while chewing a bite of the cherry cobbler I had spooned right from the oven. Vanilla ice cream melted on top. Cher pawed at her leg and was whisked to the top of the table to gobble up crumbs.

"C'mere, Baloo." Archie snapped his fingers, and the dog came obediently and got a pat on the head. Cher yapped at him from the tabletop until Courtney pulled her back by her faux jeweled collar. No treat was offered Baloo, and he walked away.

"Hey. C'mere," said Archie. Baloo returned but didn't get a treat or a pat. He ambled toward me as I sat rigid at the end of the table, taking deep breaths and fighting back tears.

"Uhh-uhh. C'mere." Baloo turned toward him, and Archie laughed. Courtney laughed. Baloo stopped, looked at them, and left again. "Hey. Hey. C'mere. The dog glanced over his shoulder and shuffled toward his bed in the corner.

I could see clearly then. That's how Archie treated me. But I kept going back when I was called. I learned from the dog. We were both trapped, but where else could we go? We loved this place.

• • •

ONE DAY rolled into another, and soon it was Thanksgiving. I had prepared the side dishes ahead of time so on Thursday morning all I would have to think about was roasting the turkey and dressing. Norman had arrived the night before and kept me company in the kitchen while I sliced apples for a pie. Archie was stationed in front of the television in the great room.

"You're looking chic, Mara. Very festive in your cranberry velour. But you better rest up for the holidays." Norman's blue eyes looked troubled as he gave me a brotherly hug. "I don't want to see you working yourself into an early grave for Archie." He poured me another glass of wine, and we toasted the season.

Louise came over in party dress, and Norman entertained us with tales of his travels in the accent he was practicing for a new role. The evening had been magical, and we were in good spirits. Norman escorted a flirty Louise home close to midnight.

Thanksgiving Day started unpleasantly with the arrival of Courtney and her annoying yap trap that immediately peed on my new holiday mat.

"You're a bad, bad dog," I snapped at Cher as I got the paper towels and dish detergent.

"Big deal," said Courtney. "You can throw it in the washing machine."

"You need to train her. Next time it will be your rug, and you won't be so amused."

Baloo came over to see why I was on my hands and knees. Cher pranced around and growled at him. Baloo gave out a single *woof!* Sharp and commanding. Cher ran. Baloo chased after her, paws skittering on the hardwood floors.

Dear Courtney snatched the little dog to her chest. "Daddy!" she screamed. "Baloo tried to bite Cher."

"What's all the racket?" Archie came into the kitchen followed by Norman nursing an early Scotch on the rocks.

"Baloo is a bad dog. He needs to stay outside." Courtney kissed her armful of fur.

"All I heard was your dog yapping and you screaming."

"You're getting deaf." She crooned to Cher. "Mara's dog is bad; isn't he, baby?"

"He's not Mara's dog, and he's not bad," growled Archie. "He's smarter and more obedient than your stupid little piece of Shih Tzu."

I turned my back to hide my huge grin. Archie stomped back to the television, and Norman held a weeping Courtney.

"Her name is Cher," she hiccupped into his shoulder.

"Time to wash up," I called out to nobody in particular. I wanted to take my plate and glass of wine out to the porch. But it was the day to enjoy relatives, the day I used the fine china and the holiday tablecloth. And wore the diamond tennis bracelet Archie was afraid I would lose. I wondered how Louise was getting along at her nephew's house.

I tried to keep the table conversation congenial.

"It was a great morning for a walk. Brisk and clear. The sky was as blue as I've ever seen it. Carolina Blue, like your fingernail polish. And your eyes." I smiled at Courtney, but there was no reaction. "Probably one of the last before the cold weather settles in."

There was no response.

I continued my monologue. "Baloo loves to prance through the woods, and he tries to catch those squirrels that are forever teasing him. He almost got one! The stupid little varmint stopped and ran in circles in front of him." Since Norman was listening, I added circular gestures for effect. "Then it dashed up a tree before the dog could sink his teeth into its neck. I think Baloo likes the chase. He didn't waste time looking up the tree." I smiled at my audience of one.

Courtney snorted.

Archie smacked his lips over a forkful of mashed potatoes. "Pass the salt."

"Uncle Norman, do you remember how much fun we had going to my ball games when I was little?" Dear Courtney looked first at Norman, then at Archie with a pert grin.

"It's true. You loved playing sports, and I loved watching you," said Norman.

"Those are our best family memories."

"I wouldn't say it was a family event." Norman's words slurred. "Your mother was a sweet lady. She didn't go to your ball games because her husband continually embarrassed her."

Archie jerked upright. "What?"

"Brother, you were always fighting with a referee or another parent. I went along to keep you out of jail."

Courtney's jaw dropped. Norman took a deep breath and briefly closed his eyes before he reached for his whiskey. Archie was sullen, tapping on my china with his table knife. His face was red and splotchy, and his mouth thin, but he kept silent.

I asked for dessert orders before he broke something. "Who wants apple pie and who wants pumpkin? Both homemade."

Silence from Archie and Courtney, and I stood up with murder in my heart.

"No, you stay seated," ordered Norman. "I don't want you to get worn-out like you did last summer. Just relax." He lurched into the kitchen.

So much for a happy holiday. I retreated into my inner world and imagined how Edith would have handled this day.

The next morning I had been happy to get back to civilization at work, even though Black Friday kicked off the busiest weekend of the year. We didn't run the Christmas specials that other stores did, but we had our share of customers. I kept busy. The following week I picked up more hours, and it seemed the more I worked, the more energy I had. Norman put ceramic tile on the kitchen floor, Archie acted grumpy, and I enjoyed being away from home.

I returned after dark one night, and Archie was putting his tools in the shed.

"What were you doing out in the garden this time of year?" I waited under the security light by the fir trees.

"I replaced the foxglove and dwarf larkspur with mountain laurel. Ten of 'em. Holly bushes behind and spreading juniper in front. All perennials so we won't have to put any more effort into that corner. Over and done." He clomped up the back steps to remove his muddy boots on the porch.

I trailed behind. The night air was bracing, and not a creature was stirring.

"And I put some peonies on the other side," he muttered.

I couldn't imagine where he got the plants. This was probably my Christmas present dug out of the woods, or a neighbor's garden. I didn't care anymore. Then I realized what he'd said. "Archie, I read last summer that peonies are toxic to dogs."

"Baloo won't bother them. He's smarter than you."

"Thanks." I followed him into the kitchen and slammed the door. I threw my purse on the counter and my parka over a chair back. The table was turned at an odd angle, and I straightened it. "Where's Norman?"

"You lookin' for a compliment on your tight pants? Why don't you wear clothes that fit your age?"

"If you are referring to the one nice comment made to me on Thanksgiving Day, get over it." The surprise on his face did me good. Working in retail sales had thickened my skin. "Where is Norman?" Baloo was whining, so I fed him. He didn't eat.

"He went back to his world of dress-up and pretend. Good riddance."

"I can't believe he left without saying good-bye." I rinsed the two tumblers that smelled of Scotch and put them into the dishwasher.

Archie paused a moment, then put a soiled hand around my shoulder. "Thanks for putting up with him. I'm sorry he was such a headache."

The camaraderie confused me. Was this an apology? I had lost count of the trespasses that required forgiveness. "I didn't take him seriously, Archie. I love you." I turned for my bear hug and saw the blood on his shirt. I kept my mouth shut.

"I know, but he was so possessive of Courtney." He kissed my forehead. "It was annoying."

"Courtney? What do you mean?"

Archie methodically washed his hands in the kitchen sink although I had told him millions of times to take his outside dirt into the laundry room. "He's her father."

I plopped down on the closest chair. Stunned.

"I didn't know that when Edith and I were engaged," he said slowly. "When she said she was pregnant, I just assumed it was mine. When you and I didn't have any kids, my doctor ran some tests, and I found out the truth. I acted the part of her father because I didn't know who was. And I love Courtney like my own." He dried his hands on a dish towel. "Norman told me today. It's all right. Not the end of the world."

My brain was numb; I spoke without thinking. "I thought Edith had a miscarriage too." It had come out before I could swallow the words.

"Who told you that?"

"Louise," I whispered, and held my breath.

Archie turned to glare at me. "I don't appreciate you gossipin' around the neighborhood." His voice was loud, and Baloo came to my side.

"Archie, don't get angry. It was an innocent conversation about ancient history." I knew our fragile harmony was balancing on a precipice, as though he was sliding down one side of a peak while I was falling off the other side.

I endured several days of total silence. Not all bad since I felt bolder. For a while.

In December the holiday season took off in full swing. In spite of being lethargic, I could see the importance of getting out of the house. Making money had once been an acceptable excuse for Archie's permission to leave during the day. Now, the more I worked, the harder Archie campaigned for me to quit my job. Three snowflakes fell, and he would use the weather as an excuse. I refused to buckle under his pressure.

Instead, I created sparks. "Christmas is in a couple weeks. Did you invite Norman and Courtney?"

"No, this year it's just you and me. If you would quit that stupid job of yours, we could take a little trip."

"Well, I'm not quitting my job. This is the season that retail waits for all year. I'm finally making a decent commission." I put my hands on my hips. "You haven't mentioned Courtney in a while. Have you talked to her?"

"Yeah. She's busy with a new lover." He left the room.

Two days before Christmas it snowed, and I couldn't drive or slide down our road. Archie had been pleased that we were unable to go anywhere. He cut a Christmas tree in the park, and we had a joyful time decorating the house with fragrant pine boughs. We invited a few neighbors over for eggnog, spiced cider, and hors d'oeuvres on Christmas Eve. Louise decorated her saffron fruit bread with red and green sprinkles, and we had a party.

"I saw Courtney over here on Saturday. She said she would be here tomorrow, but how will she make it up the hill in the snow?" Louise asked Archie. I swiveled my head to listen.

"She's not. She has other plans."

I hadn't even known she had come by, but I was glad I had been at work and missed her. I heard Louise press on.

"What about Norman. Is he coming?"

"No, it's a quiet holiday at home this year. Just the two of us." Archie reached for my hand and pulled me close in front of the group; everyone smiled except Louise.

Christmas Day I had woken up to breakfast in bed and a lovely peignoir set that I wore all morning. Louise came over in the late afternoon for baked ham and sweet potatoes. When we were alone in the kitchen, I questioned her.

"So, you saw Courtney here. Was she in the backyard by herself?"

"I didn't see her in the yard. I was at the mailbox, and she stopped to say hello. She had her snappy little dog with her. When I filled the cardinal feeder out back, I heard a commotion in the garden. I thought Baloo was chasing Cher behind the fir trees. But then it got quiet, so there must have been a truce." She lowered her voice. "To tell you the truth, I heard Archie and Courtney yelling at each other, and I went back inside my house. Please don't tell him I heard. I don't want him to think I'm a nosy neighbor."

"I'm sorry Norman didn't get to come." I hugged my friend. "I know you enjoy his witty conversation as much as I do." Her eyes had filled with tears.

Archie and Baloo walked her home in the dark. A very peaceful holiday in our white, enchanted forest.

The next day drizzle had melted the snow and made for a lazy morning. We stayed in our pajamas. I didn't have to go to work until the following day. I expected my store hours to be cut back to part-time now that the holidays were over.

Archie and I discussed plans for an azalea border around an updated patio with fire pit. The old stone outdoor fireplace could be used for a decorative plant display. We didn't use it for cooking since Archie kept a grill outside the kitchen slider under cover of the porch roof.

"I think I pulled my back out when I cleared a path in the snow," said Archie.

"Just take it easy, honey," I said. "I'll make blueberry pancakes."

"What time is it?" He asked, ignoring the mantel clock and the LED on the microwave.

"It's almost nine. I was up early, and now I'm starving." I pulled out the eggs, mix, bowls, and iron pan, humming under my breath. "I forgot to tell you about a phone call Christmas Eve. Some deranged woman who sobbed, "It's your fault she died." I hung up on her.

"Lots of people get depressed this time of year and drink too much. Did you look at the number on caller ID?"

"I didn't recognize it. And we had guests here. Obviously a wrong number." I beat the eggs slightly before adding the other ingredients. "Our backyard is going to look like a magazine cover. What about a small herb garden in front of the laurel? We could move the junipers to the other side. They need more sun."

Archie stood abruptly, upsetting his bar stool. I turned to check on him because I thought he had fallen.

"Don't touch that area. I told you. It's done," he snarled.

He stomped off. I had been at a loss for words.

When he came back into the kitchen, dressed in jeans and a flannel shirt, I put his cold pancakes in front of him, and we had eaten in silence. I imagined a collar around my neck, and he had jerked my leash, again. Dark futility expanded inside me. How long could I survive? This was like the domestic violence that had crippled my mother. I refused to be like her.

I took a deep breath and charged. "You killed Norman, didn't you?"

No answer. Just a glare.

Words just tumbled out. "Did you kill your wife too? Am I next?"

"Edith was bored to death. She hid in the house all the time. Probably dreaming about her lover. My brother."

"She was afraid of you, Archie. Afraid of doing or saying the wrong thing and enduring your temper tantrums. Her fear paralyzed her. She was just like my mother."

"Who do you think you are? Some kind of psychologist? You'd be nothing without me." He slammed his coffee mug on the table. The handle broke.

He loomed over me, but I stood strong.

"Maybe Norman poisoned her." He spat the words. "Maybe you were next, and I saved your life! Stupid bitch." Archie had stormed out of the room.

I felt very calm.

• • •

THIS MORNING I walked Baloo in the fine mist. The silent fog hunkered down on the forest. I tilted my chin upward to gaze toward the tops of the sturdy oak trunks, loyally standing guard over me and their shorter colleagues, the sourwoods and sassafras. My parka hood fell back, and I touched my diamond studs to assure myself that they were secure. The only sound was my beloved companion, tripping through the sodden leaves. All was well with my world as I communed with Mother Nature. I breathed deeply and felt her embrace. We seemed compatible. Unlike myself and my neighbor. I would never accept food from her again. Unlike myself and my stepdaughter. I wondered if she had read my dutiful e-mail of notification. It didn't matter to me. I had found peace.

Dear Courtney,

I am sorry to write this horrible news. I tried to call you but your landline was disconnected. And I can't reach you on your cell phone. I heard you changed jobs, but I don't know where you work. Archie hoped that you had finally found something you could do well.

I can't get in touch with Norman either. His touring company is also looking for him. It seems the two of you have disappeared.

I'm afraid I have to report a nasty accident that happened December 27. Baloo and I had taken our hike and were on the part of the trail that is close to the house. I heard your dad call the dog. Archie was standing across the road. He must have come home early and stopped to fetch the mail, because his truck was there with the motor running. It has a knocking noise that Archie never had time to get repaired.

Baloo bounded toward him. I heard a car coming around the curve. I called Baloo back to me so he wouldn't get run over. He stopped and looked at Archie, then at me. We were both calling him. He came to me, and Archie got angry. He charged across the street, right in front of a black SUV that looked like yours.

Louise saw the accident but couldn't get a clear view because of the fog. She told the police she didn't see any brake lights, and she thought the driver had sped up.

The funeral will be tomorrow. Of course, your father left the house to me. So sorry for your loss.

Always,

Mara

P.S. I found Cher's collar in the peonies. I didn't know it was missing. Maybe she's with Norman.

GEORGIA RUTH lives in the foothills of North Carolina. Now retired, she managed a family restaurant for ten years and worked in sales for fifteen years. Both produced rich soil for her fertile imagination. Georgia has been a member of Sisters in Crime for three years.

Imprisoned

Megan Green

"RUN AWAY," the voice beyond the wall whispered. "Escape."

"But where?"

"That's the beauty of it—anywhere."

The cherry blossoms showered down on me as I sat in the fairy circle, imagining a world beyond my towering stone wall.

The mark on my cheek where my aunt had slapped me still stung, but the injury to my pride hurt even more.

"Page?"

To escape…to see the world. But at what cost? After all, every action has an opposite and equal reaction, doesn't it?

• • •

THE MINIATURE machine wobbled in the air like a newborn doe, flying in dangerous proximity to a nearby tree.

"Blasted flying contraption!" The device dropped like a stone and tumbled through the air and out of sight. A loud crash signaled its departure into the unknown.

Wincing at the thought of what Aunt Becky would say when she found out, I started resolutely back to my bedchamber, deducing the best way to configure my next model. The servant whose sole job was to monitor my daily routines gave a barely suppressed grimace and made his way back to the house to wait for my aunt's return.

"The transmitter and receiver seem to be functioning properly. However, the specs on the motor may need work," I muttered, resigning myself to another night of building. Continuing my rambling monologue, I paused in thought just in time to avoid being smashed to smithereens. My yellow-and-white plane, out of reach only a moment ago, now landed with a spectacular *crunch* before my very feet.

"Well, I must say ,*that's* a new development." A flash of white on the back rudder caught my eye, and I bent enthusiastically forward. It was a note.

Ordinary girls would be less than thrilled at the prospect of such a small, dirty piece of parchment, but I was ecstatic. I had never so much as spoken a word to anyone outside the mansion. And besides, I didn't even know what was out there. Climbing trees was strictly forbidden, the servants were punished for speaking to me, and my aunt refused to let me get so much as a peek out the front door. I had never been told why. But one day things would be different.

Hands shaking, I slowly examined the parchment. To the girl in the orchard, the front read in a barely legible scrawl. I flipped it open.

I daresay you'll get this one to work properly. I don't think the hired help can take any more abuse.

A red flush spread across my face, and I stomped haughtily back toward the orchard wall, the piece of parchment crumpled in my fist. "How *dare* you accuse my creations of being unfit for testing?" I roared at the Wall, kicking its stone columns. When there was no answer, I yelled again, "Wall Being! I know you're out there! Answer me!"

"I'm not a 'Wall Being.' I'm a boy" came the heated response. "And I don't appreciate being nearly mauled every day by yer flying designs from hell."

Although elated about communication from Beyond, I was also terribly incensed at the being's blatant disapproval of my work. "Well, commoner, you should consider it an honor to have seen such a creation."

"Yeah—the first time. By the twelfth I had kinda gotten bored. So I decided to send it back to ya."

"Is that so?" I thundered, stomping a delicate foot on the soft grass. "Perhaps when you can return my machines securely, I may exhibit a small amount of gratitude. As it is, judging from the velocity and angle of the landing, you decided a catapult would be most effective. Quite rudimentary. What is your name, Wall Being?"

But only silence greeted my demand, and—regardless of my continued dialogue—the Wall refused to allocate any further response from Beyond. Had my smashed and smoking plane not been on the lawn I would have considered it all a most peculiar dream. As it was, I could only speculate about the event's implications.

How wonderful it would be to truly converse with beings from the Outside. Even discussions with such an impudent boy would be better than this monotonous life. Perhaps this was the opportunity I had waited so long for. Perhaps.

Day 4,809 with Aunt Becky
Day 7 after the Incident

I begin to grow weary of this prolonged wait. Communications via air continue to fail; furthermore, the note has disappeared, and the servants have been most reluctant to talk. I can only surmise Aunt Becky is the culprit.

"Miss, your tea is ready." Kimmie, my closest friend and caretaker, strode into the room bearing a tray of crumpets and cups adorned with opal flowers. Although her real name was Alexandra, I refused to utilize the name that constantly emanated from my aunt's lips. Instead, she had been dubbed Kimmie.

I slipped my stained and worn leather-bound journal into my pocket. It was one of the few things I could keep from Aunt Becky. In it I had transcribed my life events, inventions, and future successes. Had I but kept the note in there it would have remained a secret; as it was, however, the note was being chemically tested for clues as to its origins when it was stolen.

A great loss, but no matter.

"Kimmie," I said, turning toward her. "Did Aunt Becky discover the boy?" Kimmie gave a startled, frightened look my way and sent a cursory glance toward the door. "You are quite safe, my dear Kimmie; I have planted a diversion—rest assured, there are no servants present to overhear us."

"Oh, Miss." The servant's Scottish accent thickened with worry. "The lady o' the house, she's goin' to have yer hide.'

"Never mind that," I said quickly as a distant scream echoed loudly throughout the halls.

"She knows all abou' yer young lad, an' she's foired his father as punishment," Kimmie said breathlessly, her red hair cascading down her neck.

"And his father's occupation?" I asked, grabbing the tea. "What is it?"

"He's a gardener, m'lady."

A cunning grin split my face as I contentedly sipped the delectable brew. "Perfect," I said, and the door burst open.

In walked my very plump, impeccably groomed Aunt Becky. Red splotches covered her face, and her hair was dangerously close to escaping out of its usual noose-like bun.

"Hello, dear aunt. Care for a crumpet?"

The red splotches erupted like lava, and the great, glittery diamond on her left ring finger glittered ominously as she twisted it in agitation. "You are responsible, I presume?" she said, her nose lifting as though offended by a particularly nauseating smell.

"Ah, your bleak mind is far outdistanced by the art of presumption, Aunt. You'd do better simply to inquire."

Her hand rose for a slap that never occurred; without flinching, I narrowed my eyes dangerously and leaned my chair casually back onto its hind legs. "You may feel obliged to execute your anger physically, *Aunt*, but I daresay you will regret it most horribly in the days to come."

The hand lowered, but the muddy-brown eyes continued to sear with hot anger. "Miles!" Aunt Becky barked, beginning again the inevitable twisting of the diamond ring. "Take this brat to her room, and do not feed her until breakfast."

I was led through the dining room and past the gloomy sitting chambers, wincing at the large portrait of Aunt Becky above the fireplace. It was the only painting allowed in the house. After I had been safely tucked into my room, I pulled out the several crumpets I had managed to hide in my dress and opened a book discussing Einstein's Theory of Relativity.

I was sure Aunt Becky had been utterly dismayed to come home from her daily shopping only to find several toads in her toilette area, but my own emotions about the subject bordered on entertainment and satisfaction. After all, my aunt's terror of any amphibian had been one of my greatest discoveries. Too bad Einstein couldn't tell me how to magic her away into the ever-expanding universe.

Glancing outside, I nearly fell out of my chair when—far below—I saw a figure leap to the top of the orchard wall, bound onto the overhanging tree branch, and shinny its way down the trunk. As I stood to get a closer look, a small rock flew through my open window, hitting me squarely in the forehead.

"*Wall Being!*" I snarled, poking my head through the opening.

Far, far below, the figure looked up. The light from my tower room cast no rays on the unannounced visitor, but I was suddenly conscious of the sheen reflecting off my silver hair, which must look most ghastly under the light of the moon.

"I'm a *boy!*" said the Wall Being again, raising what looked like a well-boned fist. "And you got me father fired!"

The subtle Irish accent intrigued me, and I tilted my head this way and that in the dismal hope of getting a good look at this rude creature. From his position, I likely resembled a bird considering its next meal. "Your family recently moved here to get away from the shortage, then?" I asked, my tone softening slightly. The Great Irish Famine had left many in dire states, and those who were lucky enough to find jobs in America barely managed to survive.

"Tha's none o' yer business, ya nosy lass!" The Irish inflection rang loudly in the night, and I couldn't help but laugh at the outburst.

"Well, no fear, commoner! Your father will have his job back soon enough; you have my word."

Before the boy could reply, the light of a burning candlestick flickered in a nearby window, and Miles' long, thin face appeared from the servants' quarters. "Miss Everstein, did you need something?" he called across the orchard.

"No, no, Miles, I was just singing!" I shouted, casting a hasty glance at the dark ground below. But the boy had disappeared.

"A rather strange time to be singing, Miss. Perhaps save it for a brighter hour?"

"But, Miles," I said, smiling. "Great art should be enjoyed at all hours. And such a 'midnight dreary' as this is perfect for mysterious chanting. Perhaps it will draw out beings from the other realm." My discussion of fairies, witches, and the like often irritated Miles he was a man of pure logic who had never known an inkling of creativity.

"Yes, well," he said, clearing his throat. "Good night Miss."

After the light of Miles' candle had disappeared, I peered carefully down from the ivy-covered tower, but nothing met my visual inquiry save darkness.

The next morning I began preparations in my lab to fulfill my promise to the commoner; the results were most effective. The new gardener, a rude little man with small, beady eyes, could never have known that I had added superphosphate to the water he was feeding my aunt's precious rosebushes. The chemical—a mixture produced by adding concentrated sulfuric acid to powdered phosphate rock—resulted in a slightly acidic water solution. Within a week the prickly flora began to wilt, the gardener was fired, and another took his place. By the third, Aunt Becky was in a vindictive mood indeed.

"What on earth am I paying them for?" she ranted at Miles at the dining table late one evening. "My precious roses look hideous." She flopped gracefully into her chair, putting the back of one hand dramatically to her forehead.

"Oh, Aunt," I purred, my voice full of fabricated sorrow. "Your roses looked so beautiful only two weeks ago."

"I know, darling," she moaned, oblivious to my sudden interest. "And now they look just *awful*. Whatever shall my dear friends say when they come for dinner? I cannot *bear* the thought!"

"It can't be that difficult to fix the roses," I goaded gently, waiting for the epiphany that would surely arrive—and hopefully would do so that day.

"Apparently it is. All three gardeners have not been able to fix them, and they're getting worse by the day. The last time they looked normal was when—" She stopped, the brown eyes widening excitedly. "That's it! As soon as I fired that Irish buffoon, the roses began looking worse and worse. He *must* know how to fix them."

Ah, such a tortuous wait, I thought. But what came out of my mouth was

"Yes! Perhaps he would be able to nurse them; the garden has looked most dreadful since he left."

The next day Connor Boyle returned to work; as he passed me in the orchard, bucket in hand, I slid slyly by and whispered quietly, "Get a new pail, gardener. That one will only bring the roses grief." Within two days the roses had been transformed into the beautiful, bright-red entities they once were, and Becky was able to impress her equally superficial acquaintances with their stunning splendor.

That night, however, was when things started to get rather queer—and when the mystery began. Every couple of weeks I tried a new tactic to slip into the mansion's south tower, a forlorn, weather-beaten entity that no one—except Aunt Becky—was allowed to enter. Having only one entryway save for the window at its top, I had thus far failed to infiltrate the seemingly impregnable fortress. It was the only obstacle I had not yet been able to overcome in my short seventeen years. The result was a most piqued interest in its contents and a determination to discover its secrets.

The two guards at the tower entrance had long ago learned to wear helmets, remain at their stations regardless of strange, cacophonous noises, and ring for Miles as soon as they saw my small form make its way across the grounds. Regardless of my precarious journey through the gardens, around the sitting room, and through a first-story window, tonight's endeavors ended the same way they always had: with Miles grabbing me by the scruff of the neck and escorting me back to my room. Little did he know that the mystery was already beginning to unravel.

That night's escapades were unusual simply because Aunt Becky had enough zeal to punish me verbally in her own room, a feat that she had only attempted three times since my parents' deaths. Although such tirades were debilitating for her, I found them to be most uplifting. Tonight's diatribe focused on my insensitivities and need to exhaust her emotionally with my useless rule breaking.

"If only there had been another family member left," she moaned now, petulantly plucking at the sleeve of her thick, maroon nightgown. "Instead *I* was left with you." As she continued to rave about my outstanding ability to terrorize her, my eyes caught on something I had never before noticed: an attic door. This discovery so surprised me that I quite forgot the numerous accusations being sent my way.

"Page! *Listen to me when I am speaking to you.*" Becky's eyes began to crawl upward, searching for the object that had taken my interest.

"Of course. I apologize, Aunt," I said quickly, interrupting her search.

"Yes…well." She cleared her throat, and the muddy-brown eyes peered at me caustically. "Do better tomorrow; I have had a fantastic headache ever since that stupid boy was hired to do the outside landscaping. Although I must say, he's doing better than the last one."

"Boy?" I asked a little too quickly. Aunt Becky's eyes narrowed.

"No one you'll ever meet, so nothing you need worry about," she said, and began caterwauling for Kimmie.

That night I was in my bedchamber struggling to write the same story I had been working on since the age of five when a feeling so dark and heavy disturbed me that the hairs on the back of my neck stood on end. Filled with the dreadful certainty that I was being watched, I deliberately reached for my cup of tea, lifting its spoon as though intending to stir its contents. As I turned it toward the bedroom door behind me, I caught a fleeting image of what seemed to be a painfully dilapidated face; large, bulging eyes; and some dead, white substance resembling human hair. As I watched, the apparition's mouth twitched open and closed convulsively, letting out weak bursts of air that sounded like the muted whining of a teakettle.

Swiveling around, I saw skeleton-like fingers—one of which wore a small, delicate ring—disappear around the corner and out of sight. Bounding into the corridor with my candle held high, I looked left and right down the halls.

They were empty.

Down the passageway, the muffled sounds of a crying woman echoed dismally off the walls. I followed their direction and found myself in the library, my favorite place. At night, however, the towering bookcases and overstuffed chairs seemed to provide ample hiding places for all sorts of unknown creatures. As I stood contemplating my next move, the crying stopped so suddenly, it seemed as if the house had swallowed it whole.

"Miss?" I jumped. Miles stood behind me, looking rather irritable. "What are you doing out and about at this time of night?"

"Miles," I breathed, putting a hand to my fluttering heart. I peered cautiously behind him, but he was alone.

"You should go back to bed, Miss. You'll catch a cold." Without another word, he grasped my elbow and led me back toward my room.

"Miles? Did you hear a woman crying?" I asked, pulling my arm out of his grasp.

"No, Miss."

"And did you see anyone in the library?"

Miles stopped and raised a haughty eyebrow. "You must have been dreaming. Do not let such idle fantasies blur reality."

Opening the door to my room, he waited impatiently for me to enter and closed the portal; the light *click* of the lock indicated an end to my nighttime wanderings.

But tomorrow afternoon a new adventure was to take place.

• • •

THE PUNGENT odor of dust and seclusion made me sneeze. The attic had indeed been unkempt for some time. Everything was covered in a thick layer of neglect as though the maids had decided to abandon their chores one day and had never returned.

Tying my handkerchief around my face, I carefully made my way across the attic to the corner where an impressive mound of boxes sat untouched. The wood was moldy with decay and the remnants of webs, and crumbled most dangerously as I moved each container. Carefully opening a lid, I was met with a pile of papers and photographs detailing the lives of those who had lived eons ago. Their faces stared up at me without feeling, as emotionless and lifeless as the expensive china dolls my aunt kept in the drawing room.

From the pile of paperwork, a letter addressed to Abigail Everstein fluttered to the floor. It was a request from Aunt Becky for some funds to pay for living expenses. Scoffing, I threw it aside, and a small picture of a girl I could only guess to be my mother fell out. The child she was standing next to had dark hair and eyes; her name tag read SAMANTHA HOUGHTON.

Digging deeper, I pulled a newspaper clipping out of the case entitled "Daughter Loses Parents to Fire." Although it was yellowed with age, the print stood out clearly in the light from my candle:

> Page Everstein, surviving daughter of Mr. and Mrs. Kenneth and Abigail Everstein, was recently rescued from a fire that erupted at her parents' vacation house in London. The next of kin, recently widowed Mrs. Becky Winsworth of Liverpool, will be taking custody of the young lady. "I'm willing to move to America in a heartbeat for her," states Mrs. Winsworth. "This entire ordeal has been most upsetting." Firefighters are still investigating the cause of the fire.

I had been told that my parents had died of an incurable and contagious illness. Frowning, I put the article neatly in my pocket. I spotted a badly burned photograph at the very bottom of the container. Holding my candle closer, I was able to make out a young girl with long, silver hair quite like mine. Unlike the individuals in the previous pictures, her face was graced with a happy smile. To the left, her hand reached out to grasp at another's, but the image had been burned away. Who could it have been?

Aunt Becky's loud, whining voice broke the silence as she stomped into her room, oblivious to my presence in the attic above her. Gasping, I blew out the candle and slid into a corner, eyeing the cracked attic door with apprehension. Although Aunt Becky had never returned home from shopping early, it didn't take me long to deduce the reason.

"They didn't have one single hat, Miles! Not one! What's the use of shopping if I can't get what I want?"

"You have more than sixty hats, Rebecca; I don't think you need another one." Incredibly casual for addressing a superior, Miles' voice floated to my position above. "And while you're going shopping, I'm expected to watch that girl night and day."

"Yes, where *is* that girl? I didn't see her out in the orchard."

"I don't know, and I don't care. *I* want to go shopping for once."

"Oh, Miles." Aunt Becky's attempt at comforting the butler was less than heartfelt. "You know you have done so much for me; not too much longer now. *Alexandra!*" Poor Kimmie appeared. "I want my afternoon tea now, if you please."

Not daring to breathe, I waited for Aunt Becky to end her list of commands and exit to the sitting room, where she would be entertaining several guests. After the sound of her loud footsteps had disappeared, I made my way quietly to the trapdoor and out into her bedchamber.

Although I was covered in dust and grime, my mind was reeling with the possibilities this encounter had created. There had to be some sort of association, some link that connected it all.

After I closed the attic door, slipped into Aunt Becky's dressing room, and changed into the clean clothes I had put there, I made my way up the stairwell to my own chamber, where I began my relentless labor on the miniature flying machine. Today, however, the apparatus was not stimulating enough to engage my interest.

"Page!"

I winced and leaped to my feet. Miles appeared in the doorway, his horse-like face inscrutable. "Your aunt would like to see you," he said, speaking over the continued shrieks from below.

Sighing, I traipsed back down to the drawing room, where Aunt Becky met me with flared nostrils. "You told the new cook I like *cinnamon?*"

Ah yes. I had nearly forgotten about that little episode. "Why, Aunt, I always thought you had a predilection for the flavor."

"I'm *allergic* to cinnamon, you little brat!"

"Hmm, most unfortunate," I said, noticing the hives forming across her face. I had quite forgotten that, after having been forced to attend Aunt Becky's last tirade in her room, a little discussion with the cook had brightened my night considerably. "Rest assured he was simply attempting to please you, Madam. It's a feat that most find themselves unable to accomplish. Miles can attest to my story; he was with me when the conversation occurred."

Miles blubbered incoherently, looking startled. "I did not hear any such conversation," he finally stammered.

Torn between punishing Miles and accosting me, Aunt Becky settled on something much more significant: her beauty. "Alexandra!" she screeched, stomping out of the drawing room. "I need medicine *now*! I cannot entertain in such a disgraceful state."

Taking my chance, I backed out the entryway and escaped into the orchard, where my aunt's continued shouts could not be heard.

"I might go mad," I complained loudly to my usual wall, sitting in the soft circle of grass that had naturally formed there.

"Wi' yer life, I couldn't blame ya."

The voice so startled me that I jumped to my feet, but the Wall Being's presence was hidden behind the bane of my existence—the stone wall.

"I haven't seen yer flying machine," the voice said; on the other side of the stones, I could hear the scraping of a shovel.

"Is that your idea of an apology, commoner?"

There was a high-pitched whistle, and the voice said, "The name's Liam, Missie, if yeh'd be so kind as to use it."

"I understand you have found employment with my aunt?" I asked, deliberately ignoring his comment.

"Aye." The answer came carefully, as though the boy was afraid to discuss the subject openly.

"Then you know you should not be conversing with me at all. You risk losing your job—as well as your father's." The words sat in my mouth like metal; I did not want to stop talking to this strange boy from the Beyond, but I could not risk endangering his family's welfare.

"Aye," said the voice again. "My pap says that you need the company though, that it would be good for ya. Anyhow, I'm not even sure how I can hear ya through this thick wall."

I couldn't help but smile. "To your right, commoner, is a small hole in the stones that has been my only view of the outside world for many years."

"Oh, this li'l thing?" I could hear him bending over to see it, his face pressed to the ground. He let out a loud exclamation. "That's a nice dress yer wearing there."

Glaring, I stretched out on the ground and narrowed my eye toward the hole. One bright, green eye peered through at me. Grabbing a stick, I shoved it through the opening.

"Ow! What'd you do that for?"

"I am not a display made to be stared at, commoner," I snapped, and began to trudge angrily back toward the house.

"I'll see ya tomorrow then," he called through the wall, and I thought I heard a low chuckle.

• • •

SEVERAL MONTHS passed, and my eighteenth birthday approached. I conversed with Liam as often as Miles' absence would permit, and I found myself sitting in the orchard more often than not. On a number of nights I heard the woman crying, but no apparition accompanied the sad sounds save the solid figure of Miles, who seemed determined to inhibit any further nighttime explorations. Apparently *he* knew locks could not contain me for long.

In the excitement of having a true friend, I failed to ruminate on the mysteries of the attic, but they were never far from my contemplations. It was in the month leading up to my birthday, however, when the topic was brought to the forefront of my reflections once more.

"You rude little girl!" Aunt Becky had been in an increasingly poor mood lately, and her temper had been anything but controlled. "Why did I have to get stuck with you?" she wailed yet again

"Well, Aunt, to be quite fair, you also received a very large sum of money. A sum, I might add, that some would kill for." The implication hovered in the air like an uncomfortable breeze, and I was not surprised when the back of my aunt's hand met my face. It was the second occurrence this week.

My assumptions, then, were not far from the truth.

"How *dare* you! You think you can talk to me in such a manner?"

"In less than a month, *Aunt*," I snarled, my eyes boring into hers, "such a burden will be lifted from you. I intend to take charge of this house, as is my right."

"The law says otherwise, my dear," Aunt Becky whispered, twisting her diamond ring, agitated. I stared at the sparkling object in wonder, finally realizing its significance. "And so do I," she finished, and waved a hand to someone behind me.

Miles appeared as if he had been waiting all along. He spun me around—

An ideal distance for an elbow strike—balling the fist will create a smaller striking area, focusing the power and causing more damage. My elbow met Miles' face with a satisfying crunch, and I simply pushed my aunt away from me. She fell, screeching, to the floor. Scrambling away from the two, I ran across the foyer.

My next priority was ensuring that the information was spread.

I flew past the kitchen, into the pantry, and through the servants' quarters, where I snatched a piece of paper from Kimmie's desk. The exits leading outside were guarded night and day, which left the orchard and its overhanging tree. Stumbling outside, I plucked a stone from the ground, tore off a piece of my dress, and tied my hastily scribbled note around the small pebble. Diving to the hole in the wall, I stuffed the note into the crevice and made a beeline for the oak tree that towered over the barrier.

But the servants surrounded me, issuing words of apology. "Miss, we have to or we'll be fired," several said, reaching gently for me. I noticed that Kimmie and Liam's father were not among them.

"Forgive me," I whispered, grabbing a wrist and twisting its owner to the ground. Just as I had started to wriggle out of the mix of aprons, gloves, and coattails, another, much more sizable hand caught hold of me.

"Quiet, lass .Yeh need ta go fer now, but we'll be back ta get ya. Liam'd kill me if we didn't." Connor Boyle's kind face looked down at me, and before I could reply, Miles grabbed me by my hair and pulled me back into the house.

• • •

ONE WEEK passed and still I heard no word from Connor or Liam. I spent the long hours in my room, strategizing my next escape, waiting for the opportunity that I knew would eventually arrive. I was only allowed out of my room when accompanied by Miles, but his aptitude to act as a barrier for any mischief was easily overcome; slowly I accumulated the necessary equipment I would need. When Kimmie appeared with a platter of crumpets, looking even more stubborn than usual, I knew the time had come.

A grubby piece of parchment had been placed under the teacup, and the writing it held was all too familiar. Liam had written only one word: *Tomorrow.*

As Kimmie left to tend to Aunt Becky, she whispered at the portal, "Oi've about had it wi' her; someone needs ta teach that missus a lesson. An' I warrant yer the proper educator." She left, still mumbling about Aunt Becky's ineptitude for autonomy.

The next day I waited patiently for Miles to escort me to breakfast, where the real fun would begin.

As I sat at the table, silently listening to Aunt Becky's daily complaints, I waited for the typical reactions to occur. Unknown to the cook, the salt and pepper that were usually put on Aunt Becky's bagels had been given special attention the day before; Miles had been oblivious to the container swap when I reached for the tea leaves.

Aunt Becky choked midway through a sentence and stared at her swollen hands in wonder. "*Cinnamon!*" she barked, and pointed a very red, turgid finger my way.

I smiled. Looking none too pleased, Miles made his way from the corner over to my seat. Calmly standing, I gently dropped several small, clay-like lumps to the floor; their fuses sparkled as the flames ate their way down to the compact balls. As Miles reached for me, the mixture of potassium nitrate and sucrose exploded in his face; the smoke rapidly began to engulf the room and drift out the windows.

"*Fire!*" Kimmie's gleeful shriek emanated from the kitchen area, and servants from all areas of the house hurried to the doors.

Dodging Miles' blind grab, I rushed to the foyer, lit another smoke bomb that I had hidden there, and went from room to room until the majority of the house was filled with chemical fog—all the while being pursued by the most uncomely Miles.

The house quickly became utter confusion; figures traipsed back and forth in attempts to find exits, shadowy outlines flickered to and fro across the rooms, and the cross huffing of Miles ensured that he was still close behind.

I reentered the dining room just as the smoke began to clear, Miles gasping behind me.

"Is this your idea of a joke, you insolent snot?" Aunt Becky, red faced and glistening with sweat, was still on the dining-room floor. "You're never coming out of your room again!"

"I think not, Aunt," I said calmly, taking a seat at the head of the dining-room table. "You see, I have solved the puzzle."

Miles halted several steps away and stared at Aunt Becky, a look of undisguised fear in his eyes.

"And what puzzle is that?" she snapped, reaching for the ring on her finger.

"You bring attention to it now," I said, nodding toward the diamond. "You see, Aunt Becky lived a poor life and was barely able to afford her living quarters. She wrote to my mother several times asking for money while she was engaged to a Mr. Miles Winsworth, who tragically died shortly before my parents." Miles blanched. "It is unlikely the Winsworths could have afforded such an expensive ring—especially if they couldn't manage to pay their expenses."

Aunt Becky stopped fiddling with the ring on her finger, her mouth slightly open.

"But that brought me to another dilemma. Where did the ring come from, and what happened to the original? The answer came to me the night your prisoner, the real Rebecca Winsworth, escaped and sat staring into my room. On her finger was a simple ring of rather mediocre quality—the very ring that Miles Winsworth placed on her finger on their wedding day.

"Rebecca Winsworth is not the current lady of this house, but her best friend, Samantha Houghton, is." Aunt Becky, whose real name was Samantha, flinched. "At first I mistook the photograph of my *true* aunt and yourself to be one of my mother with her dark-haired little sister. In actuality it was a photograph of Aunt Becky with her childhood friend. It was a novice mistake. But the plot thickens." I leaned forward. "You took my aunt's identity, knowing that she had lived in England most of her life, thereby eliminating the chance that someone would recognize your scheme. After faking Miles' death to avoid any knowledge that you were his mistress, my parents were brutally murdered in a fire, leaving their inheritance to me, the next of kin. However, when Rebecca learned of your disgusting designs, she refused to comply, ending your hopes for a life of luxury. You then accepted me as your child and allowed Miles his share of the inheritance under the disguise of your family butler."

Smiling, I put my fingertips together. "But your attachment to your friend will be your undoing, Samantha Houghton. Rebecca Winsworth is still alive—and imprisoned in the south tower."

Samantha's face, already crimson, turned purple. "You'll never be able to prove anything, just like you'll never get out of this house."

"Quite wrong, my dear." I stood. "I hope you enjoy black and white; you'll be wearing it every day henceforth."

From the surrounding corridors and doors, policemen stealthily entered, pointing their firearms at the two murderers.

"She's lying," Samantha cried, quivering. "Why would I bother taking her in, then?"

I turned to look at her, my blue eyes narrowed in distaste. "The answer is obvious and as superficial as your own character: money."

As the charges were being read, I walked deliberately to the once-forbidden front door. As the great, walnut portal was pulled open, a lean, green-eyed figure turned to stare at me.

"Well, that coulda been a *lot* less elaborate," Liam said, and cocked his head teasingly. "Hmm, yer not quite as pretty as I thought."

"Quiet, commoner," I ordered, a smile lighting up my face. I stared toward the horizon, taking in the trees and houses surrounding me. My smile split into a grin. "Another mystery awaits."

MEGAN GREEN'S adventure into the realm of words began at a young age, when she and her mother would make up bedtime stories. Since then words have been her life, inspiration, and infinite joy. She recently graduated summa cum laude with a bachelor of liberal studies from Bowling Green State University, Firelands. She plans to continue her education in graduate school in 2014, where she would like to obtain an MFA in creative writing.

Bonus Stories

THE COMPETITION this year was fierce; and when all was said and done, there were two stories that, although they didn't make it into the top ten, just had to be included. So here they are, a bonus for our readers!

An Ordinary House

KC Sprayberry

WHAT APPEARED to be a perfectly ordinary house sat beside a hard-packed dirt road in Landry, Georgia. The home was in the current antebellum style, the modern columns sparkling white in the bright sunlight.

A beautiful young woman of eighteen years provided passersby with a glimpse of all that was right with Southern women. Her dark-as-midnight hair tumbled from a Grecian style fastened with a beaded blue clip that matched the color of her silk dress. A parasol held in her right hand twirled in the sunlight, protecting her porcelain skin. Dark lashes lowered gently and then rose, revealing bright-as-noon blue eyes. Even the mole on her right cheek added to the gentle beauty of this girl child becoming a woman. Nothing was noticeable to detract from the beauty of one of the South's greatest assets.

It was a balmy April day, the tenth, in the year of 1838. Delilah Swanson stood near the steps of her family's house and stared at the man on one knee before her. Shock riveted her tiny feet in place at what he was about to do.

Does he think he could keep his heritage from me forever? Doesn't Henri understand how powerful my family is? That we have many, many connections, even in far-off New Orleans?

He had already given her not one but two pieces of jewelry, trinkets as far as she was concerned. The first was a cameo bracelet he'd fastened around her wrist. She couldn't wait to take it off and toss it to the bottom of her jewelry box as fast as possible. The second was a gold locket with a fleur-de-lis pattern, a most boring object hanging around her neck and another item she would soon relegate to the same fate as the bracelet.

Now he was embarrassing Delilah in front of everyone strolling or driving their wagons past them on Main Street.

Goodness! This man is positively mad.

Henri DuBlucet raised his eyes to her and displayed a black opal ring surrounded by diamonds in a gold setting. The stones sparkled in the sunlight. She sneered at the opal—bad luck for any girl not born during October to wear, and Delilah wasn't one to ignore anything that might harm her luck. Paying attention to luck was what had made her the belle of Landry, Georgia. That, and the fact that every other girl in town was mud ugly.

"Chérie," Henri said in a honeyed tone, his drawl almost unintelligible. He held up the ring as if in supplication to her beauty. "This ring has been in my family for generations. A mother gives it to her eldest son when he prepares to take a wife."

He truly is mad! Delilah tapped a slipper-covered foot and adjusted her hoops to keep her skirt from flying upward in the increasing wind. *Just like Henri to ignore how the weather is making me uncomfortable.* "Henri," she said in what she hoped was a dismissive tone.

"Mama and Papa are so happy you shall soon join me at our plantation in Nah Orleans as my wife." Henri reached for her hand.

Before Delilah realized what was happening, the bauble graced the ring finger of her left hand. She stared in horror at the sparkling stones.

People will ridicule me once they see this ring and realize Henri gave it to me. "No." She backed up the steps, ignoring the look of anguish on his face. "Absolutely not." Her rouged lips pouted. "You may call yourself French Creole." Her Georgia drawl drew out the words in a cruel, cutting manner. "But everyone knows Creoles have Indian or"—the shudder that ran through her body was anything but delicate—"Negro blood. I could never marry you. It's just plain unnatural, and illegal."

Henri rose to his feet, swaying from side to side. His face took on a look of shock, as if he had never imagined she didn't feel toward him as he did toward her.

"You refuse me?" he asked in a stunned voice.

"Of course." She flipped her left hand at where he'd tied his horse. "Get off our property. Never come back, or I shall have my uncle, the sheriff, put you in the jail."

"The ring," Henri said in a faint voice. "Keep the other baubles, but you must return the ring, or I am forced to…to…" He shook his head in disbelief. "You don't want to know what I will have to do if you won't return the ring."

"This." She waved her hand back and forth, and the sunlight sparkled against the black opal with its bright shimmers of green, red, and blue. "I'll keep it, as a reminder." Her voice rose in triumph. "This ring shall serve to remind me never to let someone of such a low character bother me ever again."

Delilah, never known for her kindness to anyone she believed beneath her, moved up the wide steps until she stood on the veranda that circled the white house with green shutters. Henri started toward her, but she glared at him until he stopped moving.

"You leave me no choice." His face took up a look of resignation. "I call upon Marie Laveau, the Voodoo Queen of Nah Orleans," Henri said in a low but determined tone. "Make this spoiled child pay. Until she returns the ring, cursed are all the women of the Swanson family. They may never enter Swanson's Refuge, or they shall disappear into the half-life between death and existing with others." His voice dropped to an almost imperceptible whisper. "Once in each century, an ancestor may attempt to break this curse, but all must engage in the reunion of ring and family with an open heart, free of hatred. Once the path is set upon for righting this wrong, sunset marks the time they must finish their duty, or another hundred years shall pass before it can be tried again."

For a mad second the sun dimmed. A chill ran along Delilah's arms. She shivered and darted into the house. With a flick of her wrist, she slammed the massive door behind her.

"Truly mad." She nodded at her good sense in sending the man away from her. "Mama?" Delilah called. "You will not believe what that despicable man wanted. I should have let you stay with me. Goodness, he insulted our family so badly, I believe Papa and Uncle John should drive Henri DuBlucet out of town with a whip." Delilah tapped an impatient foot against the oak floor. "Or perhaps we should have Uncle John call a posse to rid us of this impossible man. I can't believe he thought he could marry me. He a Creole, and he believes he can rise above his station in this manner."

No one answered.

She cocked her head and listened for the usual sounds of the slaves at work or her mama speaking with the butler about errands. There was nothing to indicate anyone else was in the house. A shiver of fear snaked through Delilah. For a moment she considered that Henri's silly curse had worked.

"Oh goodness." Delilah forced out a nervous laugh. "Look at me, acting like a silly goose."

She banished the idea immediately. Delilah was far too sensible to believe in voodoo.

She glanced into the drawing room and parlor but saw no one. Delilah dropped her parasol in the stand beside the door and shook her head, searching her brain for a reasonable explanation for the silence.

"Where have they all gone? Mama didn't say a word about visiting anyone today."

Delilah peered through the tall window beside the door, taking care to avoid moving the curtain too much. To her surprise, there was a crowd of people gathered near the house. They were pointing at the roof.

"What in the world? How dare they act like that!"

A pounding on the door startled the young woman. She reached for the knob to let whoever it was in but squeaked in shock when a manservant, their old slave, Tomas, walked right through her. Not around her, nor did he shove her aside. He walked right through her, as if she didn't exist.

No! That Marie Laveau is only a myth, a Creole who didn't know her place. She can't have any powers. Henri only tried to scare me so I would give him back his silly ring.

Tomas opened the door. Mr. George Patton, one of Papa's greatest friends, rushed in.

"Louisa, James," George called. "Get out. The roof has burst into flames." He rushed toward the stairs, calling his message again. "It's most unusual. One moment Delilah's suitor was on his knee begging her to marry him and the next the roof was on fire. You must get out now. We've already sent a lad for the fire brigade, but they may not arrive in time."

Their mammy, Elsa, rushed by, shooing Delilah's four sisters in front of her. Mama hurried past carrying baby James Jr., and then Papa nearly ran over Delilah as he left the house. Delilah could hear the rest of their slaves scurrying out the kitchen entrance. Fearful this fire would harm her, she attempted to leave the house through the still-gaping door.

It was as if an invisible barrier had appeared. She smacked against it and then fell onto her bottom. Her back hoops collapsed, and her skirt flew up. Forgetting she was a lady and had to comport herself in such a manner no matter the situation, Delilah scrambled around on her hands and knees until she reached an open window. Her attempt to leave via that exit met the same result as the door.

"No!" She screamed the scream of one trapped within the horror of her own making. "Let me out, Henry DuBlucet. Undo this stupid curse. I'll burn to death."

Her only answer was seeing Henri mount his steed and ride away along Main Street. His head bent low beneath the shortened version of a top hat he'd taken to after her sage advice. Everything about Henri indicated that he regretted his deplorable action, but he never once even glanced over a shoulder as he plodded out of sight.

Delilah beat at the invisible barrier with her fists. Nothing she did released her from her prison.

"Here!" She ripped the necklace from her throat and the bracelet from her wrist. "Take them back. Just undo this stupid curse."

She threw the jewelry out the window, but the ring remained on her finger. The jewels winked at her, as a reminder of her cruel rejection of Henri.

A few weeks later, while her parents mourned her mysterious disappearance, a letter arrived from the DuBlucets. They informed Delilah's parents that their daughter's cruel rejection of Henri had caused him to take his own life.

"Now no one can save me!" Delilah sobbed.

• • •

ONE HUNDRED and seventy five years after Delilah rejected Henri and kept the family heirloom, she stood at the same window where she had remained since that day. Things had changed so much during her imprisonment; women now dressed in a most scandalous manner, and men had forgotten all about chivalry. One thing remained the same—the black opal ring surrounded by diamonds and set in gold still graced her left hand. Delilah sobbed as she observed a group of men and women setting up green-and-white tents on the lawns, the only thing left of the hundreds of acres her papa had once owned.

"Someone, please, release me from this torture," she whispered. "Let me go home. I hate what I see now."

"Oh look!" A pointy-nosed woman reached into the dirt around the old roses near the house. "Emma Swanson, look at what I found."

The pointy-nosed woman held the bracelet and necklace in her wrinkled hand. Delilah gasped and stared at the ring on her finger.

Is this what has kept me imprisoned all these years?

She tugged and tugged until the offending ring came free, and then Delilah Swanson showed sense for the first time in her life. She threw the ring out the open window and watched as it landed among the roses that had thrived since her mama planted them with such care. Not even those nasty Yankees had succeeded in ruining the roses when they occupied the house during the War Between the States.

To Delilah's horror, the unlucky ring, the thing that had caused her so much heartbreak, snagged on a branch and dangled with the black opal and diamonds hidden from sight.

Just my luck! Oh how awful. No one will find that ring now.

Nothing happened. No instant changes came about. Delilah threw herself on the seat of a chair covered in rose tapestry and sobbed her heart out.

"It didn't work. I'm stuck here forever."

• • •

KYLIE STARED at Delilah House, formerly known as Swanson's Refuge. Had she just seen a shadow moving near the open window? Come to think of it, why was the window open? No one in her family had entered the house since that day in 1838 when the eldest daughter, Delilah, had vanished and the roof had caught fire. Despite the curse rumored to have been cast by Delilah's rejected suitor, the people of Landry regarded the historic home as the crowning jewel of their Southern town.

Crowning jewel, right. Kylie shook her head in disgust, eyeing the slanting shutters and peeling paint. Delilah House is like the rest of the town: looks good from a distance, but up close, all the rot stands out.

Lifting her unruly, shoulder-length, curly black hair off her neck, Kylie blinked a few times to clear the pollen from her deep-blue eyes. She turned away from the house and walked across the grass to inspect each booth.

The Dogwood Festival, a showcase of Wallis County's finest artists and crafters, kicked off for a week-long run at noon. Before then, Kylie would have to help stock books and knickknacks, hang paintings and photos to be shown to their best advantage. Then there were the woven straw hats, crocheted scarves and gloves, and even a person making personalized t-shirts to set up, all to ensure they were ready for the crowds expected to make this Landry's finest festival in years.

Sweat streamed down her face, soaking her cotton blouse. Kylie stepped back from the last booth an hour later and smiled. So far, so good, but there was still so much to do. As the event chairperson, an honor usually given to the trust that ran Delilah House, she had to prove that, at nineteen, she was capable of organizing the show and then, wearing a period dress from the nineteenth century, appear as cool as a cucumber.

"Oh, Ky-lie!" Becky-Sue hollered, dragging Mama in her wake.

Becky-Sue raced toward Kylie on three-inch heels that definitely weren't nineteenth century peeking out from under her "belle of the ball" hoop-skirted dress of purple satin with white lace. *Does Becky-Sue realize how yellow her face looks with all that purple around it?*

Kylie silently scolded herself for the unflattering thought. It was hard enough getting people interested in these festivals, and Becky-Sue did volunteer to help at all of them, even if she wasn't very enthusiastic when she discovered she wasn't in charge.

"You just have to see what I found a-glitterin' beneath a rosebush." Becky-Sue shoved two pieces of jewelry into Kylie's face. "Why! I swear they're nineteenth century if they're a day. Don't you agree?"

Kylie had been interested in jewelry since she was a child in order to find out all she could about the pieces that had caused a French Creole man to put a curse on her ancestor's home. She studied history, but her minor was in jewelry prior to the twentieth century.

She stared in stupefied shock at the cameo bracelet and fleur-de-lis locket hanging from a broken gold chain gripped in Becky-Sue's hand.

Could it be, after all these years?

The pieces certainly looked antique, and they matched the descriptions provided by the DuBlucet family.

"They're eighteenth century." Kylie gulped and took the jewelry from Becky-Sue. "Where exactly did you find these?"

Kylie fingered the cameo bracelet, feeling the figures carved into sardonyx. She was certain of the stone, but this one was varicolored in waves of mauve, dark pink, light pink, and purple with a vein of white. Instead of a dual-layer carving of the woman's side-view face, the artisan had painstakingly done each link in a single carving, as proved by her questing fingers knocking away bits of dirt. The locket proved to be a better find, as the fleur-de-lis cover opened as if it had been crafted a week ago. She stared in amazement at the pictures contained within. The man looked a great deal like her guy, Michel DuBlucet, and the woman was a duplicate of the portrait of Delilah Swanson.

"Dear Lord." Kylie breathed in and out. "No one has seen these since 1838."

There had been many treasure hunts over the years. Everyone involved had put their all into the search, once going so far as to dig up the roses that had been nurtured since the nineteenth century. To date, no one had found a single clue.

"Where?" She turned to Becky-Sue, who was preening as if she were a cat in front of a dish of cream. "Where were these? Did you dig up anything?"

"Why, those rosebushes near the door. The anemone roses climbing the columns near the front veranda. They were in plain sight," Becky-Sue announced in a voice that indicated she would never stoop to anything as low as manual labor. "Aren't those pieces just lovely? Why, one would think they actually belonged to that poor man, Henry DuBlucet, himself. And there they were, right out in the open," she repeated. "They must have been hidden, and then they appeared after you ordered those lazy gardeners to turn over the dirt deeper this year."

She rambled on and on about this wonderful find and how the DuBlucet family would adore having their lost jewelry back, even if it was a very good replica.

"Of course they're fake," Becky-Sue gushed. "Good jewelry never would have survived being outside for so long."

Kylie's head turned in all directions. She had so much to finish before the festival opened, and she couldn't put her work off, but this find was enormous.

More than enormous, these pieces are proof that Delilah meant to return them to Henri. But we have to find the ring. That's the one thing needed to break the curse.

"Why, I bet Delilah never disappeared because of some silly curse at all,"

Becky-Sue said. "She probably ran off with another boy she had her eye on. After all"—she lowered her voice to a conspiratorial whisper—"it wouldn't have done to marry that DuBlucet boy at all. No it wouldn't. It was unnatural. And it was illegal at the time." Her thin lips pursed. "It should still be illegal."

"Did you see the ring?" Kylie asked. "It has a black opal surrounded by diamonds in a simple gold setting. The ring is why a DuBlucet is here today. It's what we need."

Becky-Sue pulled a black velvet jeweler's box from a pocket in her skirt.

"I have a ring," she said, and opened the box. "See."

The ring inside the box wasn't a black opal but rather a synthetic Australian opal, with the blue stone frosted with highlights of pink, white, and mauve. This wasn't the rare stone, nor was it in the classic setting.

"That's not the missing ring," Kylie snapped. "How dare you have some cheap imitation made up. The DuBlucets will be insulted."

"No, they won't." Becky-Sue closed the box and hid it in the skirt pocket. "Nobody knows what the stupid ring looks like." She tugged on Mama's arm. "Come on, Emma. We have to go see if there's anything else of interest near those roses."

Kylie stared at her mama's terrified face.

"Don't go into the house," Kylie warned. "Remember the curse, Mama."

"Oh, pooh!" Becky-Sue declared. "This is the twenty-first century. We don't believe in such things." She giggled. "As if some stupid voodoo could ever harm us."

She and Mama strolled toward the house. Kylie took a step after them but then remembered her duties, which right now were centered around the pavilion.

The smell of ribs and brisket smoking competed with the aroma of various barbecue sauces. Kylie took a deep whiff.

"Yum," she said with a smile, "and I get to taste test those sauces."

That was the best part of being event coordinator; she was the head of the judging committee, and she was looking forward to checking out the delicious smells wafting all around her. Right now the delectable aroma of Tennessee Hollerin' Whiskey Sauce, Columbia Gold from South Carolina, Louisiana Bayou Bite, and Billy Bob's Georgia Peach, which had no peaches in it but was a thin sauce with equal parts of vinegar, peppers, mustard, and ketchup, bekoned to her. The only one she didn't look forward to was the Alabama White, with mayonnaise as its main ingredient. Kylie wasn't sure how she would get past her revulsion of warm mayonnaise.

The cooks offered tiny tastes of their wares, from the ribs just now being bathed in sauce, to the brisket being pulled for sandwiches, to salads, breads, cakes, pies, and cobblers now gracing the tables groaning beneath their loads. Kylie graciously smiled her refusals, reminding everyone that she would be around later to judge their hard work.

"Thank goodness." She checked her watch and sighed in relief. "More than enough time to change."

Kylie hurried into the fire station across the street, where a dressing rooms had been set up for the coordinators to don their costumes. A shower, a quick styling of her hair so it hung in a reasonably neat fashion, and she pulled on the requisite undergarments before lowering the green cotton dress over her head. The fabric fell around her slim body, and she took a minute to admire her reflection in a mirror.

"Oh, Becky-Sue will be so jealous." Kylie smiled. "But this dress looks much better on me than it did on her."

Finally ready, Kylie hurried over to the historical marker and joined the others ready to start the festivities. She saw no sign of Mama or Becky-Sue, and Kylie began to worry. A man approached and touched her arm.

"Hey, Michel," Kylie said as warmth covered her from head to toe.

Michel DuBlucet was the reason she had searched so hard for the last year to locate the jewelry. He was as interested in ending the curse as she was. They had met in college, at Louisiana State University Baton Rouge, where both majored in history, with an emphasis on the nineteenth-century Southern United States. Both would finish their freshman year in two months but were here for their research on Delilah House to complete a paper on Southern mansions that had survived the war.

"Ready?" Michel's full-lipped mouth curved into a smile.

His thick black hair curled around his ears. The green of his eyes drank in Kylie in a way she found comforting. Unlike Delilah, Kylie had no problems seeing and maybe one day marrying—*Oh, I hope!*—a French Creole man. Michel had proven on more than one occasion that he wasn't at all like his ancestor, Henri, who had pursued a fickle woman that caused him untold heartache and eventually led to his suicide.

"More than ready," Kylie admitted. "I have a surprise for you later."

"What?" he asked.

"We may have found the bracelet and locket this morning," she admitted. "But I don't have them on me right now; I left them in my jeans, back in the changing room."

"But not the ring." His lips turned down into a frown.

"Not the ring," Kylie admitted. "And I hope Becky-Sue doesn't try to give you the one she has. It's not the black opal."

"Not good."

Kylie agreed, but at that moment she couldn't say a word. The Wallis

County Commissioner, Darla Munson, had arrived. She was outfitted in white from head to toe—from her white picture hat adorned with silk roses to the pure white dress straining over her rotund belly and white shoes peeping out from under the hoop skirt. Darla even carried a see-through white parasol. Her watery gray-green eyes popped behind thick, square-framed glasses.

"Who is that?" Michel whispered in a shocked tone. "She is...is..."

He coughed and shook his head. Kylie suppressed a giggle at his manners. Not many people in the county had kind words for a woman who passed herself off as a Southern belle and dressed the part on a daily basis even though she was well past seventy. Now that Darla had appeared, they could officially open the Dogwood Festival.

"Where is Becky-Sue?" Darla demanded in an irritating whine. "She promised she had a wonderful surprise for me, something I would absolutely adore. But I don't see her anywhere. This had better not be one of your wild chases to find those stupid pieces of jewelry you're always carping on in an attempt to get me to back off taking over this moldering house. The county needs to handle Delilah House so it receives the proper care."

Kylie's worry rose again. She had yet to locate either her mama or Becky-Sue. Even worse, Darla was using today to push forward one of her long-held desires: to take over the historical location.

I won't let her take the house. It will never receive any kind of funding then. But I need Mama around to handle Darla. This is not good.

While Darla took her place in front of the ticket booths and beside the historical marker, Kylie glanced around the crowd as secretively as possible. She still could see no sign of either her mama or Becky-Sue.

"And now," Darla said in her imperious voice, "we open this year's Dogwood Festival. Pick up your tickets and enjoy everything."

The crowd pressed closer, and Kylie was forced into selling tickets. All the while she scanned each face, looked over shoulders, and stared in all directions in an effort to find her mama. Her danger radar went into high gear, she was that certain Becky-Sue had something nefarious planned.

"Is everything okay, chérie?" Michel asked. "You look worried."

"Mama's not here," Kylie confessed. "And she was with Becky-Sue..." She bit back a comment about Becky-Sue's character and her determination to pass off a fake opal as the fabled one that kept all Swanson women out of Delilah House. "She just irritates me."

"How much longer before we can leave?" Michel whispered in Kylie's ear. "I'll help you find your mama. That way you won't look so worried."

He was so understanding. Kylie flashed a brilliant smile in his direction, but it faded to a terrorized gasp when an ear-piercing scream rent the air.

"That's Becky-Sue," Kylie managed to say. "I'd know her scream anywhere. What's happened?"

Hoping it was nothing more than a garter snake arguing with her for its place in the rose garden, Kylie spun around. Her heart leaped into her throat.

There, in the doorway to Delilah House, Mama pounded against an invisible barrier. Kylie lifted her antebellum skirt to her knees and raced toward the house, determined to stop this insanity once and for all.

"*Chérie*! Stop." Michel grabbed her arm. "You can't go in there. You can't even step on the threshold."

"That's my mama!" Kylie screamed. "She's caught. We have to get her out."

The festivalgoers ignored the delicious food and attractive arts and crafts to gather around the steps to the house.

"Hey, Danny," a woman said, "someone's pretending the curse is real. I told you this was all a scam."

The man beside her laughed. "Sure looks real enough to me. Look at how that woman's hands keep stopping at the exact same spot."

A few others speculated on the possibility of playacting to extract more money. Kylie fumed. She'd long believed in the curse and that Delilah had brought her troubles on herself, but this was going too far.

"Becky-Sue," Kylie called. "Where are you?"

With Michel at her side, Kylie pushed through the throng and mounted the steps. Becky-Sue cowered behind one of the anemone rose–decorated columns, her hand trembling over her mouth.

"We just needed some more serving spoons," Becky-Sue said. "I made Emma go after them. I didn't believe…believe…" She choked and began sobbing.

"It's done," Kylie said, staring in disbelief at the young woman sidling up beside Mama.

That has to be Delilah!

The woman, clad in a sky-blue dress that was made of miles and miles of fabric, was almost a clone of Kylie. If they stood in front of a mirror, the only thing that would be different was the mole on the woman's cheek—in the same place Kylie had a mole removed at sixteen.

"Lord help me, she looks exactly like you," Michel said. "Is that who I think it is?"

"I'm betting Delilah has shown her face for the first time in one hundred and seventy-five years," Kylie said. "I need to find that ring."

"Ring. Ring." Becky-Sue seemed to come out of her trance. She rummaged through her skirt pocket and pulled out the fake. "Here's the ring, you fool. Now, let Emma out of that house."

She shoved the synthetic Australian opal ring into Michel's hand. He stared at it for the longest time.

"Not that ring!" Kylie knocked the ring out of Michel's hand. "It's a fake. You'll only make things worse, Becky-Sue, unless you find a way to get these people away from here and let us fix this."

"But it's the real ring," Becky-Sue protested. "I swear it is."

"It's not." Kylie slammed the fake against the railing and then turned it over. The "stone" had a few scratches, where if it had been a real opal, it would have shattered. "It's not even a good fake."

"Well," Becky-Sue huffed. "I just don't know who you think you are, Kylie Swanson. I am trying my best to right things. Give it to me, and I shall end this game now!"

"Not with a fake," Michel said. "You do not understand, Miz Becky-Sue. Not only must the ring be the same one my ancestor Henri presented to Miz Delilah, but Kylie or her mama must be the one giving it to me. And it must be done with a charitable feeling in their hearts."

"Are you sayin' I'm not charitable." Becky-Sue straightened. "I'll have you know I give to many, many charities, most of them for those poor children on the west side of town."

Kylie rolled her eyes and jerked her head toward the back of the house. Becky-Sue was on a rampage now, and she wouldn't stop talking about the tea parties she gave year-round to raise money for the children in West Landry.

Michel grinned and followed Kylie around the building.

"She won't hush for hours now," Kylie said. "And we don't have that kind of time." She glanced at her watch. "I have to be over at the judging tent in an hour. The only clue I have as to where Becky-Sue found the locket and bracelet is that she mentioned the anemone roses. They're only around the columns."

Michel groaned. "There are eight columns," he said. "Four here in the back and—"

"Four in the front," she said. "I know. I know. It's an impossible task, but I want my mama out of that building. That won't happen for another hundred years unless we find that ring before sunset."

Both knew the curse well. Henri DuBlucet had not only punished Delilah; he had provided a way to reverse what he'd done—but only if the people involved weren't bigots.

"Then we'll each take a column until we find the ring," Michel said. "Love you, dah-ling."

Kylie suppressed a delighted shiver. When he talked like...Stop thinking about Michel. I have to find that ring and formally present it to him to release Mama and Delilah.

Although a thoroughly modern, twenty-first century woman, Kylie firmly believed in any kind of curse attributed to Marie Laveau. She had been very strong in the voodoo arts throughout her reign in New Orleans during the nineteenth century.

Shaking off any thought but locating an ancient ring, Kylie searched the columns, concentrating on the area around their bases. She scratched her arms on the rose thorns, going so far as to rip open a long cut on her hand when she thought she'd located something of importance, which turned out to be the pop top of a soda can.

"Anything?" Michel called as they approached the last two columns on the house. "We don't have much time."

He stooped down to begin their final search but straightened as an announcement came over the speaker system.

"Will the judges please report to their tent," Becky-Sue said. "We need all the judges at the tent. That means you, Kylie Swanson."

"Oh, good grief." Kylie stared at the scratches on her hands and the long cut on one of them. "What do I do about this?"

"Here." Michel whipped a large handkerchief from his breast pocket and wound it around the cut. "Now I understand why men wore these awful suits back then."

He had purchased a planter's suit, complete with string tie and the heavy coat, just for today. Kylie thought Michel looked quite handsome in the nineteenth-century outfit.

"Milady?" He held up an arm. "Shall we put everyone else to shame?"

Laughing, Kylie draped her hand near the elbow and walked beside him through the crowds. People stopped to admire them as they passed, until she reached the judging tent.

"There you are," Becky-Sue said. "Whatever took you so long?"

"We were busy." Kylie sat on the folding chair and adjusted her skirts. "I'm sure you know why."

"I haven't a clue." Becky-Sue motioned for the contestants to begin bringing in samples of their food. "Remember, judges, only a small taste of the food. We don't want you full before the final round."

The next two hours passed in a haze of tasting food and writing down her opinions. Kylie kept glancing at the house, where Mama and Delilah stared at her as if begging for their immediate release.

I'm doing the best I can, Mama. Kylie waited patiently for the last round: desserts. She already knew how she'd vote but had promised to be fair. For all her faults, Becky-Sue makes the best peach cobbler I've ever tasted. I just have to get her recipe.

"We're now ready for desserts," Becky-Sue said. "And I'm proud to announce, after much discussion with all those cookin' for us today, we will have a cookbook available for those interested in how we make such delicious food. If you want one, there's a sign-up book behind the pavilion. They'll only cost five dollars, and all money collected will be given to the Children's Center, to pay for school supplies." She grinned at Kylie. "Miz Kylie Swanson, the lovely young lady who organized this event, will hand out the prizes after the judges come to their decision."

It was nearly three, and Kylie only had until sunset, somewhere between six and seven this time of year. She had to get back to the house and find the ring, but her responsibilities kept her occupied for most of the rest of the festival.

An hour later, after much argument about the best dessert—*Who would have thought Gene Patton would have liked Mama's rhubarb/strawberry pie better than Becky-Sue's peach cobbler!*—Kylie took the microphone and stared out at the people standing before her.

"First, the barbecue sauce," she said with a straight face. "Although it has no peaches, which Billy Bob will have to explain after he submits his recipe for the book, first prize goes to Billy Bob's Georgia Peach Sauce."

A smiling Billy Bob Jackson elbowed through the crowd to receive his blue ribbon and a small trophy.

"Ain't no secret to it," he hollered. "Everyone knows Georgia peaches are always the best! And they don't need to be fruit to be a peach."

Kylie thanked him and continued with the awards, keeping a worried eye on the sky as the sun began to sink on the horizon.

"Finally, the dessert competition," she said. "And for the fifteenth year in a row, Miz Becky-Sue Patton wins with her peach cobbler. Becky-Sue, you have to tell us how you do that biscuit topping with pecans now."

"I surely do." Becky-Sue accepted her prize. "And then I'm a-gonna retire my cobbler recipe and work on something new."

She launched into a speech about her pride-and-joy cobbler and what she had planned next. Kylie sneaked away and joined Michel near the rear of the crowd.

"I don't think she'll stop talking any time soon," he said.

They moved with as much stealth as possible until they reached the porch. The festivalgoers returned to the activities, and Kylie was able to relax enough to concentrate on the task at hand.

Where would I hide if I were a ring?

She knelt on the ground, ignoring the damage that could be done to the dress, and began to paw through the loosened dirt. Then Kylie stopped.

Her heart racing a million miles a minute, she reached for a dull gold ring hanging off a branch.

"Michel," Kylie said. "I think...I..." She pulled the ring free and gasped. "I've found it!"

Michel raced over to look for himself. Both of them stared at the gorgeous black opal with the veins of green, red, and blue glowing in the setting sun.

"Come with me," he said, and led Kylie to the stairs. "Ladies." Michel glanced at Mama and Delilah, and then KyLe. "We must all go through this with goodness in our hearts. None of us can believe they are better than anyone else."

Kylie stood on the second step from the bottom and held out the ring.

"Michel DuBlucet, on behalf of my ancestor Delilah Swanson, I return this ring to your family, where it belongs."

"*Merci beaucoup*," Michel said. "And I accept this ring as a token of the generosity with which you give it."

His lips twitched into a smile. Kylie had to work hard not to laugh. Both of them had thought the staged words were far too funny for anyone to say, but a book she'd read had said they had to follow the procedure formally to break the curse.

"May everyone return to where they belong," Kylie said, and laid the ring into Michel's cupped hands.

There was a loud clap of thunder. Everyone at the festival ducked and looked at the sky.

"You did it!" Mama cried. "Oh, Kylie, you've broken the curse."

"But I'm still here." The deep drawl was full of disdain.

Kylie stared at the woman who had rejected a man who loved her. Delilah shrank from the last rays of the sun and shook her skirts into place.

"You have one more thing to do," Michel said. His voice was full of patience for the woman history had recorded as a heartless bigot. "I am ready, Delilah Swanson."

"Oh, must I?" Delilah asked. "It's far too humiliating."

"Unless you want to spend another hundred years inside that house," Kylie said. "Quite frankly, I don't care if you do, but I want my mama free."

"Oh, well." Delilah heaved a huge sigh. "I guess I could have been nicer." Her form started to fade from sight.

"I apologize to Henri DuBlucet," she said. "I didn't mean to insult him."

Her voice sounded as if she meant the words. Seconds later, Kylie knew her statements were true. Delilah Swanson vanished from view.

"Hey, Mom," a child yelled. "That sure looked real to me."

"It's just playacting," a woman answered. "I'm sure they did it with hidden cameras."

Michel and Kylie walked back to the festival. Both were laughing.

"I'm glad she cooperated," he said.

"So am I." She snuggled up against him. "And I will never again volunteer to help out with this festival."

"Why?"

"Do you know, I don't think I've had a wink of sleep over my whole spring break." Kylie stared up into his face. "And I forgot the one thing I promised myself I'd do if we did break the curse."

"Go inside the house?" Michel asked.

"Yes."

He turned her around, and they walked up the stairs to the house. Kylie's hand shook as she stood in the doorway. Michel stepped inside first, and then she put her foot onto the oak flooring that had survived almost two centuries.

"One more step," he urged.

She took that step, and then he scooped her into his arms.

"The curse is broken!" Kylie cried.

KC SPRAYBERRY juggles her writing in between a son in the band, a loving husband, a reformed barn cat, and an excitable black Lab puppy determined to play all day long. She lives in northwest Georgia and often uses local settings, such as the one in "An Ordinary House," in her stories. Her first love in writing is for young adults, be it historical, contemporary, sci-fi, or fantasy, a short story, or a full-length novel. She has been featured in *Mystery Times Ten 2011* and *Mystery Times Ten 2012*.

Website: kcsprayberry.com

Blog: outofcontrolcharacters.blogspot.com

amazon.com/author/kcsprayberry

Confidence in the Family

Paula Gail Benson

AS HE drove up the circular driveway to the Reed mansion, Fred Parker had only one thing on his mind. His earliest memory.

He was seven years old, standing in the back alley behind Madd Prancks Pizza Shoppe. He didn't remember how he had gotten there or how he had stolen the paper that listed Madd Prancks as the last-known address associated with his birth mother. He only knew he had to escape the orphanage and find out where he belonged in the world.

That's when he first saw Mona. She was exiting Madd Prancks to put a bag of trash in the Dumpster. She had been turning to go back inside when she saw him. Their eyes locked.

For the first time in his life, Fred had a sense of inner calm. A feeling of belonging. Mona looked at him as if she recognized him. As if she knew who he was.

Now, twenty years later, he wondered if that recognition was personal or potential. If Mona had seen him as her family or as part of a future con.

• • •

HE KNOCKED at the door and was admitted by the maid, who escorted him to the den and left. Grandmamma Reed asked why he didn't use the key she had given him. He just smiled and kissed her cheek before turning to greet the newspaper reporter and photographer. They were there to get information and a photo for a story about how Fred and the Reeds had been united as a family just in time for Thanksgiving.

Fred knelt beside Grandmamma Reed, whose right hand reached beneath his chin so her thumb and index finger could cup his cheeks, giving them a squeeze. Her left hand extended in the opposite direction to touch a picture of her deceased son, Brighton, in a silver frame on the antique table beside her.

Grandmamma told the reporter about baby Brighton's first Thanksgiving meal ending with a rush to the hospital. The doctors had said that Brighton had a rare but severe allergic reaction to cranberries and must never eat them again.

Unfortunately, many years later, on the night he was elected to Congress, Brighton had eaten something containing cranberries at his victory party. He had gone into anaphylactic shock and died.

Not all the Reeds believed Fred was Brighton's illegitimate heir; but thanks to Mona, Fred had medical records documenting his history of allergies, including penicillin and cranberries, just like Brighton. Fred convinced Grandmamma he was her offspring, and that was what counted.

What Fred wondered was whether it was true. Or had Mona really orchestrated the biggest con of her life?

• • •

ON THANKSGIVING Day Fred Parker sauntered down the corridor of the Branwell Rehabilitation Center. When he saw Darla working on the computer at the nurses' station, he began to whistle the theme from *The Andy Griffith Show*. Even though Darla's eyes remained focused on the screen, Fred saw the left corner of her mouth rise, and he knew he had her.

She had once told him he looked like Opie Taylor, only all grown up and with a full head of red hair. He kept cultivating that image because he never knew when he might need Darla's help. Although he felt secure in his current situation, a con man could never tell when the floor might fall out from under him.

Besides, charming Darla kept him in practice. True, she was probably in her fifties, at least twenty-five years his senior, but so were a lot of female voters in town. He seemed to be doing well with mother and grandmother figures these days. He needed to continue to do so if he decided to follow in his presumed father's footsteps and run for office.

"Hey, Darla. How's she doing today?"

Darla looked up from the computer. She gazed at him. For a moment he flattered himself into thinking adoringly. Then her expression sobered. "Mona's been a little down lately. Hip replacement's been giving her a lot of pain. She's complaining the therapy's brutal. But seeing you will perk her up." Darla's nose wrinkled. "What have you brought with you?"

He put a pizza box on the counter. "Our Thanksgiving tradition. Mona's and mine. A cheese pizza with sun-dried tomatoes, and"—he leaned closer—"anchovies."

Darla grimaced. "How is that a Thanksgiving tradition?"

Fred feigned amazement that she didn't make the connection. "Those are premium pizza ingredients. We could only afford them on special occasions."

Darla shook her head. "To each his own, I guess. I hope it will tempt her appetite more than the tray that came up a while ago. I just looked in on her, and she hadn't touched it."

"You know why that is," Fred said. He winked conspiratorially.

Darla moved within inches of his nose. "Why?"

He sent a gust of hot breath against her cheek. "Hospital food is never good until it has time to congeal."

Darla pulled back, rolling her eyes. "You're *so* bad. Do something useful and bring a little joy into Mona's life."

He snapped to attention and saluted. "I choose to accept that mission. Please don't self-destruct before I return."

"*Mission: Impossible* was off the air before you were born."

"But I've seen the reruns. And the movies."

He felt Darla watching him as he took the pizza and headed down the hall. He figured she had read the article, because the morning newspaper was folded on the counter showing a portion of the picture with Grandmamma and him.

• • •

MONA SAT upright against two pillows, ignoring the tray on the portable table that fit over her bed. She faced the window with its blinds half closed. Not looking outside but living inside her thoughts. Dangerous territory.

She had loved Fred from the moment she saw him, aged seven, in the alley behind Madde Prancks Pizza Shoppe, clutching the address he had torn from his file. The only information with him when he was left on the church doorstep as a baby.

When he was found at the church, social workers had questioned everyone at Madde Prancks, trying to find a connection to the abandoned child. Max owned the place then, with Mona waitressing. No way could she care for a baby.

She looked for a new way of supplementing her income. When Max caught her stealing from him, he threatened to fire her if it ever happened again. But at the racetrack, the bettors were more careless. She got very skillful at picking pockets and gradually bringing the cash into her income stream as if it were coming from tips.

When Fred found her, she was ready to claim him. Initially she had returned him to the orphanage. There she learned that his potential adoptions kept falling through because Fred was excessively ill as a baby, and too sullen and rebellious as a child, so she went through the process of qualifying to be his foster mom. Had her apartment inspected, her life scrutinized, and her employer interviewed. So much trouble, and that was before she had to contend with the fractured child. Gradually she gained his confidence and weaned him from his surrogate family, the TV.

And she taught him something else. How to pick pockets, her alternative-income source. But she made him promise not to use the skill. Little con jobs followed. All along, she prepared him for the "con" that would make his life, and she dreaded the day when that con would be put into place.

• • •

FRED PAUSED as he reached the door of Mona's room. The interior was dark. He glanced at the TV mounted on the wall and recognized the giant turkey float that led off the Macy's parade. The bed next to Mona's was stripped. Her roommate had been sprung for the holiday, Mona had told him when he had visited the previous weekend.

She had the same expression she had worn the first time he had seen her in the alley behind Madde Prancks. Her short gray hair, perfectly cropped by her own hand, still gave her a regal appearance. But he noticed the lines around her eyes and the creases leading down to her lips. Mona had broken in the last year. The fall had contributed, but it was more her spirit than her body that had begun to betray her ever since he had connected with his "new" family.

"What's happenin'?" Fred asked, entering the room with a few jaunty steps, the pizza held high, trying to imitate the character from the seventies' TV series *What's Happening!*

Mona turned to face him. For a moment her lips curved into a tight smile. Then, like a curtain concealing a stage, her countenance changed. Her right eyebrow arched, and her mouth relaxed, reminding Fred of Mr. Spock. "I don't know why you remain mired in old TV shows."

"It seems the logical thing to do," he replied, making an attempt to mirror her expression. Unfortunately, his eyebrow twitched more than arched, and the corners of his lips kept darting upward, spoiling the effect. He gave up and continued, "Growing up as an orphan, you make your traditions where you can find them. The TV was always good company and, as far as I know, never harmful."

"Except when it kept you from doing your homework."

"That's where you came in to hound me. One of the perks of the foster care system."

"Obviously, I'm a saint." She eyed the box suspiciously. "What have you got there?"

He replaced her dinner tray with the pizza box, then, perched on the edge of her bed, he lifted the lid.

"Our Thanksgiving tradition," he said, closing his eyes, savoring the delectable aroma. "Ready to dig in?" When he opened his eyes, he saw her cross her arms and frown. "Has rehab made you lose your taste for pizza?"

"Fred, what are you *doing* here?"

"I'm visiting my former foster mom for the holiday." He leaned back with a smirk. "Now who's the saint?"

She sighed. "It's your first year celebrating Thanksgiving with the Reeds. You've got to focus on being one of them."

"I'm not worried."

"You should be. The family will be looking for any error or discrepancy to throw you out. Not everyone's as gullible as Mrs. Reed."

"I told *Grandmamma* Reed I would be a little late getting to Thanksgiving dinner because I was visiting you. Made her even more certain that I'm Brighton's son."

Her eyes narrowed. "Why?"

"As Grandmamma put it, 'Just like my Brighton, bringing joy to the less fortunate before having his own dinner.'"

Mona snorted. Fred wasn't sure whether it was at his mimicry or the sentiment, but at least she seemed to be coming out of her doldrums.

"I remember Grandmamma Reed's darling boy coming to Madde Prancks," she said. "I didn't notice him having the generosity Grandmamma attributes to him."

"What was he like, Mona?"

"Like any wealthy, good-looking boy growing up in the most well-known family in a small town. Full of himself. Convinced, by his mamma, that he'd be in Congress before he was thirty."

"A prophetic woman. Grandmamma says all the girls ran after him."

Mona grunted. "I remember one he chased. Fortunately she got away and made her own opportunity."

"Was she beautiful?"

Mona's eyes had focused on the edge of the table. "You've seen her picture."

"So I have." Fred looked around the room. "Didn't you bring it with you as a memento of the Shoppe?"

"It's in the nightstand drawer. Too much clutter around this morning when they brought the bath pan."

Fred raised a slice of pizza, took a large bite, and chewed. After a moment he said, "Grandmamma wasn't really surprised Brighton had a child out of wedlock. I have to admit, it's the best con you ever planned."

"Quiet," Mona whispered, looking toward the door. "You never know when someone might come in. That nosy nurse is always spying on me."

"Darla just wants to help speed your recovery. As a matter of fact, I do too. So you can be welcomed into the bosom of my new family."

"I told you, Fred; that's not going to happen. I warned you. Take this one on and you're stuck with it for life. You'll have to leave your past behind. Permanently." Her lips twisted at the last word.

"C'mon, Mona. That's the beauty of it. It's not fabricated. It is my past, or close enough, so I don't have to lie about it." He finished his last bite of pizza and licked his fingers.

Mona's hand snaked out to take a slice. She bit off the point and chewed thoughtfully. "Not bad."

"Of course, you could make better." His face was all innocence, but his tone had a hint of sarcasm.

Mona gave him an indignant glare. "You don't spend thirty years at a pizza joint making an inferior product."

"I thought you spent at least half that time waitressing at Madde Prancks."

"Until I had the funds to buy it outright."

"From your *side ventures* that supplemented your income."

"Don't be impertinent."

"I'm not. I'm very respectful of those side ventures. You picking all those tourists' pockets at the track benefited me as much as you. I just wish you had taken me with you."

"And how would I have explained that to the Foster Care Review Board?" She took another bite. He selected another slice.

"Watch out not to get it on your fancy new duds," she warned.

As he lifted his arm, he noticed her eyes focus on his wrist. The cuff links engraved with *BR.*

She had always been attracted like a crow to gleaming metals. From coins in the cash register to more substantial quarry, like a Rolex on a tourist's arm. He would watch her focus on the target like a laser beam, and in his head he would hear that Burl Ives song from the Rudolph program. "Silver and Gold." The con would be on. Mona could never see a gleaming accessory without reaching for it.

"When did she give you those?" Mona asked.

"Last night. Pretty, aren't they?" Fred put down his slice and held out his arms for inspection.

Mona observed the cuff links without touching. Her restraint surprised Fred. Usually her hands moved, almost involuntarily, toward a shiny object. She had finished her pizza, and her hands lay still in her lap. Not even a finger twitched.

"Grandmamma must have told you a story about them," she said, an acid tone lingering on the *Grandmamma.*

"Yes. A sad tale."

"No sadder than the one you told her."

Fred shrugged, watching as his cuff links glimmered in the florescent light. "As Grandmamma says, at least my story has a happy ending."

Mona pushed the table toward him. "I'm tired of hearing about your grandmamma. Why don't you go spend Thanksgiving with her?"

"Because, for the moment, I'm spending it with the woman who took me in when I had no place to go. Who cared for me, raised me, and made me into the man I've become. For better or worse. The woman who"—he leaned forward and whispered—"devised the perfect con." *Fortunate*, he thought as he realized his lowered voice coincided with Darla's entrance.

"Wonderful," Darla said, her eyes looking from the open box to the tray. "I see Fred got you to eat some pizza. Can I warm up your dinner?"

"Actually," Mona replied, "I prefer cold turkey. Let's switch back to the tray now that I've had my appetizer."

Fred took the pizza box, and Darla returned the tray to the table.

"I'm so glad the kitchen used real cranberries instead of that gelatin mixture this year," Darla said. She looked at Fred. "Of course, I don't want you trying it."

Mona frowned. "Why do you say that?"

A furrow developed between Darla's eyebrows. "I read the story in the paper this morning."

"What story?" Mona's eyes shot daggers at Fred.

"About Fred and his dad sharing an allergy to cranberries."

Mona continued to pin Fred with her stare. "So it's a news story?"

"Didn't they bring you a paper this morning?" Darla looked around the room. "I'll have to get you one. It's a great story. Hard to believe Brighton died from an allergic reaction the night he was elected to Congress."

"Grandmamma said he had a lot of allergies," Fred explained. "I was just lucky Mona got me to the doctor immediately when I ate cranberries as a kid."

"Lucky that the hospital still had the record on file so you could show the Reeds," Darla commented. "Well, enjoy your visit." She headed for the door but turned back as she reached the threshold. "Mona, where's your daughter's picture?"

"I put it away."

"Let me know if I can get anything for you." This time Darla turned and was gone quickly.

Fred crossed his arms and stared at Mona. "Your *daughter's* picture?"

"She could have been," Mona replied. "I seem to have a habit of picking up strays, as you well know. Besides, that's what the nurse thought when she saw the picture. She assumed it was my daughter. It was easier to agree than to get into a long conversation."

He glanced at his cuff links. "I'd like to see that photo."

"I'll get it." Mona turned to open the nightstand drawer.

Fred watched her. "If the girl in that photo was your daughter—and my mother—that could explain how you were able to set up this supposed con."

Mona looked him straight in the eyes. "Careful, Fred. A con only works when the con man doesn't confuse the truth with the story he tells his mark."

"But what if the story is true? Let me see that photo."

"All right. I'm getting it."

She took a few moments, fumbling with the items in the drawer before producing the framed photo.

Fred grabbed it, studying the girl's face.

"Since I took you to the doctor as a boy that first Thanksgiving we spent together, you've never eaten cranberries, have you?" Mona asked. "The reaction you had was terrible. Remember?"

"I remember your pal Nelly saying she couldn't fake it with makeup. They would check for that in the emergency room."

"So I relied on your allergy to penicillin. I had some tablets left from a prescription I had for amoxicillin. I mashed one up and stirred it into your cranberry sauce. Then I took you straight to the hospital so you wouldn't be in danger."

"Why didn't you tell me?"

"I didn't want to frighten you. Besides, I knew what I was doing. I read up on the allergies. They both have the same symptoms. I told you it would pay off in years to come." When he continued to stare at her, she said, "If you're so sure you're Brighton's son, why don't you take a spoonful of cranberries off my plate? Might as well try them here where you have medical help close by."

Fred glanced at the red clump.

Mona frowned. "While you're considering, was Grandmamma in the vicinity when you ordered the pizza?"

"I had it delivered to the house."

"Was she alone with it?"

"I left it in the kitchen while I got my coat."

"Hand me that pizza."

When he gave her the box, she began pulling a piece of pizza apart. Triumphantly, she held out her hand.

"Recognize these? Dried cranberries. They look very much like sun-dried tomatoes. And the salt of the anchovies would mask their sweetness."

Fred stood with his hands on his hips. "Are you saying Grandmamma planted them?"

Mona gave him her sweetest smile. "I'm saying you should watch out for Grandmamma. She might still need some convincing that you're her grandson."

• • •

A FEW minutes later, Fred left Mona's room. He felt like whistling but didn't want Mona to hear. Since he had gone to the Reeds, Mona had been pushing him away. He thought she no longer wanted him in her life, but he was wrong. Somehow she had put those dried cranberries in the pizza. He couldn't help but share his elation with Darla as he passed by the nurses' station.

"Don't tell her I know," he whispered, "but she *loves* me!"

He could feel Darla watching him as he continued down the hall.

• • •

BACK IN her room, Mona held the picture Fred had wanted to see. A picture of her own daughter. She thought she had lost her family forever when she'd given custody of her baby, Iris, to her ex-husband and the society dame he had married. With them her beautiful flower could go to good schools, meet the right people. Not until Mona met the fourteen-year-old Iris dining alone in Madde Prancks did she understand her mistake. Iris lived a miserable, lonely, loveless life with a father and stepmother too caught up in themselves to realize that Iris needed their attention.

Because Mona had terminated her parental rights, she couldn't tell Iris who she was, but she reached out to the girl. She had recruited her actress-friend, Nelly, to teach Iris makeup and poise. Soon the wallflower had blossomed. The brash young Brighton Reed, Iris' classmate, noticed her transformation and had included her with his tagalongs to Madde Prancks. Mona had worried but convinced herself that she saw mutual love and respect in the young couple's eyes. Brighton finished college; Iris flourished in modeling; but Mona had underestimated the influence of Brighton's mother.

One night Iris came to Madde Prancks with a glossy photo of herself wearing a designer gown and holding gold cuff links engraved with *BR*, initials for Beau Richards Jewelry.

"They're going to use it in their national ad campaign," Iris had told her. "They gave me the cuff links for my boyfriend with the same initials."

"Wonderful, baby. Your future's made."

Iris had shaken her head as she signed the photo. "This is for you. The money will give Brighton and me a start. You see, I'm going to have a baby."

Mona's heart had sunk as she listened to Iris. When Brighton entered, Iris had run to hug him and pull him to their secluded booth. As Mona took their order, Iris had still bubbled with excitement, but when Mona brought the Hawaiian pizza, Brighton's favorite, Iris seemed withdrawn. Brighton left a few minutes later, placing the Beau Richards' box in his pocket before he went out the door.

By the time Mona reached her, Iris had been in tears. Brighton's mother wouldn't let him ruin his political career by marrying a pregnant girl. Iris' father and stepmother had barely raised her; they would be useless with an infant. Mona had offered Iris the little money she had set aside, but Iris assured her she would manage.

Mona never saw her again. She heard about Fred's birth in the news story about him being left on the church steps, and talked with the social workers about the baby when they came asking questions at Madde Prancks. Then, four years later, she had read about Iris' death at twenty-four of a drug overdose. Mona's ex-husband never called. Apparently, he and his socialite wife knew nothing of Iris' child.

Finding Fred behind Madde Prancks brought family back into Mona's life. She thought about what had just transpired between the two of them.

Something had told her to hang on to that box of dried cranberries when the nurses' aide had passed them out last week. She had planned to use it as a hiding place to stockpile pills, hoping to accumulate a lethal dose. But now the cranberries had come in handy for a better purpose. She'd palmed a handful when Fred insisted on her getting the photo from the drawer. Maybe she did need to hang around for a while, if for nothing else than to convince Fred that his precious grandmamma wasn't all she seemed.

No one paid enough attention to older women. After her daughter's death, Mona had become involved with the Reed campaign for Congress. No one ever suspected that she had arranged for those dried cranberries to be on Brighton's favorite Hawaiian pizza on election night.

Yes, maybe she needed to stick around to look out for Fred. Besides, there were probably a few more things Mona could palm off on people.

AUTHOR

PAULA GAIL BENSON, a legislative attorney and former law librarian, belongs to Mystery Writers of America, Sisters in Crime, and Romance Writers of America. She enjoys attending writing and mystery conferences, moderating panels for the South Carolina Book Festival, and writing and directing original plays and musicals for her church's drama ministry. In February 2014, she will be a featured author at Murder in the Magic City in Birmingham, Alabama, and Murder on the Menu, in Wetumpka, Alabama. With other authors, she blogs at writerswhokill.blogspot.com. Her personal blog is littlesourcesofjoy.blogspot.com.

More Books from Buddhapuss Ink

Mystery / Thrillers

The Last Track: A Mike Brody Novel
by Sam Hilliard

IMAGINE IF being late meant a child disappeared forever. That's the fear that drives Mike Brody, the man you want when the one you love is missing. He's more than just a master tracker. An ex-Special Forces operative, Smoke jumper, and now extreme adventure tour guide, he also possesses a unique ability to tap into the memory and emotional state of those he pursues.

Some say his gift is supernatural; others consider it a curse. To Mike Brody, it's a penance.

Available in paperback and Kindle editions.

MYSTERY TIMES
Mystery Times Ten 2011

CHOSEN FROM more than 200 submissions, these ten mystery short stories come from new and established authors alike. Never before published, they are gathered together in our first annual Mystery Times YA collection.
This collection includes Barb Goffman's *Truth and Consequences*–nominated for the 2012 Agatha, Anthony and Macavity Short Story Awards!

Mystery Times Nine 2012

LEGEND HAS it that a cat has nine lives, but this cat has nine tales: tales of murder, mystery, intrigue, and revenge. Written by both new and established authors alike, they are gathered together in our second annual Mystery Times collection.

There's something here for every mystery fan, from hard-boiled to paranormal, each one a small bite of mystery to satisfy and delight even the most discerning of readers.

Both books available in paperback and Kindle editions.

Contemporary Fiction / Romance

The Stone Trilogy by Mariam Kobras

The saga of Jon Stone, international rock superstar,
and the woman he loved, lost, and found again.

All are available in paperback and Kindle editions.

The Distant Shore, Book I
Winner 2012, Bronze Independent Publisher's Book Award

THERE'S NOTHING like receiving a letter from a
teenage son you knew nothing about, but that's what
happens to international rock star Jon Stone. He drops
everything to find the boy and his mother, the girl he
loved so many years ago who left him when his rock 'n'
roll life became too much for her to bear.

Under the Same Sun, Book II
Winner 2013, Silver Independent Publisher's Book Award

THERE COMES a time in life when you realize that
neither fame nor wealth will carry the day. It's the moment when all that matters are love and faith.
  Stand with Naomi on a lonely beach as she faces
her greatest threat and discovers that nothing is more
important than her love for Jon.

Song of the Storm, Book III

WHEN DREAMS come true for some and worlds crash
for others, when friendships are tested and true love is
found at last—that is the Song of the Storm.
  The conclusion of the award-winning Stone Trilogy
brings the love story of Jon and Naomi full circle; with
some things lost and some things gained, they discover
the true value of love and family, and the high cost of
survival in our world today.

Emerging Voices Imprint

Sweet William

by Martie Odell Ingebretsen

EACH OF us carries the seeds of good and evil. It's William's turn to choose. Will he remain locked in his cold prison of anger and loss, or reclaim the key to peace held for safekeeping by two angels?

Since the tragic deaths of his wife and young son, William has been trapped in a circle of depression, grief, and homelessness. When he is picked up on suspicion of child molestation, it appears to be just more bad luck; but it's the catalyst that allows him to open the door to the past and, at long last, accept it, and the love of the people around him.

COMING IN 2014

Message From a Blue Jay
Love, Loss, and One Writer's Search for Home

by Faye Rapoport DesPres

WHEN NATURE writer and essayist Faye Rapoport DesPres turns forty, nothing about her life fit the usual mold. Join her in her travels as she reflects on a modern life marked by a passion for the natural world, a second chance at love, shocking loss, and her search for a place she can finally call home in this beautifully crafted memoir in essays.

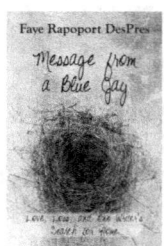

And the highly anticipated prequels to
The Stone Trilogy:

Waiting for a Song, Naomi's Story (Spring 2014)

and

The Rosewood Guitar, Jon's Story (Fall 2014)